THE BOY WITH NO BOOTS

THE BOY WITH NO BOOTS

Sheila Jeffries

**SIMON &
SCHUSTER**

London · New York · Sydney · Toronto · New Delhi

A CBS COMPANY

First published in Great Britain by Simon & Schuster UK Ltd, 2015
A CBS COMPANY
Copyright © Sheila Jeffries, 2015

3 5 7 9 10 8 6 4

Simon & Schuster UK Ltd
1st Floor
222 Gray's Inn Road
London WC1X 8HB

www.simonandschuster.co.uk

Simon & Schuster Australia, Sydney
Simon & Schuster India, New Delhi

A CIP catalogue record for this book is available from the British Library

Paperback ISBN: 978-1-47115-228-3
EBOOK ISBN: 978-1-47113-766-2

Typeset by Hewer Text UK Ltd, Edinburgh
Printed and bound in Great Britain by CPI Goup (UK) Ltd, Croydon CR0 4YY

Chapter One

THE TREACLE JAR

Annie waited at her garden gate, an earthenware jar clutched in her swollen red hands. If she stared deep into the landscape, she sometimes glimpsed the shine of Freddie's hair as he bobbed along the lane below the tall elm trees. Her face was hot with anxiety. Under the stained apron, Annie's heart was dark with guilt. A woman of your age, Annie. Dependent on a seven-year-old child! But that's what she was. And only Freddie knew why.

Freddie had rescued her when she'd been clinging to the railings outside the Post Office, too terrified to move. He'd led her home on her stone feet, plod by

Sheila Jeffries

plod, and stilled her trembling with his bright unwavering gaze.

On that October afternoon, Freddie's footsteps were slower and slower as he trudged home from school. His face was purple, half of it a bruise from where Mr Price had thrown a book at him for daydreaming, and the other half a brighter purple from the blackberries he'd been eating. His four pockets bulged with wet beechnuts, and he smelled of autumn. Blisters scorched his small feet from walking a mile to school and a mile home in a pair of wooden clogs.

'Don't you dare take them off,' Annie had warned.

'No, Mother.'

'If you do, then you take your socks off, too, and walk barefoot, and I'm not darning them, Freddie. Understand?'

'Yes, Mother.'

He dreaded being given the job of darning his own socks with the long bodkin threaded with scratchy grey wool, the smooth wooden darning egg, and the hours of misery, weaving and picking and unpicking, and being scolded as he worked in the square of light from the cottage window.

Freddie paused in the lane. He didn't want to go home. It wasn't that he didn't want to see his mother. It was what she would make him do.

2

The west wind was swishing the elm trees, their oval leaves flickering through the blue air to assemble in thick drifts that filled the lane with gold. Freddie sighed. If only he could paint it. What he longed for most was a paintbox and a brush, but where would he get paper? Tonight he had to do his homework on lavatory paper, a roll of thin tracing paper, shiny one side and dull on the other.

He sat down in his favourite gateway, sinking into the inviting toastiness of fallen leaves. He scruffed them up with his small hands, covering his knees until he had completely buried his legs. Like a Babe in the Wood, an afternoon babe. Perhaps he would nod off to sleep in the drowsy sunshine. Freddie leaned back against the elm trunk and studied the colours on the wooden gate, a glaze of lime green, little hoops of silver, burning blotches of mustard-coloured lichen. This hot and tex-tured colour framed the Somerset landscape with its lines of pollarded willows notating the fields like a page of music dip-dyed in the mystic blue of the Mendip Hills.

Freddie decided to eat ten of his precious beechnuts to fill the ache in his stomach. He counted them out carefully, laying them in a line along the lower bar of the gate. Then he peeled them, the brittle cases gleaming

3

auburn in the sun, and cupped the tiny triangular nuts in his hand. He put them into his mouth all at once. That way they tasted nuttier and made more of a mouthful. Freddie liked autumn. He liked the mellow sun and the apple orchards, and the morning puddles curled with interesting ice. Autumn was full of ripe berries and hazelnuts. One morning Freddie had found a mushroom the size of a dinner plate growing in the field. Annie had fried it in goose fat and seven of them had feasted on it.

He sat for longer than it took to eat the ten beech-nuts, licking the crumbs from his teeth, and picking 'old man's beard' from the hedge. His blue inquisitive eyes stared into its tendrils, wondering at the wisps of fluff protecting the clustered dark seeds. He picked a rose hip and twirled its leathery scarlet fruit thoughtfully between his finger and thumb. He noticed that its black top was a perfect pentagon, and Mr Price had drawn a pentagon on the blackboard that day for them to copy on their slates.

'Like a haystack,' he'd said. 'A pentagon. Like a haystack.' That was before he threw the Palgrave's *Golden Treasury* at Freddie's head.

'Stupid boy – daydreaming again! Is that how you're going to live your life?'

The bruise ached and his eye hurt when he blinked. The longer he sat buried in the golden elm leaves, the drowsier Freddie became. The bees buzzed deeper, and the starlings began their four o'clock twittering, filling the half-bare poplars with a black rippling as if someone had scattered them into the light. Freddie listened, and through the mosaic of the starlings' song, he could hear Annie calling him.

'Freddie! Fred!'

A little wind-blown voice from such a huge woman, the cry was a blend of anger and genuine desperate need. Freddie sighed and shoved his feet into the hated clogs.

'Coming.'

He clumped down the lane, hearing the church clock striking four. Why was he late? He could see the cottage now with its sagging thatch. He heard the chickens muttering and smelled the coke oven. Tiredness draped its threadbare cloak over his small shoulder blades. He longed to go inside and creep to the brown corner by the window and read his brown book, and disappear into the brown comfort of home.

But his mother was there, as he knew she would be, standing at the wicket gate, brandishing the dreaded jar. She was like the earthenware jar, solid as fired clay, but

5

old, the glaze cracked, the smile chipped, the knowledge gone stale inside. In that moment, Freddie felt glad he had a mother to soak up his tiredness. He leaned on her, his cheek against the heavy damp apron, which smelled of cheese. He could sometimes make her be a proper mother, even when she didn't want to be. He made cracks in her earthenware armour.

She pushed him away.

'Get on down the shop,' she said. 'They've got some treacle.'

'I want a drink.' Freddie turned on the garden tap and guzzled the cold bright water.

'Hurry up. The queue will be long. Don't come back until you've got some.'

It was no use appealing. Freddie digested Annie's expression as he took the jar with both hands. He saw the frustration in her eyes. Then a spark, a frown of concern.

'Freddie?'

'Yes Mother.'

'What happened to your face?'

'Mr Price threw a book at me.'

'What for?'

'Daydreaming.'

'Serves you right. You go on now and get that treacle.'

Freddie turned and walked off as smartly as he could, his little back square with anger. Not again. Please not again, Mother. Every day I have to stand in that queue. Why me? I'm tired out from school. I'm starving hungry. I get cold in the queue. Do I have to? Why can't I have boots? Why is there a war? I didn't want the war, did I?

The sunlight was lengthening bars of amber gold as Freddie reached the village. He walked past the blue-lias cottages with their scrubbed hamstone sills, past the church with its monster yew tree covered in mistle thrushes squabbling over the berries. The street was full of leaves. Freddie could hear the queue even before he saw it, an aggrieved babbling. It was long, wrapped around the market cross like a knobbly scarf, mostly women in long skirts and shawls, a few children. There was no playing, but only queuing, and shuffling forward.

Between shuffles, Freddie ate beechnuts, leaving a trail of husks behind him. He stood there frozen for what seemed like hours, but the church clock was striking five by the time he reached the shop, terrified it would close and send him home shamefaced with an empty jar.

He could see the Hessian sacks on the floor of the

7

shop, and the shadowed eyes of Mrs Borden as she ladled the gleaming sepia-dark treacle into people's jars. She was reaching deeper and deeper into the barrel, and counting the queue as she looked out of the shop. People were grumbling as they came away with less and less treacle. Freddie knew why his mother wanted it so much. Black treacle was the only kind of sugar you could get in the 1914–18 war. She used it to sweeten the baking, and for making hot drinks, or for something to spread on the thick yellow cornbread. It was as bitter as the cornbread was bland, but better than nothing. Freddie felt those words had been stamped on his head the day he was born. Better than nothing.

'There's just a spoonful left, Freddie.' Mrs Borden looked at him with a face like a squashed apple. 'It's so difficult to judge it right, and you were last in the queue.'

'I can help you scrape it.' Freddie leaned over to look in the barrel, his heart already pounding with anxiety about how to face his mother with nothing.

Mrs Borden handed him a wooden spatula and he reached into the barrel and scraped the dark streaks from the sides.

'Don't get it in your hair, dear. Such lovely blond hair you've got.'

Together they scraped the ladle, and the handle of the ladle, and around the lip of the barrel. Finally he had a pathetic dollop of treacle, which hardly covered the base of the earthenware jar.

'Better than nothing.'

'Yes. Better than nothing, Freddie. Come earlier tomorrow, dear. We've got corn meal coming in.'

Freddie nodded. He couldn't speak. Mrs Borden patted him on the shoulder with a hand deeply ingrained with dark treacle, and smiled at him kindly. He backed away in case he cried. It seemed to Freddie that no one was allowed to cry because of the war. Everyone beamed stoically, especially the women.

His tiredness deepened as he trudged home, as if he dragged its cloak through heavy mud. The afternoon had darkened and the sky shone like the inside of a saucepan lid. Flocks of yellow hammers fluttered along the hedges, and barn owls circled low across the fields, their plumage cream and silent.

Freddie felt giddy with hunger and anxiety as he pushed open the door of the cottage. Annie was stoking the coke oven, her huge arms glistening in the firelight. On the table was a bowl of something she had mixed, waiting for the treacle. Freddie stood in the doorway, close to the heavy curtain, its fusty folds comfortingly

9

dark. Suddenly the firelit room rocked like a boat. He fell forward onto the stone floor. The earthenware jar smashed, and so did his head. He heard Annie's scream fly past him and disappear into the whirling darkness.

Chapter Two

LIES

Doctor Stewart threw his bike against the hedge, unlatched the wicket gate and reached Annie's cottage door in brisk strides. Sparrows chirruped in the thick ivy that covered the walls, its tendrils catching in his shock of white hair as he pushed open the door. He was used to this place. In his younger days he had delivered all four of Annie's children in the polished attic bedroom, and he'd spent some rowdy evenings playing cards with Freddie's dad, Levi, the two of them hunched over a green baize table while Annie pounded dough in the kitchen.

Delivering Freddie had been memorably different from most of the births Doctor Stewart had managed.

The first song thrush was singing on a crystal morning in February when Freddie had emerged easily and quickly.

'An angel,' Annie had gasped when Freddie was put in her arms, not crying, but staring into her soul with eyes the colour of blue cornflowers. And when Levi held his new baby son for the first time and stroked the quiff of blond hair with a gentle, grime-encrusted finger, Freddie's intense gaze had moved the giant of a man to tears.

'He's – different,' he'd mumbled. 'Different from the others. He's . . .' Levi had wanted to say 'heaven-sent' but it seemed an unmanly sort of comment. Gruffly he handed the baby back to his beaming wife.

'I got to work now.' Then he'd gone out and flung his hat high up into the morning sun. 'A boy! A boy! After two girls, I got a boy!'

Freddie would be seven now, Doctor Stewart thought, as he pulled aside the heavy brown curtain. The kitchen floor was splattered with blood, and the broken treacle jar. He raced up the stairs.

'Where are you, Annie? It's Doctor Stewart.'

'In here. In the front bedroom.'

Visibly trembling, Annie sat at Freddie's bedside, a blood-soaked rag in her hand.

'Calm down, Annie, he's not dead.'

Numbly she moved back and let the doctor examine her precious son who lay unconscious in his little iron bed with its horsehair mattress and coarse grey and red blanket. He examined Freddie in a methodical silence, frowning over the child's bruised face and swelling nose. Then he peeled back the blanket and saw the boy's thin scarred legs and blistered feet.

'Look at the state of his feet. How did they get like this?'

Annie hung her head. 'We've no shoes for him, Doctor.'

'These blisters are going septic.'

Everything he said sounded like an accusation to Annie. Raising Freddie with the Great War going on had been difficult. She'd wanted a happy childhood for him, wanted him to be rosy-faced and robust like her other children had been, carefree and healthy.

'Have you got salt in the house, Annie?'

'Yes, a block in the larder.'

'You must bathe his feet in warm salty water. Every day. Twice a day.'

'Yes, Doctor.'

'And he's very thin. Undernourished.'

Annie sat absolutely still, afraid that any small

13

movement she made might produce another curt diagnosis. But the fat tears kept on running over her cheeks, and the suppressed need for a good cry manifested a hot pain in her throat.

'Will you tell me how this happened, Annie?'

She blurted out the story to its bitter end, only omitting the real reason why she had sent Freddie to fetch the treacle.

'Is he going to die?' she asked finally.

'Not yet. But he's seriously concussed, malnourished and, I would say, exhausted.'

Freddie's eyelids flickered open. He stared at Doctor Stewart who shook his head and smiled reassuringly.

'It's all right. You'll be fine. Just a bump on the nose and a little cut on your head that bled a lot. You be quiet now, Freddie. I'll come and see you again in the morning. No school tomorrow.'

'Mr Price threw a book at my head,' said Freddie clearly, 'and it was Palgrave's *Golden Treasury*, and it's got a poem I really like in it. Shall I say it to you? It's about . . .'

'That'll be the Innisfree thing,' said Annie. 'He knows it by heart.'

'No, Freddie. Not now. You go back to sleep.'

Annie sat holding Freddie's small hand in her red

fingers, watching his eyes closing. Doctor Stewart folded his stethoscope into its wooden box. 'Is it worth a jar of treacle?' He laid a kindly hand on Annie's humped shoulder, looking into her face in the October twilight. 'I'm telling you Annie, you mustn't expect Freddie to do so much when he's undernourished.'

'I know, I know.' Annie began to rock herself to and fro, the gentle rhythm easing the pain of her guilt.

'You can go to the shop, Annie. While he's at school, can't you?'

Annie nodded, avoiding Doctor Stewart's probing eyes. Her darkest secret was the terror she felt at going out, the way her heart hammered and the elm trees swayed towards her, and the road spun like a slow spinning top. She wasn't ill. It was how her mother had been. Housebound. Perpetually afraid. Agoraphobic. But tell the doctor? Never. He'd have her locked up in a mental hospital. Things would have to go on as they were. She'd find a way of giving Freddie more food, and a pair of boots.

Yet Freddie knew about her phobia, though she hadn't told him. She depended on Freddie, on his inner light, his depth and compassion. He's only a child, she thought now, a frail child. He might die.

'Why does he get hit so often at school?'

15

'He daydreams, Doctor.'

'Is that all?'

'That's all, as far as I know.'

'I'll go and see his teacher. That's a nasty bruise, too near his eye. Keep him warm and quiet, and let him sleep for as long as he wants. No school tomorrow. And . . .' Doctor Stewart frowned at Annie, 'Pull yourself together, Annie.'

She rocked harder. I'm not that kind of woman, she wanted to scream, not a wartime woman, cheerful and heroic. I'm a lump. A frightened housebound lump.

'I'll see myself out.'

'Thank you, Doctor.'

Annie sat with Freddie through the pink of evening watching the changing sky from the square of window. On the deep stone sill were all of Freddie's possessions. Two books, his collection of stones, conkers and cones, his precious wooden spinning top, three green marbles, and a sepia photograph of his Gran in a tiny silver frame. She thought about how she could make him some shoes by sewing leather onto socks, and the possibilities of making cakes without eggs so he could have a boiled egg for his breakfast. She longed for her girls, Betty and Alice, who were all living in lodgings and working at the glove factory in Yeovil. Only George, her eldest, came to see them on his motorbike. He worked at Petter Engines making shells for the war. Occasionally on a Sunday he brought one of his sisters home in the sidecar.

Levi worked long hours in the corn mill, coming home grumpy and stinking, capable of nothing but sitting by the fire in the rocking chair. He wouldn't read. He wouldn't chop firewood. He just sat, staring endlessly into the bright flames.

'Freddie's took sick,' Annie said tonight as he hung his stinking coat on the back of the door.

'Oh ah, what's up with him?'

'The doctor says it's exhaustion. And he's undernourished.'

'Ah.' Levi stuffed tealeaves into his pipe and gazed into the fire for long minutes before his eyes sparked into life.

'You had the DOCTOR?'

'Sally from down the farm sent her son to fetch him. Freddie's been hit again, a nasty bruise near his eye. For daydreaming.'

'Ah.' Another lengthy pause while guilt, anger and helplessness sorted each other in Levi's mind. 'He'll have to learn to pay attention then, won't he? Or end up useless like me.'

'You aren't useless, Levi. Don't talk like that. Just because they turned you down for the war. It's not your fault you've got arthritis.'

Freddie woke slowly after a long sleep. Bees hummed and fussed outside his window and the smell of cooked apple drifted up the stairs and through his open door. The cottage was strangely silent and Freddie sensed a new emptiness about it. The clock chimes were icy cold in the apple-flavoured air. He counted ten. Ten o'clock! He ought to be in school!

Freddie got up quickly and ran barefoot down the stone stairs where he found his clothes hanging, stiff and crusty by the stove.

'My beechnuts!'

To his relief she had emptied them into a dish and put it on the table. Next to it was his plate with a slab of yellow cornbread thickly spread with dripping and the unexpected white gleam of an egg, boiled and shelled. A piece of firewood was next to it with 'Freddie's breakfast' written on it in black charcoal. And the broken treacle jar had been pieced together with some kind of glue. Freddie smoothed his fingers over it, doubting that it would hold together for all the journeys it had to make. He climbed into his clothes and sat at the table to eat breakfast hungrily, finishing every single crumb. Then he found his tin mug and filled it with hot water, lifting the heavy kettle with two hands clutching the string-wrapped handle. 'Mother?'

With his hands around the tin mug, Freddie walked into the scullery, pausing to sip the steaming drink. She wasn't there. Still barefooted, he padded into the garden. 'Mother?'

The garden flickered with late butterflies, Red Admirals and Tortoiseshells sunning themselves on the cottage walls or feeding on the Michaelmas daisies. Freddie listened. There was hammering from far away, a robin singing, but no one was talking. Where was his mother? Annie had gone out when she shouldn't go out. Only Freddie knew that.

Freddie pulled on his scratchy socks and the heavy clogs. Where would she be? Was it his fault for breaking the treacle jar?

Levi hesitated outside the schoolroom door. He could smell smoke from the stove, and the only sound was the occasional cough from a child or a creak from the floor-boards. Had he been inside the schoolroom, he would have heard the steady squeak of thin chalk sticks on little black slates as fourteen children aged from five to twelve years old worked silently at their arithmetic.

Once again Levi mentally rehearsed what he intended to say, and how he wasn't going to be intimidated by the likes of Harry Price. He knocked on the heavily varnished door and pushed it open, the dented brass knob cold in his hand. Fourteen heads turned to look at him. The children smelled of damp socks and rice pudding. Harry Price sat on a small platform at one end, stuffing tobacco into a curly pipe.

'Work,' he barked, and the children's heads snapped back into position. Levi took off his cap respectfully.

'I'd want a word.'

Harry Price took a used match from a St Bruno tin on his desk and carried it to the stove, opened the door to a cloud of smoke and lit it from the roaring flames inside. He sucked and puffed at the pipe, almost disappearing into curling smoke while Levi stood awkwardly. 'Outside.' Harry Price wagged a grizzled finger at his class. 'If anyone moves or speaks, I shall know.'

The two men stood in the brown corridor outside, looking squarely at each other's eyes.

'I've took time off work for this,' Levi said. 'It's about my boy.'

'Frederick?'

'Ah, Frederick.' Levi thought about the bruise he'd seen on the sleeping face of his small son, and the words jostled in his throat. 'He ain't strong. And I want to know why he's being punished so often. Is he a dunce?'

'A dunce! No. On the contrary he's clever, very clever.' Harry Price's eyes looked uncomfortable. Doctor Stewart had already admonished him for his treatment of Freddie and he'd disagreed, of course. Boys had to be kept in line. How would Doctor Stewart cope, shut in a room all day with fifteen village kids? No matter how well they behaved, Harry Price could sense their frustrations and their simmering energy waiting to engulf him if he once slackened his defences. Worse, he sensed their hatred of him, the way they stormed out at home time like a basket of pigeons released into furious flight. And that Frederick always looking right through him with those eyes, as if he could see right into the secret rooms of his head.

Once Freddie had said something that had deeply disturbed Harry Price.

'Sir, who is that lovely lady standing next to you?'

'What do you mean, boy? There's nobody here!'

'Oh but there is, Sir,' and Freddie had described his late wife, who he'd never seen, with breathtaking accuracy.

'Don't you dare tell me such lies, Frederick. Sit down and get on with your work or you'll feel my cane. Shame on you boy!'

But no amount of shouting and blustering would erase from Harry Price's mind the clear and startling picture of his late wife. From that day he feared and hated Freddie.

'So what does he do?' persisted Levi. 'If it's just daydreaming, does that warrant such punishment?'

'He does daydream. But . . .' Harry Price raised his bushy eyebrows at Levi. They were stained yellow from the pipe smoke. 'I'm sorry to say he tells lies.'

There was silence while Levi's blood pressure soared and his expression changed from concern to anger.

'LIES,' he shouted. 'My boy tells LIES.'

'Oh yes, daily.'

Levi could have sworn that Harry Price looked pleased with this information, as if it were a trump card.

'What kind of lies?' he thundered.

Freddie hurried along the lane to the village, checking inside every gateway. He paused by a stile, which marked a footpath leading to the woods, thinking his mother might have gone looking for mushrooms or hazelnuts. He checked the stubble fields in case she was gleaning for any remaining grain, a hopeless task as the sparrows and finches had probably scoffed it all. A few uncut heads of barley nodded in the hedge, and that was treasure. Freddie picked them happily, tearing off the stalks and cramming the bristly heads into both his pockets. Annie would add them to the soup, boiling them until they were glutinous and soaked with the taste of beef broth.

Freddie ran towards the distant church, his clogs in his hand, his head aching again. He found Annie sitting inside the lych gate, gripping the blackened timber. She was gasping for breath and whimpering like a puppy.

'Come on, Mother, I'll take you home.' Freddie unfastened her fat red fingers one by one from the gate until he had all of her hand in his. 'Come on.'

Annie looked at her small son in the deepest gratitude. She didn't think she could possibly get home, but she stood up, rigid and shaking. 'You're hurting me,' said Freddie, and she loosened her grip just a little. Her eyes searched for something to hold.

'Touch the wall, Mother. Hold the wall.'

Annie set her mouth in a purple line that turned down at the ends. She wasn't going to tell Freddie how the solid wall seemed to be swaying, and the flagstone pavement turning like a roundabout.

'Come on, take a step,' he encouraged. 'One small step. That's it. And another. Just keep moving.'

Freddie spoke gently, walking backwards in front of her so that they had eye contact. Annie held him so tightly by the hand, he had to keep reminding her not to pull him over. Step by step they progressed along the wall and the iron railings bordering the churchyard. The lane was more difficult, with nothing to hold but brambles. Freddie needed all his strength to support his mother's shuffling steps. He understood that fear had a strange power over her body and he thought she might die of fright.

'Just keep moving. I won't let you fall.'

Still walking backwards, holding her with both his hands, Freddie noticed a man in a cap coming up the lane, his head bobbing above the hedges, marching with loud boots as if he was angry. Annie stiffened and pulled herself up proudly.

'It's Dad!' cried Freddie. 'Where has he been? He looks grim.'

Chapter Three

BROKEN CHINA

Levi fumbled with the brass buckle of his leather belt as he strode towards the cottage. The boy deserved a good strapping. He'd never tell such lies again; Levi would beat it out of him. The Barcussy family didn't tell lies. Now Freddie had brought shame on the family. Levi had always known his last son was different, and clever, Harry Price had said. Levi had swelled with pride, momentarily, then the lies had come scorching in, spoiling it, burning it black like a slice of good bread accidentally dropped from a toasting fork into glowing coals.

He was close to the cottage now, his throat hot with

rage. He could see Annie's face watching him over the hedge like a rising harvest moon half hidden under the navy blue hat that loomed on her head. Wait until she heard what Harry Price had said about her precious son.

The rage festered in his boots as he covered the last strides to the cottage gate. His swollen feet wanted to stamp and punish the whole earth until his bones rang with the pain. The sight of Freddie's pale quiff of hair and luminous eyes stopped Levi in his tracks as the boy darted towards him, smiling with a radiance so disempowering that Levi could only stand locked into his fury.

'Hello, Dad. I'm better. And look what we found.' Under Freddie's small arm was a bristling sheaf of golden barley.

'He's a good lad,' crowed Annie, looking down at him fondly. 'He's helped me all the way home. I had a – a turn. Proper bad I was. Shaking. And he got me home, bless his little heart.'

Levi stood, powerless, hands clenched at his sides as he felt his limited supply of language escaping, the words swirling away from him like tealeaves down a plughole.

'What's the matter with you?' Annie stared at him,

her eyes suddenly dark with alarm. 'Lost your job or something?'

'What's wrong, Dad?' Freddie hovered in front of him and Levi glowered into the child's eyes. He took hold of Freddie's shoulder and steered him into the cottage with Annie bustling behind. She took the rustling barley sheaf from Freddie's arms and stashed it against the kitchen wall.

'Your hand is shaking, Dad,' said Freddie, and Annie swung round, pausing in the middle of taking her hat off. A strand of grey hair fell across her cheek.

'Levi,' she said in a warning tone. 'You haven't been drinking, have you?'

Levi sat down heavily at the scrubbed wooden table, his head in his hands. Still the words refused to assemble. He raised a knobbly fist and banged it down on the table with such force that the nearby dresser shuddered and the china tinkled. Two willow pattern plates rolled along the shelf and perched precariously. Annie moved towards them, and the sight of her arm reaching out, and the disapproving frown on her face unlocked Levi's anger.

At first the words came slowly, like shingle tumbling.

'You. Boy. Stand up straight and look at me.'

27

Freddie responded eagerly, his back straight, questions shimmering in his eyes.

'I've been to see Harry Price,' rasped Levi. He fingered the buckle of his belt again. 'Look at me, boy.'

'I am,' said Freddie, shivering now as he saw the colour of rage seeping up his father's stubbly throat, over his chin and up his cheeks until, when it reached his eyes, it was crimson.

'I've never laid a finger on any of my children,' whispered Levi. His eyes bulged with pain. 'But you've been telling LIES.'

Freddie stared hotly back at him.

'I have not.'

Levi lunged forward and caught Freddie's threadbare shirt by the sleeve, his angry fingers tore a strip out of the material. Annie gave a cry, and Freddie's bottom lip started to quiver.

Levi's other hand was on his belt, undoing the buckle, the wide leather strap trailing to the floor.

'So help me, God, I'll thrash you, boy. Any more lies. Do you hear? Do you?'

'No, Levi!' screamed Annie. 'He's not strong, Levi. You'll kill him.'

Freddie stood motionless. His calm eyes inspected Levi's tortured soul with sadness and understanding. A shell of light seemed to be protecting the boy, and Levi couldn't touch him. He raised the belt high and hit the table with it, again, and again. He worked himself into a frenzy, his lips curling and spitting, the smell of the corn mill and the stench of sweat emanating from him into the room. Freddie backed away and climbed onto the deep window seat, his favourite corner, shuffling himself back behind the brown folds of curtain. Annie just stood, her hat in one hand, her face like a stone lion.

Levi heaved the table over with a crash, kicking it and roaring in wordless fury. The tinkle of china from the dresser, the chink of anxiety in Annie's eyes, and the sight of Freddie hunched in the corner with his torn shirt and bony knees and eyes that refused to look shocked, enraged him further. One by one he seized every plate, every china cup, every jug and teapot from the dresser and smashed them on the stone floor. When he had finished, he collapsed into his fireside chair and cried. The rage was spent, purged into a mosaic of winking china across the flagstone floor. Now the last dregs of it sobbed out of him like ripples, further and further apart until finally Levi was still.

'I'm sorry,' he said. 'I'm so sorry,' and he began to weep again until his eyes were red and his rough cheeks soaking wet. 'I'm sorry.' He looked across at Freddie, surprised to see him sitting calmly, watching.

'Don't you ever,' Levi said. 'Freddie, don't you ever be like me.'

'I won't,' said Freddie. Throughout his father's display of rage, Freddie had sat quietly, looking across the room at his mother's frozen eyes. It wasn't the first time in his young life that Freddie had witnessed Levi's uncontrollable temper, watched him smash things then cry with shame, as he was doing now, stooping to pick up the two halves of a cream and brown teapot, holding them tenderly in his hands.

'I can mend this. I'm sorry, Annie. I'm so sorry. I'll make it up to you.'

Annie moved then, picking her way through the fragments of china. Her mother's willow pattern. Auntie Flo's jug. The gold-rimmed bone china cups which were her pride and joy. She went to Levi and put a comforting hand on his shoulder. She said nothing but her silence was powerful. It healed Levi's battered psyche like nothing else. She looked at Freddie, and he crept out to be part of the silence, both of them nursing Levi as if he were a hurt animal.

Levi glanced up at the fragile radiance of his small son.

'I'm sorry, lad. I'm so sorry,' he said again, in a grating voice, and his red-rimmed eyes checked the pale moon of the clockface over the hearth. Right on cue it breathed in and started to chime its Westminster chimes, and each melodious note seemed to vibrate through the smithereens of china.

'I gotta go to work,' said Levi. 'I took time off to . . . to . . .'

'All right dear,' said Annie, steering him away from the subject of Harry Price and Freddie's lies.

'My arthritis. 'Tis bad.' Levi stood up unsteadily. 'But—' He looked at Freddie. 'We gotta talk about this.'

'After tea,' declared Annie. 'We'll sit round the table and sort it out. Now – help me pick up this table before you go – and Freddie, you get the brush and sweep up.'

Freddie swept the shattered china into a rusty dustpan.

'I could make something with this,' he said.

'No you couldn't,' Annie replied. She was stripping the grain from the barley sheaf, putting it to soak in a deep bowl.

'I could, Mother. I could make a sailing ship.' Freddie collected the white and gold curved fragments of cup, holding them up and turning them thoughtfully. He could see in his mind the billowing white sails and the idea of making a model ship excited him. The broken

31

curves of Auntie Flo's jug would make the base of the ship. He planned to get clay from the streambed and work it into a boat shape. Then he'd set the broken china into it. Or he'd make a bird. An owl with big eyes.

'No Freddie. You'll cut your hands,' warned Annie. 'You put that china in the bin.'

But Freddie just looked at her. He took the dustpan outside, where he quickly picked out the bits he needed for his sailing ship and his owl and hid them inside a hollow log at the back of the coal shed. He tipped the remainder into the dustbin. When he went back inside, he saw that Annie was touching the empty dresser, and he planned to make the ship and the owl in secret and stand them up there to fill the empty space. He wasn't going to let his parents stop him.

After a tea of thick yellow cornbread spread with dripping followed by baked apples, Levi slumped into his fireside chair, looking apprehensive.

'We gotta sort this out.'

Annie sat on the other side of the bright fire, darning a grubby grey sock with brown wool, and despite her apparent indifference, Freddie was glad of her solid presence as he faced his father. He dreaded another outburst, but Levi was calm now, his voice and eyes flat and defeated.

'Now, Harry Price told me you was clever,' he began. 'And I were proud, Freddie. I were proud of you.' His eyes glistened with disappointment. 'Then he said you told lies, Freddie. And it weren't just one lie. Now what have you got to say about that?'

'I don't tell lies,' insisted Freddie. He squared his shoulders and directed his candid gaze into Levi's confused eyes.

'But Harry Price says you do.' Levi wagged a crusty old finger and put his face closer. 'He says you told him you saw his wife standing there, and you described her, and she's dead, Freddie. Dead. So how can you see her? Eh?'

'But I did see her. I can see people who are dead,' said Freddie.

Annie gasped and her darning needle paused in mid-air, the long brown strand of wool slowly slipped out of the metal eye and trailed over her lap. Freddie turned and looked at her.

'Can't I, Mother?'

Levi looked flummoxed, the colour spreading again from his collar and over his neck.

Annie leaned forward, the darning needle still in her

hand. Her bust heaved with the dilemma she now faced. Pacify Levi, or protect Freddie, or tell the truth? She took a deep breath.

'Levi,' she said. 'He's got the gift.'

Levi sank back into a confused silence.

'It's in my family,' Annie said. 'My mother had it, and my Nan. Whether you like it or not, Freddie's got it. He can see people who've passed on. It's a gift, Levi. A gift.'

'Tis wrong,' shouted Levi. 'I'm telling 'e. Wrong. Bad, that's what. And I don't want no son of mine doing it. I don't want no fortune-telling or mumbo jumbo in this family. D'you hear? I won't have it. I might be poor, I might work in a corn mill, but I'm honest. I don't tell no lies.'

'Tell him, Freddie,' encouraged Annie. Freddie was edging nearer and nearer to her, backing away from his father, glad of Annie's warmth and support.

'I do really see people,' he said. 'Not all the time. Just now and again. But why is it wrong to see nice people? They aren't bad just because they're dead, Dad, are they?'

Levi didn't answer. Instead he took out his pipe, tapped it on the hearth and started stuffing a fruity mix of tobacco into it. He lit a dead match from the fire and disappeared into the curls of blue smoke. Then he coughed convulsively, growling and retching. Words had abandoned him again, leaving him spluttering like a clogged engine. Exhaustion, frustration, the war, the corn mill, all of it loomed between him and his longing to be a good father. Levi was fighting his own war, and he wasn't winning. All he could do was put up barriers of discipline, whether he agreed with it or not.

'Now you listen to me,' he drew Freddie close again, noticing the torn shirt and yesterday's bruises. 'I forbid you ever to speak of this again. D'you hear? If you do see people, as you say, then you are not to speak of it. Not to me, or your mother, your sisters and brother, or Harry Price.'

'And not Doctor Stewart either,' added Annie.

'Or the vicar.'

Freddie studied their frowning faces in the firelight. From now on his life would be ring-fenced. Secret. A secret life. That's what he would have. He'd say yes and no, and go to school, and stand in the queue for the shop, and carry his dreams in a secret golden box inside his head. But when I'm grown up, he thought, things will be different. No one will tell me what to do and what not to do.

Chapter Four

GRANNY BARCUSSY

Twice a year Freddie was sent on 'his holiday', a mile across the fields to where Levi's mother lived alone in her farmhouse. He didn't have much to pack, a few matchboxes, a pencil, a tobacco tin and a precious fishing net. This time he had something extra.

'When you give a present, you wrap it up in something,' Annie had said. 'Brown paper and string, and sealing wax. But we haven't got any of that now the war is on. Wretched war. I'll be glad when it comes to an end.' She rummaged in the kitchen cupboard and fished out a piece of butter muslin. 'Here you are. Roll it up in that.'

Freddie took the soft butter muslin and wrapped the present for Granny Barcussy, and tied it round with a frayed blue ribbon.

'I used to wear that in my hair, when I was a girl,' said Annie, taking the ribbon and tying it in a bow. 'There. That looks like a present now. But don't you let your father see it. He'll . . .'

Freddie nodded. 'I know.'

'What the eye doesn't see, the heart doesn't grieve over,' said Annie, and she packed it into the old carpetbag with Freddie's pyjamas, and a dead pigeon.

'Do I have to carry that?' asked Freddie, looking at the iridescent greens and purples in the pigeon's neck, and its head flopped sideways, the eyes closed under white lids.

''Course you do. Don't be so silly. I've got to send something for you to eat. Granny will make a pigeon pie.'

Freddie looked at his mother anxiously.

'How are you going to go out, Mother? When I'm not here.'

'I shan't need to.'

'But what if you do?'

'I'll manage. Now don't you worry, Freddie. You like going to Granny don't you? Just remember she's

38

eighty-one. You get the wood in for her and feed the chickens – and don't go playing by the river – and don't loiter about daydreaming. Go straight there.'

Freddie still worried about his mother as he waved goodbye and set off across the fields which were wet and squishy underfoot. He knew the way well. Over the sheep pastures, through the woods and down towards the river valley. The baby lambs and the song thrushes cheered him up, and the thought of a holiday, and the present tucked in his carpetbag under the wings of the dead pigeon. And he had another surprise, hidden in one of his matchboxes.

He was climbing the stile into the woods when a strange feeling crept over him like a warm wind blowing on his skin. Something, or someone, was inside the woods, waiting for him to jump down from the stile. Freddie perched on the rail, the carpetbag clutched in his hands looking, searching the flickering twilight of the woods. He could smell the primroses and the moss, and he could smell the person who was waiting. He smelled of sweet meadow hay and boot polish.

Freddie got down from the stile and started to walk over soft pine needles on hushed footsteps. It was silent under the tall conifers, but he could hear the whisper of soft-treading feet padding beside him, and the swish of a cloak brushing his skin. He stopped under a lime tree, and the other feet stopped. But still he couldn't see anyone, even when he sat down against the cool trunk of the lime tree, and searched the space with his eyes.

The sun had gone behind a cloud and the lights of the wood vanished into translucent gloom. Around his legs were the amber spirals of young ferns uncurling from dark leaf mould, and pale mounds of primroses which seemed to shine with a light of their own. The light that appeared in front of Freddie was prim-rose-coloured, a tall shimmering shape. He reached out and touched it, and it felt like velvet, indescribably smooth and lingering, a sensation that infused his skin with secret energy.

Freddie closed his eyes and visualised the space around him, something he practised doing often. The scene came instantly to life. First he saw the energy of the sap rising from the tree roots below the soil like fountains of glistening light, green gold and lemon gold, branching into thousands and thousands of arteries that trickled through the new young stalks and leaves. He listened and he could hear the subtle high-pitched music of growth; each tree sang with a different voice, the voice of its growing. The sky between the leaves rang with the hum of honeybees in the lime flowers.

'The bee-loud glade,' Freddie thought, remembering the poem he had learned at school. 'This is like Innisfree. I'll live alone in the bee-loud glade.' He loved the poem because to him it was about a man who wanted to live alone where no one could tell him what to do.

With his eyes still closed, and believing himself to be alone, Freddie decided to say the whole poem aloud, say it to the singing trees and the dancing lights of the wood that were coming alive in his vision. He took a deep breath and began:

'I will arise and go now, and go to Innisfree
And a small cabin build there, of clay and wattles
made:
Nine bean rows will I have there, and a hive for the
honeybee
And live alone in the bee-loud glade.'

Preoccupied with his recital and his vision, Freddie didn't hear the very real footsteps coming through the wood. Softly and briskly they came, winding between the ferns, a long black skirt swinging, snagging on brambles, a forked hazel stick hooking them away. A person so small and light inside the black skirt and shawl, she could move over the ground like a whisper, not shaking it. She could pause like a hoverfly over a flower, and listen undiscovered to Freddie's clear boyish voice under the canopy of the lime tree. With a benevolent swish she sat down on the other side of the tree trunk and waited.

Freddie emerged from his dream very slowly. To be slow was real luxury, and he could only do it when he was quite alone. Even now, Annie's words were hammering insistently in his head. No loitering around daydreaming. Or Harry Price's barking voice. *Wake up, boy. Wake up.*

But now he was on holiday, under a lime tree. A time to stretch and yawn out loud, and open his eyes a slit at a time, allowing the rich colours of mosses and tree roots to come in gently. The backs of his knees were embossed with the patterns of twigs and grass, and he rubbed them back to life, brushing leaves and scraps of bark from his socks. Then his hand touched a different fabric, a fabric that wasn't his, smooth and cottony, draped over the tree roots. His eyes opened wide, following the swirl of black fabric round the tree.

'Granny Barcussy!'

'My Fred.'

She never called him Freddie. Too babyish, she declared, for an old soul like her grandson.

'How are you, Granny?' said Freddie politely.

'Eighty-one, and still dancing, my luvvy.'

Granny Barcussy only had three teeth, one at the top and two randomly spaced at the bottom, but her eyes more than compensated for the dark cave of a smile. Eyes that danced with secret knowledge, eyes that made Freddie feel grown up and trusted, and loved. He studied the pattern of wrinkles on her face and saw her as a line drawing, if only he had a sharp enough pencil and a clean square of paper.

'I got you a present,' he said.

'A present! And it 'tidn't me birthday, Fred.'

Shoving the dead pigeon aside, Freddie extracted the butter muslin parcel from the carpetbag. His heart began to thud excitedly as he put it into her hands.

'Ooh. 'Tis a cheese,' she cried, sniffing it.

'No,' said Freddie. 'Unwrap it. Go on.'

''Tis heavy. What can it be?' She looked at him sideways under her silver eyebrows. 'What have you been up to?'

Freddie was so excited he felt his stomach trembling as she slowly untied the blue ribbon and he watched her old hands unrolling the muslin parcel in the woodland sunlight. At last it was out, and he saw it again, the owl he had made from the broken china.

Granny Barcussy gasped. Speechless, she stared down at the owl. Its eyes, ringed with two gold cup handles, winked back at her, cleverly made with black and white china flowers. Its breast feathers, set in the clay, were made from the splinters of Annie's china cups, the wings from fragments of a brown and cream jug, the feet from more curly bits of handle.

'Where did this come from, Fred?'

'I made it. For you.'

Now he'd said it. Freddie had looked forward to this moment all the winter. He'd worked on the owl in secret, digging clay from the streambed, moulding it and rolling it, keeping it wet and pressing the china into it. Some of his blood was in it too; he'd cut his fingers and got into trouble for it, but he wouldn't be stopped, and he'd kept the owl hidden under a loose floorboard in his bedroom. And each time he took it out he'd imagined how Granny Barcussy's eyes would shine when she saw it. He wasn't disappointed.

'Oh, but 'tis beautiful. Beautiful,' she murmured, the words surfacing from somewhere deep in her chest. 'You made this. You clever, clever boy.'

Freddie soaked up the praise. It was something he so rarely had, and he stored the feeling away to sustain him in harder times. He'd made a treasure out of a disaster.

But Levi wouldn't see it like that. It would stir up guilt and shame, and Annie had deemed it wiser not to show it to him.

'It's got some of my blood in it,' he said cheekily and Granny Barcussy laughed out loud and gave him a hug.

'Then I shall love it all the more,' she declared, and her eyes looked at him shrewdly. 'And don't think I don't know where this broken china came from. Enough said. Come on now, Fred. I've got our dinner ready. We're having BACON and potatoes.'

Granny Barcussy's place was full of chickens. They sat up on the back of the old leather sofa, and on top of the oak sideboard plumped together in sociable little groups, coming and going as they pleased through the square-window which was always open. They weren't allowed in the kitchen.

'I've only got nine left,' she said. 'That old fox had my lovely cockerel; lovely bird he was, used to boss the hens about, rush them inside if the buzzard came over. They don't lay many eggs now, now he's gone. Fox had him in broad daylight. Now, mind you don't sit on an egg, Fred. They lays them in funny places. You might hatch it!' Granny cackled with laughter as if she was a chicken herself. She darted around the cottage, talking non-stop.

Freddie was quiet. He had found Millie, a glossy black chicken who would sit on his shoulder, or settle on his lap like a cat. He loved the warmth of her on him, the mysterious depth of her plumage, the motherly crooning sounds she made in her throat. And he loved being allowed to just sit there on the sofa and watch the life of the cottage. Sparrows came in and out with the chickens, and high on one of the beams were two corpulent spiders who had been there for years and their webs were old and dust-covered, festooned with the flies they had caught and wrapped in gossamer. Now one of them had a pale orange cocoon attached to the wall. Freddie watched her fussing over it and wondered what it was.

'That's her family,' said Granny Barcussy. 'All her hundreds of children in there. Waiting for the right moment to be born.'

'How are they born?' asked Freddie, fascinated.

'The cocoon explodes, not like a gun, gently over a few hours, and the baby spiders float out the window on long strings of gossamer. 'Tis a miracle, I think.' Her eyes were alight with the magic of it. 'Spiders are so organised,' she continued. 'We can learn a thing or two from them.'

While she was talking, Freddie was absorbed with

stroking Millie and looking at her bright eyes and orange beak. He imagined himself in a cocoon, and Granny Barcussy's voice was wrapping threads around and around him until he was again in his own special sanctuary. The dark interior of the farmhouse grew bright, a hazy, primrose yellow light drifted in through the wall and settled itself right in front of Freddie. He smelled it – sweet meadow hay and boot polish, and suddenly a man stood there in a cream robe, the man who had walked beside him through the wood. The glow of his brown eyes was hypnotic. The man came close and sat himself down on the sofa next to Freddie, and Millie cocked her head to look at him.

'Are you real?' asked Freddie.

''Course I'm real. What a funny question,' said Granny Barcussy sharply.

'I wasn't talking to you,' said Freddie. 'I was talking to him.'

'Who?'

'The man sitting next to me.'

'What man?' Granny Barcussy dragged a rickety music stool across the floor and sat on it, staring intently at her grandson. 'Describe him, can you?'

Freddie looked at the man carefully. 'He's got brown eyes, and a moustache, and he's wearing—' He was going to say 'a long cream dress' but as he looked deeper into the shining robe he saw the man's clothes. 'He's got shiny brown boots and breeches with buttons up the side of his knees, and a tweed jacket like the one Dad's got, and a white shirt, and a waistcoat with one button missing, and he's got a watch in his pocket on a gold chain. And . . .'

'Go on.' Granny Barcussy's cheeks were wet with tears. The tears ran into the deep wrinkles and made her skin glisten.

'Don't cry, Gran.' Freddie was alarmed. What had he done? Then he remembered he wasn't supposed to talk about the spirit people he saw. His father had forbidden it. 'I'm not allowed to—'

Granny Barcussy saw the shadow steal into Freddie's eyes.

'Don't you be afraid. You can tell me anything. Anything you like.'

But Freddie looked at her as if he was peering out through prison bars, the sparkle gone from his eyes.

'You saw my William,' she said warmly. 'He's often around. William, your grandfather. He's been dead a long time, before you were born. Oh he'd have loved you, Fred. He liked to make things with his hands like you, clever he was, and a heart of gold. Heart of gold.'

Freddie was silent. He looked again at the seat next to him, and the man had gone. 'I've got it wrong,' he thought. 'Grandfather William wanted to say something to me and I didn't listen.'

'There's nothing wrong with seeing a spirit,' said Granny Barcussy. 'I can see Levi's been hammering you down – and that schoolteacher, he's a pig. Don't you let 'em bring you down, Fred. You're a good 'un. And I'd fight for you, I would.' She clenched her fist and grinned. Freddie smiled at her gratefully. William would come back, he knew it. If he went to sit under that lime tree again, or if he sat quiet and waited. It was the first time he'd seen a spirit person who belonged to him, and the feeling clung around him like a blanket.

'I like coming here,' he said. 'I feel happy.'

'Good. You deserve to be happy.' Granny Barcussy was still on the music stool, giving him her undivided attention, another luxury he wasn't used to.

'Mother and Dad don't think so,' said Freddie. 'They think everybody's got to suffer because of the war.'

'Pah!' said Granny Barcussy passionately. 'Never mind the war. Let 'em get on with it. Nothing to do with me. Yes, there's poverty, but there's beautiful life all around us.' And then she said something that Freddie never forgot. She tapped her heart fiercely with one finger, and her eyes were full of fire. 'I make my happiness inside myself, in here, in my heart, and nothing and nobody can take that away from me.'

A golden bubble drifted through the silence that followed, and came to rest in Freddie's soul.

Then Granny Barcussy jumped up and whirled around, turning the music stool over with a crash. She pointed at Freddie's feet.

'You still got those blimin' clogs!' she cried. 'How big are your feet? Big, aren't they, for a seven-year-old? I've got some BOOTS for you!'

She tore upstairs, startling the chickens from the bottom step, pulling herself up energetically with the banister, and Freddie heard her crashing around upstairs. Then he heard a cry.

'Got 'em! The little beauties.'

She reappeared, clambering downstairs with a pair of black boots in her hand. They looked new, the soles thick and clean, the long laces unfrayed. Freddie eyed them dubiously.

'Are they girls' boots?'

'No. I wouldn't give you girls' boots, Fred. These were mine, yes, but they were men's boots my William got me for working on the farm, and I never did wear them, too tight they were. But I've looked after them, kept rubbing in the saddle soap, kept the leather nice and soft. Go on – try them.'

Her excitement was infectious. Freddie beamed as he slipped his feet inside the boots and stood up. Immediately he felt taller and more important. He gave Granny Barcussy a hug.

'Thank you.'

'Are they too big?'

'A bit.'

'Right – that's a good thing. You'll grow into them. And if they're too big we'll stuff 'em with sheep's wool.'

She produced some of that, too, from a box next to her spinning wheel, and soon Freddie was marching around in the garden, feeling as if his feet were in bed. He felt like a normal person who was worth something. He wanted to stay with Granny Barcussy forever.

'When I'm grown up,' he said, 'I want to find a wife just like you. She'll have long black hair and her name will be Kate.'

Chapter Five

A RED RIBBON

Freddie had always given horses a wide berth. He didn't dislike them, he was just wary. Annie often told him the story of how her brother had been killed in a horse-and-cart accident. The horse had bolted through the market, scattering pedestrians and overturning traders' stalls. Annie had been there and she relished the telling of the story, each time adding a detail and exaggerating more. The horse went faster each time, the screams were louder, pots and pans and boots and shoes from the overturned stalls were strewn far and wide, the fruit barrow toppled and hordes of apples rolled wildly down the street. When the cart finally crashed, her brother was thrown even higher into the air and was even more dead when he landed. Freddie always listened, wide-eyed, fascinated not so much by the story but by the effect it had on Annie's normally dour appearance. Telling a story brought her to life, her eyes sparkled and her cheeks flushed redder and redder as she galloped through the story. There were pauses too, crisp silences where Freddie held his breath, his eyes fixed on Annie's face.

The storytelling became a ritual. Round the fire on a rainswept evening, or under the apple tree on a balmy afternoon. Despite his difficulty with communication, Levi had stories too, and when he started in his gravelly voice, Freddie was transfixed. Most of Levi's tales were funny, but Levi never smiled or laughed. He would tell the story, po-faced, and his silences were longer than Annie's. Being part of one of Levi's silences was like pole-vaulting over the river, that moment of uncertainty in the air when you didn't know which way you were going to fall. Then Annie and Freddie would scream with laughter while Levi remained po-faced, only the occasional spark of pleasure straying into his eyes. Finally he would add, 'I don't know what you're laughing at. 'Twere true as I'm sitting here.'

Some of Levi's stories involved horses, usually casting

them in a negative role, and Freddie's wariness of horses evolved from the storytelling rather than from actual experience.

So when he found himself facing a massive Shire horse in a narrow lane, Freddie's heart almost stopped.

Annie had sent him to the village of Hilbegut, a two-mile walk, with a cracked white basin in his hand and some pennies tied in the corner of his hanky. The faggot man was coming to the village. He had a barrow piled high with pork faggots which disappeared rapidly as soon as he started selling.

'Get three, if you can. And don't drop them,' Annie had said. Now that he had boots, Freddie was sent on longer and longer errands to neighbouring villages. He was eleven now, and still wearing Granny Barcussy's boots which were now too tight. There were holes in both the leather soles, letting in the water and the stones, and his feet were again sore and blistered. It was November now, nearly time for Christmas. He was hoping for a present, just one, and what he wanted most was a penknife, his own knife so that he could whittle sticks and carve owls and monkey faces out of the wood he'd collected.

'If I run, I'll drop the basin,' thought Freddie, so he stood still, facing up to the Shire horse. It appeared to be loose in the lane with only a leather halter on its head. Freddie looked at the horse's knees, which were the size of two dinner plates. Its coat was a lustrous black, with four creamy white skirts of long hair around its hooves and a white stripe down its face. Its mane was so thick that he could hardly see the eyes, but he knew the horse was looking at him. He considered flinging the basin in the ditch and making a run for it.

The horse tossed its head and gave a reverberating sneeze, and a few drops of spray reached Freddie's face. He had three options: jump over the wide ditch which was full of water, reverse into the prickly hawthorn hedge on the other side, or sneak past the horse with his basin, past its tree-trunk legs and massive rump. What if it kicked him? One kick and he'd be dead.

Freddie was scraping up his courage to try the sneaking past option, when he heard a strong bright voice from behind the hedge.

'You stay still, Daisy. I'm just shutting the gate.'

Daisy? What a name for a giant with dinner-plate knees. Freddie backed into a prickly hawthorn tree and peered through its berry-laden twigs, his mouth open in astonishment as a little girl emerged from a gateway and marched up to the horse with a confident swagger, her long dark hair swinging. She wore a red dress with a white ruffled pinafore over it, tightly laced boots and a rather tatty red ribbon in her hair. But what Freddie noticed was the glow in her dark eyes and the way she skipped happily up to the big Shire horse and picked up the trailing reins. The horse bent its huge head and blew softly out of velvet nostrils. Obviously it loved and trusted the tiny girl who was so absorbed with it that she didn't notice Freddie standing against the hedge.

What she did next took his breath away. First she kissed the horse's soft muzzle. Talking all the time in a voice like a chirruping robin, the little girl persuaded the horse to turn around, its metal shoes scrunching on the gravel. She led it back and coaxed it round until it was standing alongside the gate. Then she climbed energetically up the bars, stood on the top bar, and leaped expertly onto the horse's bare back, opening her legs wide to stretch across the broad withers. She had sunburnt little knees as if she was used to hitching up her long dress and racing about in the sun. She looked relaxed and at home on the horse's back.

High in the air, she rode past Freddie, her eyes alight, her plume of hair blowing in the breeze. She didn't notice him at all. Freddie thought she was beautiful. And he saw how carefully the big horse plodded away down the lane with its precious cargo. He watched the little girl's straight back and the horse's shining rump disappearing with the slow clop-clop of its hooves, and he wished he had spoken to her. He could have asked her name.

Quickly he put the basin down and climbed a nearby ash tree to watch where she went. He thought she might be a Romany gipsy. She had the same bold manner and vibrant eyes of the gipsy children he had seen. But no, she was heading down a farm track between post and rail fencing, the Shire horse still moving placidly. She lived on a farm. A proper farm. Round golden haystacks, barns with red roofs and a farmhouse with several groups of cream-coloured chimneys. The horse and the little girl disappeared through the entrance gate which had two tall stone pillars with carvings on the top. The sun was shining on them and Freddie could just make out what they were. Animals with curly manes and fierce faces. Were they dogs? Or lions? Freddie had never seen a lion for real, only a picture of one, and he'd read about them in Rudyard Kipling. He knew that lions represented power. What kind of girl would live in a house with two stone lions guarding it? A rich girl, he thought.

Beyond the farm, half hidden behind a blaze of copper beeches, he could see another intriguing building with turrets and minarets. Hilbegut Court, he thought, awed. He had heard of Hilbegut Court and the squire who lived there like the king of the village. A flock of jackdaws evidently lived there too, he noticed as they flew up, chack-chacking, and a flight of white doves circled glittering against the sky twisting and turning in formation.

The little girl probably lived at Hilbegut Farm, he concluded.

The sound of voices wafted over the fields, he could hear her robin-like voice, and the laughter of the children playing. He longed to go nearer and peep, and, more than anything he wanted a closer look at the stone lions. It excited him to think of them sitting up there staring into the sunlight, glaring into the night, shrugging off the rain and the wind, appearing on winter mornings with icicles hanging from their jaws and hoar frost capping their manes.

There were so many things Freddie wanted to do. He wanted to go fishing, he wanted to carve wood with a penknife he didn't have, he wanted to go to the cemetery and spend time studying the stone carvings there, the sweet faces of angels and the ornate letterings, the exciting gargoyles round the edge of the church roof who snarled down at him and made him shiver. He wanted to go pole-vaulting over the river like the boys he'd watched one day as he'd crossed the bridge on one of his endless errands. They were boys from his school, big boys, and they laughed at him and called him 'snowball' because of his white blond hair.

Now he wanted to go to Hilbegut Farm and feel the burning gaze of the stone lions. He wanted to sit in the sweet meadow hay and smell the summer, hide and keep watch to see that girl with the red ribbon. He tucked her away in his mind, putting her top of all the treasures he'd stored in there, to think about on his long cold walks. He'd paint a picture of her, riding the majestic Shire horse with her hair blowing in the breeze, if only he could have a piece of paper. At school they were allowed one piece each per week, for the art lesson, and Harry Price usually arranged a few bottles and an apple on his table.

'Draw that,' he'd bark, and stalk around the classroom criticising their efforts. They were never allowed to do a picture of their own. So strong was Freddie's need to do the picture in his head that he actually considered stealing a piece of paper. Today it was November the 11th. Christmas wasn't far away. He might hope for a drawing book instead of a penknife.

Still sitting in the ash tree, he heard shouting and

three boys came running round the corner. They were yelling and jumping, pushing each other and throwing their caps in the air. Freddie climbed down quickly to grab the white basin which he'd left in the grass. He expected the boys to stop and ask his name and what he was doing there, but they clattered past in their rough boots, and one of them waved and winked at Freddie.

'Come on!' he cried, and ran on.

Puzzled by the exuberance, Freddie followed at a distance, the basin under his arm. It was an awkward, slippery, heavy thing to be carrying in his small fingers.

Approaching the village where the faggot man traded, he noticed the church and people milling around it. Something was happening. Instead of standing in a miserable queue, men and women were dancing and shouting, waving strips of cloth and throwing their hats in the air. Freddie stood against a wall, watching, half afraid of the unfamiliar riotous scene. He was used to misery. Now the whole village seemed to be going mad.

Suddenly a forgotten sound jangled across the countryside. The bells. The church bells. Ringing and ringing. Freddie could feel the stone walls trembling under his hands and down the backs of his legs. The clangour of the bells lifted his mind into mysterious halls of wonder, a place where everything was spun from gold. He'd never been to a party, and now a party had come to him, filling the sky with music.

The whole landscape seemed to shiver with the unaccustomed revelry. Flocks of finches and yellow hammers bobbed along the hedges with extra bounce, and the trees threw down the last of their leaves in swirls of gold. The cows started to gallop, bucking and twisting, with their ridiculous tails in the air, their hooves squelching. In the next-door field the sheep clumped together and stampeded. And all the dogs of Hilbegut village and beyond were barking like the symphony of a thousand dogs.

Some children scuttled past him, rolling hoops of rusty metal. Freddie grabbed at a boy's coat.

'What's happening?' he asked.

The boy gave Freddie a wild toothy grin.

'Don't you know?' he said. 'The war is over.' He clenched his fists and shouted at the sky, 'The war is OVER.'

Freddie absorbed this information in silence. He didn't know how to dance and celebrate and throw his hat in the air like the boy was doing.

'Do you know where the faggot man is?' he asked.

'The faggot man? I dunno. Ask me mum,' said the boy, and his eyes lit up. 'We ain't gonna need no faggot man now. No more queuing, see? They'll be shops, proper shops with things in 'em. Want a go with my hoop?'

Freddie shook his head, looking at the metal hoop the boy held out to him. He'd never played with a hoop. In fact he'd never played at all, except with Granny Barcussy. He'd never even had a friend.

'Come on, Jack!' yelled another boy further along the road.

'Gotta go.' With another toothy smile, the boy ran off to join his friends.

The war was over.

And suddenly it hit Freddie. The loneliness. The overwhelming loneliness. The hard work, the hunger, the long cold walks to school, the worrying about his mother. What difference did it make to him that the war was over?

Freddie slid to the ground, wrapped his arms around his knees and hid his face from the world. An old and merciless sensation was erupting from the middle of his chest into his throat like boiling water. He hadn't cried since he was very little, and Annie had reprimanded him for it. 'Stop that noise,' she'd barked, and he'd learned how to swallow the sobs deep into his being. But they were still in there. All that crying he hadn't done, and now he couldn't stop. It was massive. Stone after stone, shaking his thin body like a bombardment. The autumn sun was warm on his hair, he could hear the bells and the cheering, but all he wanted to do was cry. He cried and cried until his body felt boneless like a fungus clinging there against the wall.

'What's the matter with me? I'm useless,' he said aloud, and then Levi's words came marching into his mind. 'Don't you EVER be like me' and he'd said, 'I won't be.' But was he?

The following Wednesday at school, Freddie realised the effect the end of the war was having on everyone. Even Harry Price. A stiff smile had cracked his leather face, and he had a cardboard box on his desk with sweets in it.

'The war is over!' Harry Price had bellowed, and he'd seized a handful of sweets and flung them at the children.

'Well go on. Eat them,' he'd laughed as the children sat in stunned silence, not daring to touch the sweets that twinkled tantalisingly. 'If you don't want them I'll take them back.' Harry Price took a step forward, his eyes mischievous, and the children moved, scrabbling for the sweets. Freddie had three of them, a boiled raspberry, a striped humbug, and a toffee. He didn't dare eat them but stuffed them quickly into his pocket to look at later.

'Now,' said Harry Price when the excitement had died down, 'it's time for the art lesson. And just this once, only once, mind, you can do any picture you like.'

Freddie's heart soared. He took his rectangle of clean white paper and smoothed it on his desk in disbelief.

'And you can use these crayons,' Harry Price was saying, 'I've been saving these for a long time.'

A battered tobacco tin appeared on Freddie's desk with stubs of wax crayons inside.

'Work carefully. And don't break them. And don't get the paper sticky. And don't . . .'

Freddie heard no more. For the next hour he was completely engrossed in his picture. He did the Shire horse first, starting with its head, and even though Daisy had only been wearing a halter, he drew an elaborate bridle with studs and curly patterns on the leather. He did her eyes black, leaving a tiny crescent of white to make them look shiny. He did a set of horse brasses dangling down her chest, each one different and intricate. He drew her four enormous legs with the long skirts of hair, and her orangey-gold hooves peeping out. He drew the metal shoes with the little triangle at the front, and the seven nails hammered in and bent over each hoof.

Harry Price strolled around, smoking his pipe and making observations on the children's drawings.

'I'm surprised,' he kept saying, 'surprised what you can do.' When he came to Freddie he stood for a long time in silence, and Freddie tensed, but he went on drawing confidently, working his way round the Shire horse, making its body rounded and sleek, drawing each crinkly hair of its mane and tail.

'A horse is the hardest thing to draw,' said Harry Price, and he picked up Freddie's picture and held it up. 'Look what Freddie's done.'

The whole class gasped, and suddenly Freddie was the centre of attention; children who had teased him were smiling at him admiringly.

'I haven't finished it yet, Sir,' he said anxiously, and Harry Price put the picture down and moved on.

'Only quarter of an hour left,' he said, and the children groaned.

Freddie got to work again. Could he draw the little girl with the red ribbon in such a short time? His pencil moved swiftly, surely, as if an invisible hand was guiding him. Freddie started to tingle with excitement. His grandfather was there again. He was holding his hand over Freddie's small one, steering the pencil, drawing the little girl's vivid face, her long hair flowing in the wind, the curls of it, the red ribbon fluttering. Then her straight back, the ruffles on her pinafore, her leg gripping the horse's back. Freddie rubbed out part of the back so that she would look real, as if she was really sitting there. He paused to see what he had drawn, and was unexpectedly overwhelmed by it. Had he really drawn it? It was good. He had captured something precious. And he wanted to keep it.

Harry Price loomed. He always collected the children's artwork and they never saw it again. Freddie wanted his picture to keep forever, to show Granny Barcussy and his parents. He wanted it on his bedroom wall to look at before he went to sleep. He thought quickly. Waited until Harry Price walked away. Then he picked up his picture, crept past the hot stove, right to the door, opened it stealthily with one hand, and made a run for it.

It was raining hard. He tucked the picture under his jacket and ran with his heart pounding at his ribs, across the wet playground, splashing through muddy puddles.

'COME BACK HERE, BOY,' he heard Harry Price roar after him.

Freddie struggled with the iron latch of the gate, throwing it open with a squeak of hinges. He bounded down the steps and ran hard, feeling the picture crumpling against his body, the rain plastering his hair, the puddles filling his boots.

And he knew he could never go back.

Nor could he go home.

Panting, he paused under the shelter of the lych gate by the cemetery. It had two benches inside and he sat on one, ready for flight if anyone came chasing after him. He was steaming hot and his breath rasped painfully. But he had the picture. He took it out and looked at it, thrilled; it made him smile. Where could he hide it? And how could he keep it dry? Already it was puckered and limp. Reluctantly he folded it into four, then once more, and stuffed it in his jacket pocket.

Harry Price would complain to his dad again, and Levi would go into a fury. He'd make Freddie take the picture back and apologise. The injustice of it stung. The only option was to hide it and pretend he hadn't got it, and take it out years later when everyone had forgotten about his crime. There was only one person he could trust. Granny Barcussy.

Freddie set off on the two-mile walk in the pouring rain. Mud sucked at his boots, his socks hung round his ankles like sodden sponges, and the water seeped down the back of his neck and trickled inside his jacket. He kept his hand over the pocket where his picture was, trying to keep it dry as he walked and ran alternately, across the squelching sheep fields and into the wood. Imagining Granny Barcussy's face when she saw the picture kept him going. She'd give him soup and dry his clothes and let him tell her what had happened. And she'd hide the picture for him in a secret drawer she had in her bureau.

Under the lime tree where his grandfather first appeared in his haze of primrose light, Freddie lingered just long enough to remember that summer day and the warmth of Granny Barcussy's greeting. Now he was sopping wet, starving and frightened by what he had done. She would be better able to deal with it than his mother.

He trudged on across the carpet of sodden leaves, out of the wood and down towards the river. The water was brown and swirling, washing sticks and foam against the bridge as he ran over. Now he could see the round terracotta chimney of Granny Barcussy's place, and it struck him as odd that no smoke was rising from it.

A strange feeling hovered around the farmhouse, a thick silence that seemed to reach out towards him, pushing him away. Freddie walked slower and slower, his hand over the picture in his pocket. He wondered if Granny Barcussy knew the war was over. He'd tell her. And he'd give her one of the precious sweets in his pocket, the humbug he thought she'd like. Then he'd chop wood and light a fire for her.

With those bright thoughts he ran the last stretch to the farmhouse door, undid the latch and pushed it open. It smelled musty and the fireplace was full of ashes, cold and unlit. He touched the empty rocking chair and it creaked, rocking a little on the flagstone floor.

'Where are you, Granny?'

Leaving wet splodges of footprints Freddie went to the kitchen, surprised to see the door swinging open. He peered inside, and saw the worn soles of Granny Barcussy's boots facing him on the floor. She lay there, on her side, her white hair, unrolled from its usual bun, spread out across the stone floor. A stain of blood, now old and dark, oozed from under her neck. Her cheeks and lips were blue-white, her eyes closed under eyelids that had the cold sheen of marble.

The nine chickens were clustered around her, cuddled together along the length of her frail body and in

the crook of her arm, roosting there quietly, like guardians.

Shocked, Freddie touched the black knitted shawl that covered her shoulder. She felt strange, like a log broken from a tree. He touched her blue hand. It was stiff and icy cold.

Freddie sat down on the floor and stared at her. He stared until he realised he could no longer see the bright aura that had always shone out of her. The light had gone out. And then he knew.

Granny Barcussy was dead.

Freddie felt oddly calm. First he took a cream wax candle from the jar, set it in the metal candlestick and lit it with a match. The glow flickered warmly in the rain-darkened room, moving the peachy light up the damp walls, making shadows of the kettle and the pots and pans, lighting the wise eyes of Freddie's china owl which stood on the dresser.

Then he fetched the red tartan rug from the back of the sofa and arranged it gently over her, right over her face and hair. The chickens murmured but didn't move. Then Freddie lay down on part of the rug beside her, cuddled up to her in his wet clothes, and closed his eyes.

Chapter Six

'SHADES OF THE PRISON-HOUSE'

Levi stared into the solicitor's eyes for a long time. They were dark brown and unwavering over the top of a pair of round gold-rimmed spectacles. The lower lids were red and pimply, the skin sagging into half-moons of shadow, giving Arthur Warcombe a look like that of a bloodhound. He didn't suffer fools, and he wouldn't wait much longer for Levi's decision. His black fountain pen gleamed in his hand, a minute bead of Quink on the gold nib, waiting above the document on his desk.

'I've never, in my life, taken a risk like this,' Levi said.

'Well, now is the time, my man. Now. It won't wait.'

'Ah.' Levi thought about Annie and Freddie waiting for him at home. "Tis my missus, see. She can't manage no more. Can't go out – won't go out. And my younger lad, Freddie, twelve he is and clever. The village school can't teach him no more, he's learned it all, and now he's bored. Two more years he's gotta go there, wasting time. I gotta show him how to make a life. That's what I gotta do. And this – well 'tis an opportunity.'

'He'd be better off in school here – it's just down the road, a good school from what I hear.'

'Ah,' said Levi again, his mind moving several squares ahead, seeing Freddie as a young man leaving school at fourteen, and Annie, hiding indoors. He loved their cottage, but it would be better for all of them to live in town.

'I've known you a long time, Levi, and your father before you,' said Arthur. 'And I wouldn't give you this advice if I didn't think you could handle it.'

Levi thrummed his fingers on the desk, looking out of the window at a cherry tree in full blossom, its white petals drifting down the street like snowflakes. People were walking past the window along the pavement. To Levi they looked energetic and smart, not downtrodden

and defensive like Annie. He saw a boy pedalling past on a bike with shiny handlebars; the boy looked purposeful and in charge of his life. Levi wanted Freddie to be like that, not forever white-faced and exhausted as he carried buckets from the well and chopped wood for the fire.

'Well then – now – I'll do it,' said Levi, and Arthur handed him the fountain pen.

'Good man. No, don't sign yet. We need a witness.'

He rang a brass bell on his desk and his secretary appeared, standing stiffly at the door in her stone-grey suit and shiny black shoes. She watched importantly while Levi signed the cream-coloured document, wrote his name and address and the date. Arthur lit a match and took a stick of red sealing wax from the tray on his desk, melted it over the flame and dropped a neat round blob onto the paper. He pressed a seal into it before it dried.

'There. Congratulations, Mr Barcussy. You are now a baker, and a landlord. Good luck.'

Levi shook his hand, the rare spark of a smile in his eyes. A baker, and a landlord. He began to shake, deep inside his stomach, uncontrollably, and, feeling it spreading down to his painful knees, he stood up and left the office, leaning on the polished knob of his walking stick as he hobbled down the steep stairs. Outside in the street he put his cap on, then took it off again, threw it up in the air, and allowed a smile to unlock his face which had been tightly closed for years under a florid mask of resignation.

He strutted down the street, past Monterose Post Office and the church, the graveyard and the Board School. Through the cattle market and down the next street which had houses one side and tall elm trees on the other. At the end of it, Levi saw the roof of his new property coming into view, and it felt like the sun rising. Leaning on the garden wall he savoured the strength of the stones, sun-warmed and inlaid with intricate lichens, yellow stonecrop and toadflax. Inside the wall on the sunny side was a mass of pink and white valerian covered in butterflies. It was a long time since Levi had even glanced at flowers and butterflies, but now he gazed, his soul hungry for beauty. This was his garden. His paradise garden. Annie would love it.

His eyes moved down the overgrown path to the door next to the shop window and looked up at the dilapidated sign. A new one was needed. Barcussy's Bakery. It sounded grand. Freddie would help him paint the big letters. Annie would be inside that big window in an apron as white as a goose, welcoming people into the shop, while he and Freddie made the loaves and rolls, the currant buns and the lardy cake. Levi could smell it cooking as he stood there. Freddie would have the sturdy bicycle with the delivery basket on the front and he'd go out, cleanly dressed and confident with his cargo of fresh bread.

Levi got over the wall and walked across the over-grown lawn. He stood looking at the rest of the terrace which consisted of two cottages, each with a garden. Suddenly he could smell the musty interiors, feel the heavy sag of the red tiled roofs, the collapsed chimney at one end and the bulging crop of ivy which housed a colony of sparrows. He peered through one of the dark window panes and saw a room lit by a hole in the roof. On the floor were big puddles, and in the fireplace a group of rats sat up with stiff whiskers looking at him knowingly, as rats do. This is our place. Not yours. It belongs to us rats, and the jackdaws in the chimney watching with their blue eyes, and the ivy tearing the stones apart with sinuous creepers. It belongs to the rain and the wind and the mould and the frost. Don't think you can change it, human.

Levi's exuberance was totally eclipsed.

'What have I done?' he said to himself. 'How am I

going to cope with all of this? And my money's all gone. All of it.'

Freddie had a plan for his life.

First he had to endure school until he was fourteen. He did his work diligently in beautiful copperplate writing that he was proud of, he did his arithmetic accurately and with relish, and read the books he was told to read. None of it challenged him now. Sitting in a class whose ages ranged from five to thirteen, he'd heard the same history and geography lessons over and over; he'd sung the same old songs and heard the same old Bible stories. He developed strategies to deal with his boredom, and dreaming was top of the list. He felt useless and imprisoned, except on the rare occasions when Harry Price asked him to help the 'little ones' or mark the register or clean the blackboard.

He longed to be fourteen. On his birthday he would leave school forever and learn to be a mechanic. Then when he was sixteen, old enough to drive, he planned to buy a lorry and start a haulage business. And he'd save every penny to buy tools and paints for the art he wanted to do. In his mind he had a queue of pictures waiting to be painted and sculptures waiting to be carved. He grew increasingly resentful of his wasted time in school. At home he had no time to himself at all, always out on errands or helping with the endless tasks that needed to be done. Sometimes he stayed up late in his bedroom making models by candlelight, as quietly as he could. His latest was a model of a queen wasp which he'd found hibernating in a fold of the curtains. He'd caught her under a glass jar and studied every detail of her stripy body, then he'd made a model using an acorn and a hazelnut shell. The face was a tiny triangular piece of wood cut from a clothes peg and drawn in ink, the legs and antenna from bits of wire found in the hedge. The yellow paint he'd begged from the sign-maker's work-shop in the village, a precious spoonful in a tobacco tin, and the brush he made from a chicken feather. The wings were two of Annie's hairpins.

Annie was thrilled with the model. She made Freddie take it to school, but Harry Price wasn't interested.

'So that's what you waste your time on is it?' he mocked. 'Making silly models of wasps.'

Freddie thought carefully about what he was going to say in reply. He tucked the anger away in a corner of his mind, looked Harry Price in the eye, and spoke slowly.

'I need to practise making models,' he said calmly, 'because one day I'm going to make aeroplanes for the war and I think that's important, don't you, Sir?'

The mole on Harry Price's right cheek began to twitch, and the pupils of his dispassionate eyes became small pinheads.

'Well, Frederick – and what war are we talking about?' he asked. 'The war ended years ago, or were you too busy making models to notice?'

Again Freddie allowed a silence to hover as the words dropped into his mind like aniseed balls from a jar.

'When you are an old man,' he said, 'I'll be a young man, and World War Two will come. And I'm not going to fight. I'm going to make aeroplanes. About the nineteen thirties, I would say.'

'Oh, and how do you know this? You can see into the future now, can you?'

'Yes.'

'Yes, what?'

'Sir.' Freddie searched Harry Price's eyes and discovered a sea of fear lurking behind a barrage of anger.

'And stop staring at me like that, boy. Insolent. That's what you are. And arrogant.' Then Harry Price lost his temper, as Freddie had known he would, thumping the desk so hard that a tray of pencils jumped in the air and scattered, some rolling onto the wooden floor.

Freddie wasn't fazed. Quietly he picked up the fallen pencils and put them back.

'Arrogant. That's what you are,' shouted Harry Price. 'Look at me when I'm talking to you, boy.'

'Excuse me – Sir –but you just told me to stop looking at you,' said Freddie quietly, and he strolled back to his desk, lifted the lid and put the model wasp inside.

'I've got better things to do than talk to a boy who thinks he can see into the future.'

Ignoring Harry Price's blustering and the extravagant curls of smoke that suddenly puffed from his pipe, Freddie opened his copy of *Treasure Island* and tried to read. He was aware of the other children glancing at him as much as they dared, and he felt a sense of kinship with them. But the words on the page blurred into a mist. All he could see was a vision of a fleet of aeroplanes lined up on a vast airfield in the rain. They weren't like the ones he had seen. These were small, elegant planes with rounded wing tips and rounded noses lifted towards the eastern sky. The clouds rolled back and he heard the roar of the brave little planes, as they took off one by one into the dawn. And he saw himself, a grown man, standing watching on the airfield, wearing dark blue overalls, a spanner in his hand.

The vision made him feel strong.

★   ★   ★

When he got home from school, Freddie was surprised to see his father there, sitting under the apple tree. Annie was with him and the two of them were talking animatedly.

'Now, you sit yourself down, Fred. I got something to tell you,' said Levi in a rather ominous tone, and Freddie sat down on the grass, and looked at his father, puzzled by the unusual sparkle in his eyes.

'Now,' said Levi again. 'You take this in, Fred. 'Cause this is what your life is gonna be in a few years when you leave school. I got a job, and a business all lined up for you. What do you think of that?'

Freddie didn't answer. He felt a shadow creeping over his shoulders, the shadow of a great wall which his parents would build to keep him in confinement.

Levi rushed on, anticipating a smile on his son's face, a light in his eyes, gratitude.

'I bought a bakery,' he said proudly. 'And it's got all the equipment, the ovens, the recipes, the big bicycle with the basket on front. In town, it is, near the railway. We're going to live there. There's a school just down the road you can go to.'

'And a shop at the front,' said Annie. 'You and Levi's going to be making the bread, and I'll be behind the counter selling it.'

'And – I haven't finished,' said Levi. 'It's got a terrace of two cottages. We'll live in one, and let the other – just need a lick of paint, they do – and that will bring in some money, plenty of money. What with that, and the bakery, you'll have a ready-made job to go to when you leave school, Fred, and one day, when you're old enough, you'll take over the business.'

A bolt of pain shot through Freddie's mind. A baker. They wanted him to be a baker.

'I done it for you, lad, and for your mother,' continued Levi, puzzled by the way Freddie was staring stonily at the sky.

'She can't go out much. Now she won't have to. There's work for all three of us, years of work. I done it for you.'

Annie was frowning at Freddie. 'Say thank you,' she mouthed.

'Thank you.'

''Tis a risk,' said Levi. 'Cost me all my money, it did.'

'Granny Barcussy's money?' Freddie's eyes stung with the threat of tears.

'Ah. Granny Barcussy's money.'

Freddie stood up. Even the soles of his feet burned with anger. But I won't be like Dad, he thought. I won't lose my temper. I won't. I will not. His face went hard with the effort, hard as glass, and his fists ached in his pockets. He looked at Levi who was sitting with his back against the apple tree, his hands idly collecting petals from the fallen blossom, scooping them into his palm and blowing them playfully at Annie.

He's got no idea what I want, Freddie thought. I'll have to tell him, somehow.

And then he saw her. Granny Barcussy. Floating like steam, and radiant as sunlight, in the air next to Levi. She wore a robe that glistened with the colours she'd loved, he could smell the honeysuckle and lavender she had grown, and sense the warmth of her. She didn't look haggard and old now, her skin was smooth and her eyes full of life and compassion. She looked directly at Freddie and her smile melted his anger. It was the same mischievous smile she'd always had, and now she held a finger to her lips and shook her head. He heard her voice.

'Don't tell him,' she said. 'Not now. You keep the peace.'

She disappeared gently, like salt dissolving in water, and Freddie became aware that Annie was looking at him with an alarmed expression on her face. He wasn't allowed to tell her, but she knew, Freddie was sure. The hours of eye contact he'd had with his mother on those long difficult walks, the way their souls had been linked by her panic, as if he was her anchor forever chained to her, and she was his lifeboat, safe, but blotting out the light.

'I'll talk to him,' she said to Levi. 'He just needs time to think about it.'

'Aye. 'Tis a big thing. For a lad,' Levi nodded, struggled to his feet and brushed the apple blossom from his trousers. 'I'll leave you to it.'

Freddie sat down again, close to his mother's bottle-green dress and the white apron she wore so proudly. They were better dressed since the war had ended. He had a new shirt and shorts, socks without darns and new brown boots, a warm jacket and a cap.

'Did Harry Price like the queen wasp?' asked Annie.

'No.'

'More fool him,' said Annie. 'The old misery. Well, now you can wave him goodbye. You can go to a new school in town. They've got four teachers there, and one of them is a lady. A Miss Francis. She takes the top class, and they say she's very nice, and clever.'

'But Mother – I don't want to be a baker. I want to make aeroplanes.'

'I know.' Annie put her arm round Freddie. He was twelve now, tall for his age, his white blond hair had darkened a little. She looked at his long fingers. 'You've got hands like your dad. Do you know what he wanted to do when he was young?'

'What?'

'He wanted to be a jeweller.'

'A jeweller?' Freddie stared at her in surprise. 'Why wasn't he, then? What stopped him?'

'His hands were too big. He couldn't do the delicate work, so he had to give up his dream. Just as I had to give up my dream.'

'Your dream? You had a dream? What was it?'

'I wanted to be florist – to grow flowers and make them up into bouquets and wreaths. I was good at it. But then the family came along, needed me to do the washing and the baking and the scrubbing and the nursing, and then the war came. We've all had to make do, and do things we don't want, Freddie. And you will too. This bakery idea, it's perfect for your father. He won't have to go out in the cold and the wet with his arthritis, he can work at home in a warm dry bakery. It's perfect. We've gotta help him, Freddie. Give it a chance.'

Freddie sighed.

'But all my life I've been doing things I don't want to do.'

'I know,' said Annie kindly. 'But your turn will come. You'll see.'

'It hasn't so far.'

Freddie looked gloomily at his mother. Her grey curly hair was scattered with apple blossom petals, her red cheeks shining with excitement. The hope in her dark blue eyes was underlaid with layers and layers of old fear and old pain going deep into the distances of her soul, and right at the far end was a little child full of love who only wanted to pick flowers. He felt sorry for her.

'You've had a hard life,' he said.

She nodded slowly. 'But the hardest thing,' she said, 'is my fear, Freddie. Night and day it's with me. I'm a strong woman, got to be, but that fear is stronger than me. It's like an illness, but it's invisible. No one knows, Freddie, only you. No one knows what I go through.'

'Isn't there a medicine for it?' Freddie asked.

Annie shook her head vigorously. 'Even if there was, I daren't tell the doctor, daren't ask for it.'

'Why?'

'Because – he'll think I'm mad, and they lock you up, in these terrible places. Asylums, they call them. I'm not going to one of those, ever. I'd rather be dead,' she said fiercely, wagging her finger at Freddie. 'And don't you let them take me.'

''Course I won't. I'll take care of you,' said Freddie, now feeling the weight of the shadow that hung over his shoulders, darker and denser as he thought about what was to come. A shadow over his dreams. Instead of making aeroplanes he was expected to be a baker and he couldn't bear the thought of standing there making bread, shut away from the world. Instead of marrying a brave bright girl, like the girl on the horse, he'd have to be his mother's guardian. For how long?

People kept telling him the war had been fought, and all those soldiers had given their lives, so that he, Frederick Barcussy, could be free. But he wasn't free. He wondered if God had got it wrong.

He undid his school satchel and took out a piece of paper which he unrolled and showed to his mother.

'We had to copy this poem,' he said. 'It's a long poem but we've got to learn this verse of it by heart and say it to Mr Price. Shall I read it to you?'

'Yes please. You know I like poetry.'

Annie sat back to listen. She loved to hear Freddie read.

'This is another William,' he said. 'William Wordsworth.'

'Oh – Daffodils?'

'No. This is different. Listen.'

Freddie spread the paper out and began to read, the words falling like the apple blossom petals into Annie's troubled mind. But as he read on, he got tense and emotional, hardly able to read at all.

> *'Our birth is but a sleep and a forgetting;*
> *The Soul that rises with us, our life's Star*
> *Hath had elsewhere its setting*
> *And cometh from afar;*
> *Not in entire forgetfulness*
> *And not in utter nakedness*
> *But trailing clouds of glory do we come*
> *From God, who is our home:*
> *Heaven lies about us in our infancy!*
> *Shades of the prison-house begin to close*
> *Upon the growing boy . . .'*

Freddie stopped, unable to continue.

'That's it then. Isn't it? Shades of the prison-house – that's my life – and yours.'

Chapter Seven

THE GOLDEN BIRD

The young girl with the red ribbon in her hair carried the billycan of fresh milk out through the gates where the two stone lions watched her pass below in the September sunlight. She crossed the road and walked up the village street until she came to another stone gateway, two pillars with a coat of arms carved on each and painted in blue, black and gold. Inside the gates a magnificent avenue of copper beeches led to Hilbegut Court, residence of the Squire of Hilbegut.

Built from Bath stone, with turrets and minarets between the tall golden chimneys, it was an ornate and imposing place. Although fully occupied by the Squire and his servants, it still seemed to belong to the hordes of jackdaws who nested in the complex chimneys and cubbyholes of the roof. At dusk, the blue-eyed birds performed a spectacular ritual of formation flying, swooping to roost and covering the entire roof with their fluttering black bodies. Today they knew, by the arrival of the girl with the billycan, that it was nine o'clock in the morning, and just before the clock tower reverberated with its nine chimes, they flew down and strutted around the lawns.

The young girl bustled up the steps to the oak door which stood in its own archway of golden stone. She pulled the white porcelain knob of the doorbell and waited, listening to the bell jangling deep inside the house, and the tap-tap of footsteps. A flustered-looking maid opened the door.

'Hello, Miss Kate. The Squire's waiting for you.'

'Hello, Millie.'

With her back very straight and her long hair swinging, Kate stepped through the porch and into the great hall of Hilbegut Court. At the far end the Squire of Hilbegut sat at his breakfast table, his legs in brown riding boots stretched wide, his pipe in his hand. His expression was gloomy, but when he saw Kate his eyes lit up and he gave his moustache a tweak. Captivated by her radiance and her confidence, he watched her coming down the hall towards him. She was only a child from the farm, the daughter of his tenant, bringing his milk, but she walked like a princess and smiled like a nurse. He could have had the milk delivered straight to the kitchen, but he wanted to see the child. Sometimes her mother came, or her sister, and then he was disappointed. It was Kate he wanted to see. He loved the way she tried so hard to behave but her eyes had a wicked, expectant sparkle.

'I've brought your milk, Sir.'

'Is it fresh?' he asked, not because he wanted to know, but because he wanted her to talk to him. She always had some bright tale to tell him.

'Oh yes, Sir,' said Kate. 'It's Jenny Lu's milk. She's a Jersey cow, and I milked her myself. Ethie helped me. We sat one each side on two three-legged stools and we got the giggles.'

'The giggles?' The Squire raised his ginger eyebrows, pretending he didn't know what the giggles were, just to engage Kate in more conversation.

He was rewarded with the radiant smile which brought such warmth and cheeriness into his neglected heart. The child trusted him like no one else did.

'The giggles,' she announced, putting the billycan on the table, 'is when you can't stop laughing.'

Since he rarely laughed, that sounded like a song from a party to which he hadn't been invited. Taking the lid off the billycan he poured the fresh milk into a waiting tumbler, and took a long drink.

'Beautiful,' he said. 'More of that tomorrow, please.'

Kate's eyes had turned solemn.

'Well – this is the last time I can come,' she said. 'Tomorrow my mum will bring it for you.'

'And why is that?'

'I'm going away. To boarding school with Ethie. I'm eleven now,' said Kate, and for the first time the Squire thought he saw a cloud pass through her sunny eyes.

'Ah,' he said, hiding his disappointment. 'So you're growing up now, are you? And how do you feel about boarding school? Won't you miss your mum?'

The cloud rushed through her eyes again, but Kate seemed to have an internal light switch. She lifted her chin and gave him a smile that made him feel the whole world was all right, God was in his heaven and all would be well.

'I'm going to enjoy every minute of it. Especially –' Kate leaned forward and whispered dramatically, 'the midnight feasts.'

The Squire put his hand into the pocket of his clean tweed jacket, and fumbled with the coins in there. He took out a silver half-crown and pressed it into Kate's small hand.

'Thank you,' she gasped. 'That's very kind of you.'

'You get some chocolate. For your midnight feasts. And I want to hear all about it when you come home.' He managed a smile, or what he hoped was a smile. 'Goodbye now.'

Kate knew she was supposed to walk out of Hilbegut Court in a lady-like manner, but the half-crown was so exciting that she tucked it in her pinafore pocket, lifted the skirt of her red dress and skipped away down the hall, turning once to wave at the sad old Squire who was staring after her. She would have liked to tickle him under his arm and round his ribs and make him laugh out loud like she did with her father, but she knew her mother wouldn't approve.

She danced all the way home, in and out of the copper beeches, the leaves crackling like cornflakes under her laced boots. Scooping armfuls of leaves from the hollows around the tree roots, she flung them into the air, whirling and laughing as they fluttered down into her hair. At the end of the avenue she paused and took a last look at the turrets and chimneys of Hilbegut Court, and the jackdaws flew up, chack-chacking as if saying goodbye.

It was to be a day of last looks for Kate, and her older sister Ethie, but Ethie was used to it. Ethie was thirteen and bored with it all, and she spent a lot of energy trying to be responsible. This morning she'd said scathingly, 'You don't have to say goodbye to each individual chicken, Kate.'

But Kate loved every animal on the farm, even the massive Hereford bull steaming and stamping in his well-barricaded corner of the barn. She wanted to touch the bristly backs of the pigs and watch their ears twitch as she told them her news; she wanted to look into the velvety faces of the sheep, and smooth the coat of every cow. And Daisy, the Shire horse, she'd already said goodbye to about six times, her arms wrapped around the horse's kindly face.

Kate didn't want to grow up. She didn't want to get cross and busty like Ethie. She wanted to stay eleven for the rest of her life.

As she skipped through the gate between the stone lions, it began to rain in a silver downpour. Kate ran for the swing which was set in the barn door on two scratchy ropes. She loved to swing backwards into the high dusty interior and sail out into the glistening rain, and sing: 'Out in the rain and in again, out in the rain and in again.' The squeak of the ropes, the rush of air on her face, the extravagant rhythm, created a time to sort out her thoughts, chuck out the bad ones and keep the good.

Tomorrow morning the half past ten train would carry her away, like a log on a swollen river. Her father would turn the pony and cart round and drive home at a brisk trot, without her.

But it didn't work out quite as expected.

Kate got down from the swing and ran into the kitchen where her mother was making butter at the kitchen table. Her cheeks were tense and pale, and instead of greeting her daughter in her usual peaceful way, she said, 'We'll have to change our plans for tomorrow morning, Kate. Your father's not well, and I'm afraid he's too poorly to drive to the station. I'll have to do it, or Ethie will.'

'What's wrong with Daddy?' asked Kate, watching her mother's eyes.

'We don't know,' said her mother shortly.

Kate sat down at the oak table and rested her chin on her two hands, studying her mother's face. Sally Loxley was giving nothing away. She went on beating and beating the milk in a round white basin; she wouldn't stop until it turned to butter and then she would separate the whey, and work the butter between two wooden butter pats, over and over, working the beads of moisture out of it. She'd won prizes for her butter-and cheese-making and the certificates were displayed inside a glass cabinet, along with several silver cups. The largest of these was inscribed with 'Best all round Farm', awarded to her husband Gilbert Loxley, Bertie.

Sally was a sturdy woman, energetic and calm. She'd raised four children, two boys who had both married and emigrated to Canada, then after a ten-year gap, Ethie had come along, and finally Kate. The two girls had grown up at Hilbegut Farm among the cider orchards and peat-cutting areas of the Somerset Levels. Bertie ran his own tenant farm as well as overseeing the farms and cottages owned by the Squire. The good wages and abundant crops had continued even through the war, and now the family had sufficient wealth to send Ethie and Kate to boarding school on the Dorset coast.

It was rare for Sally to look worried, but she did now, and it alarmed Kate. Something bad had happened, on this last day before she went away to school. She never remembered her father being ill. He was up at first light, organised and hard-working, but always made time to talk to his children. Kate adored him. He'd played games with her, read her stories, and showed her how to love and care for animals, trusted her to fetch the gentle Shire horse on her own, let her care for orphan lambs and piglets. He often said, 'Our Kate – she could run the farm on her own.'

'Where is Daddy?' she asked now.

'In bed.'

'In bed! So what is it, Mummy? The 'flu?'

'No. We don't know, dear, 'til the doctor comes. But he looks bad.'

'I don't want to go to boarding school when Daddy is ill,' said Kate. 'I've made up my mind. I'm going to stay and look after him.'

'No, dear. No, you've got to go. You can't miss the first day, it's so important.'

'But Daddy is important, to me.'

'I can look after him.'

'No you can't, Mummy. And you can't run the farm on your own. Who's going to milk the cows?'

'Don't tell me what I can't do, Kate. You go up and see your father, see what he wants you to do.' Sally looked wearily at her daughter's assertive expression. She didn't need a battle with her now. 'And don't twist your father round your little finger – madam,' she added, in a good-humoured way.

Kate flounced up the stairs, her cheeks hot with

determination. She pushed open the varnished wood door to her parents' bedroom and swanned up to the bed.

'Daddy?'

What she saw extinguished her enthusiasm like a candle-flame being snuffed out. The man looking at her from the bed was a pale ghost of the father she knew. The sparkle had gone from his eyes, they looked like two bubbles surrounded by shadows, and his skin was a sickly yellow. Even the whites of his eyes were yellow. He tried to smile, but it didn't convince Kate. Obviously her father was seriously ill.

Shocked, she sat down in the green Lloyd Loom chair beside the bed, and reached for his hand, which lay limply on the satiny brown eiderdown. Her hand looked pink against his yellow skin.

'What is it, Daddy?'

'I don't know,' he whispered. 'Not 'til the doctor's been.'

'I'm going to stay home and look after you. And I'll milk the cows,' said Kate firmly.

Her father put his arm round her as she sat on the bed, and his fingers twiddled the ends of her hair.

'My Kate,' he said. 'You're a good girl.'

'I'll do anything you want, Daddy, to help you get better.'

'Now you listen to me,' said Bertie, and his eyes shone out of his sickly face. 'What I want, Kate, is for you to go to school. You put that smart uniform on in the morning, and you go, without any fuss, and get a good education. That's what I want.'

'But Daddy—'

'No buts. And no argument, please. Ethie is going to stay, 'til I'm better. She's older and stronger than you, Kate.'

Tears of frustration ran down Kate's face.

'It's not fair, Daddy. I'm a much better nurse than Ethie. I'll cheer you up. Ethie is so cross and grumpy.'

'I know, but Ethie will do her best, Kate. Come on, you do your best for me, go to school and that will make me happy.'

Exhausted, Bertie sank back against the stack of lavender-scented pillows Sally had arranged for him. Kate gazed at him, her lips twitching with the conflicting feelings in her mind. She held her father's hand tightly while he dozed, and she could feel the love and the ebbing strength he was sending her through those work-worn fingers. She felt as if she was part of him. She was the bright love and encouragement he'd given her all her life. She was the beaming smile that lived inside Bertie's soul, a smile more powerful than the sun.

Kate had come upstairs determined to refuse to go to school. She felt old enough and well capable of nursing her father, giving him back some of that love, making him smile. She would put a rose on his breakfast tray on the snowy white cloth. She'd cover his boiled egg with a cheerful red and green cosy she'd knitted. She'd write jokes on a square of paper, fold it into sixteen triangles, and hide it in his napkin for him to find. Then she'd sit on his bed and chatter. Kate knew what her father needed, better than Ethie did. It wasn't fair. Or was it?

Ethie had almost finished her education, begrudgingly, now she only wanted to leave school and work at home. She was perfectly capable of running the farm, making butter and cheese, making clothes on the treadle sewing machine. But she worked mechanically and joylessly, only laughing when Kate was with her.

It didn't take Kate long to change her mind.

'All right, Daddy. If that's what you want,' she said, 'I'll go to school. I was looking forward to it.'

Bertie opened his eyes and saw her smile.

'That's my girl,' he said huskily. 'My golden bird.'

Kate's face lit up.

'Tell me again, Daddy – about the golden bird,' she begged. 'Please, Daddy.'

'Come here then.'

Kate snuggled onto the bed, curling her legs up, her head resting on Bertie's shoulder. She could hear his heart going faster as he started to talk, his breath rattling a little. His voice grew stronger as he told their favourite story, his hands twined in his daughter's wavy hair, enjoying the bright energy of her presence.

'When you were born,' he began, 'here in this room, 'twas a scorcher, one of the hottest days in the summer. The cows were in the shade under the elm trees swishing their tails, and the horses were standing in the river up to their bellies. I was downstairs making cheese in the kitchen, and listening to the midwife walking about upstairs, I could hear the ceiling creaking and squeaking. It was scary, for me down there, listening. When Ethie was born, she didn't come easy and there was a lot of noise, but when you were born your mother never made a sound. It was a surprise. I heard one scream, at three o'clock, and it wasn't a scream of pain, it was a scream of joy.' Bertie stopped for breath and Kate glanced up at the yellow skin of his face, thinking that already a hint of pink was returning to his cheeks.

'Then –' he continued. 'The clock struck three – one – two – three chimes, the door opened, and the midwife called me to go up. Oh I went up those stairs three at a time, wiping my hands on—' He paused, waiting for Kate to giggle as she always did at that part of the story. He looked at her bright eyes.

'On the seat of your trousers!' she squealed.

'Yes,' fuelled by her ringing laugh Bertie continued, lowering his voice as he approached the magical part of the story. 'Well, I went in, and there you were, bright as a button in your mother's arms and she was sitting up in bed with her face round and smiling like a dinner plate.'

'Was I crying?' asked Kate.

'No. You weren't. You were lovely. The midwife wrapped you in a cream shawl and put you in my arms. I carried you over to the window, and there, outside, on a branch of the walnut tree, was a golden bird.' He lowered his voice to a whisper. 'And none of us had ever seen a bird like it before. It was bright orange-yellow, sitting there in the tree, and it stayed there, singing. It stayed in the garden for the rest of the day.'

'What was it?' Kate asked, even though she knew the answer.

'A golden oriole,' said Bertie. 'We asked old Mrs Barcussy and she knew; she looked it up in a book she'd got about birds, and showed us a picture of it. It came over from Europe, she said, and a very rare visitor, it was. So that's why I called you my golden bird.'

'And my name,' said Kate. 'Oriole Kate, that's why.'

'That's why.' Bertie closed his eyes again and the breath rattled in his chest. 'Oriole Kate.'

They rested, each thinking about the golden bird. The effort of talking had drained Bertie, but he was struggling to tell her something else.

'There's a legend,' he said, 'that if a golden bird appears when a baby is born, it . . .'

His voice faded away and he sank deeper into the pillows, his eyes fixed on Kate's eager face. Then the door opened and Ethie came in with a bucket. She looked sourly at her younger sister curled on the bed.

'You shouldn't be in here, Kate,' she said curtly, 'Daddy's too ill to cope with you bouncing around.'

'I'm not bouncing around, I'm cheering him up.'

'That's MY job now,' said Ethie fiercely. 'I'm staying here and you should be packing, shouldn't you?'

Kate felt that Ethie wanted to drag her off the bed, the fierce jealousy in Ethie's eyes made her uncomfortable. She smiled, but the smile only made Ethie look even more draconian. Kate wanted to keep the peace, so she got off the bed and kissed her father on the cheek.

'I'm going to pack right now,' she said, 'and I'm going to enjoy it.'

Chapter Eight

PLAYING TRUANT

Monterose was a small Somerset market town, centred around the railway which curved its way through cuttings in the hills and over viaducts and embankments. The town was half on a hill and half in a river valley, the lower part of it flooded for much of the winter. Boats were rowed along the streets and wild swans, ducks and geese swam in and out of gardens and cottages where the occupants lived upstairs from November to March. The top half of the town had a busy market square and a capacious church with the loudest bells in the county.

The railway station was a magnet for Freddie. The

thrilling power of the steam engines fired him up as if he had swallowed a furnace. When he wasn't making bread or going to school he ran down the street to the station and hung around watching coal being shovelled, wild-eyed cattle being loaded into trucks, and the spectacular cauliflowers of steam erupting from the saddle-back engine as it shunted to and fro. He was fascinated by the fire inside it and the glimpses of sooty-faced men working in the cab, the white gleam of their eyes as they shovelled and shouted. Freddie spent so much time there that his clothes started to smell of coal, and Annie complained. So did his father, and Freddie was given a brush which was kept outside for him to brush himself down before being allowed back into the bakery.

He soon discovered there was money to be earned at the station by carrying luggage over the cream and brown footbridge. Passengers put their hands in their pockets and gave him tuppence, or thruppence. Freddie made friends with the other boys who went racing down the hill after school to earn money at the station. At first he watched and listened, soon figuring out that it wasn't always the pushy boy who got asked to carry luggage. It was the cleanest ones, the strongest-looking and most respectful. Freddie soon learned how to doff his cap and call people 'Sir' and 'Madam', and how to look after his money. He memorised the times of trains and found out which trains would have the wealthiest passengers.

Every morning he rose at 5 a.m. to help bake the bread. By then Levi was taking the first batch out of the three coke ovens and Annie loading the shelves in the shop or cleaning the window. By 7 a.m. the whole street smelled of fresh bread and Freddie stacked the bicycle basket with loaves for the round he had to do before school. Usually he had breakfast, a big chunk of lardy cake and a cup of cocoa before setting off. Once he'd discovered the station, he took his lardy cake with him to eat while he waited for trains. If he did his bread-round quickly, he managed to be there for the eight o'clock and the eight-thirty trains, and still get to school at nine.

He liked the teacher, Miss Francis, but despite being in the top class there seemed to be very little for him to learn. He was far ahead of the rest of the class in reading, writing and maths and there were no workbooks to take him further. Sitting at the back of the class, Freddie spent a lot of time daydreaming, drawing, and reading his way through a set of *Encyclopaedia Britannica* and the works of Dickens and Robert Louis Stevenson. Miss

Francis told his father Freddie should go to university, but the thought of more study filled him with horror. He wanted to get out there and do real work with engines. He didn't want to be a baker, and he didn't want to waste his life sitting in school.

One September morning he decided not to go. He'd be there for the ten-thirty train to Weymouth. It wasn't a decision he'd taken by himself. Granny Barcussy had appeared to him in a dream, and she was unfolding a piece of drawing paper, holding it up to show him, and it was his picture of the little girl on the Shire horse. Annie had extracted it from Freddie's wet jacket, ironed it under a cloth and put it in an old picture frame on top of a photo she didn't like. It hung on the wall halfway up the stairs, and even though Freddie protested that he could now draw much better than that, Annie insisted on keeping it there, as if she wanted to cling to a relic of the child he had been.

In the dream, Granny Barcussy had shown him Monterose station and pointed at the clock. It was ten thirty. She wanted him to be there. So he went, pretending he was going to school as normal, then running round the back of the bakery, through an alleyway and down the hill to the station, his breakfast wrapped in a cloth under his arm. He prayed he wouldn't be found out. Deceiving his parents wasn't something he enjoyed, but lately it had become an essential part of his life.

Annie never went out, and Levi spent most of his time working in the bakery. Freddie felt oddly calm about what he was doing. He thought about Miss Francis calling the register at school, questioning why he was absent, but he didn't care.

He was a tall boy now, taller than anyone in his class, and he felt awkward at school. Living in Monterose had been his education. At weekends and holidays, when he escaped from the bakery, Freddie had hung around watching men at work. He watched the wheelwrights and was allowed to help occasionally, and he learned everything he could about motorcars. If he saw one with the bonnet open, he would go and ask questions, finding people were usually proud to explain the workings of the engine to him. Freddie's favourite place was the stonemason's yard where he sat wistfully on the wall looking at the statues and tombstones being made.

In long strides he headed for the station, thinking there were two other trains due, and he'd have no competition. He felt jaunty and independent, a new feeling in his life, one that he wanted to cultivate.

With one and fourpence safely in his pocket from the two early trains, Freddie climbed up the grassy

embankment and sat there to eat his lardy cake peace-
fully in the morning sun.

'Shouldn't you be in school, lad?' the stationmaster,
Charlie, paused to shout up to him.

Freddie shrugged.

'Playing truant, eh?' asked Charlie with a wink.

'I'm too big for school,' said Freddie. 'And I need to
earn a bit of cash.'

'What you gonna spend it on then? Eh?'

'A lorry.'

Charlie laughed loudly. 'Ah, you'll be buying a whole
load of trouble. I don't like those petrol lorries. Stinking
things. I suppose you'll be meeting the ten-thirty
Weymouth train today? They'll be plenty of wealthy
folk putting the precious daughters on there, sending
'em off to that posh boarding school.'

Ethie had always been savagely jealous of Kate. From
the moment Kate had been born, Ethie had felt
unwanted and her sadness had curdled into a thunder-
cloud lurking over her life. Sally had tried to treat her
two girls exactly the same, but the contrast between
Kate's exuberance and Ethie's negativity made such an
ideal impossible.

Today Ethie felt smug that she, not Kate, had been

asked to stay at home and run the farm while her father was ill. She hoped Kate would have a hard time, as she had done, starting at boarding school on her own. Ethie felt creepily adult as she headed off to catch the pony and harness her into the cart, proud that her parents trusted her to take Kate to the train.

The bay pony, Polly, was known to be 'cussèd'. Once caught and harnessed she behaved beautifully, trotting with her neck arched and her toes pointed like a dancer. Loose in the field, Polly was reluctant to relinquish her freedom. She didn't much like Ethie, so that morning Polly chose to be awkward. Round and round the field she trotted, snorting, her nose in the air. She came close and snatched the square of bread Ethie held out to her, then spun around and galloped off.

Ethie got more and more exasperated.

'WILL you come here?' she called. 'You wretched PIG of a horse.'

Furious, she ran after Polly, hoping to head her off and get her in a corner, but time after time the pony kinked her tail and cantered off to the opposite corner, where she stood tossing her mane and looking triumphant. Ethie got hotter and hotter, dressed in her farming gear, heavy breeches, boots and jacket. The sound of the Hilbegut Court clock chiming nine was the last straw. They'd agreed to leave at nine, allowing plenty of time for the pony and cart to reach Monterose station. Polly should have been caught, groomed and harnessed by now.

Ethie could have cried with rage, but she wasn't good at crying. She'd seen girls at school who cried daintily into lace hankies with hardly a sniff. But if Ethie cried, it was ugly. Loud and snorty and convulsive, so embarrassing that people pushed her away instead of comforting her. So Ethie had turned her tears into anger, stamping about for hours with her face set rigid like a cardboard mask.

As the clock chimed, Kate appeared at the backdoor with her mother, dressed in her new grey and scarlet uniform. She looked good in it, her hair plaited in two thick braids, each with a red ribbon, one over each shoulder, the round grey hat just at the right angle over her expectant face. She was chattering as usual, and she and her mother were standing by the cart waiting.

'I can't catch this infernal damned pony,' Ethie roared. 'How am I supposed to harness her if she won't be caught? She won't. She WILL NOT. I've finished with her. I'm not doing it. She's the most impossible, stupid damned awkward animal in the whole of this farm. It'd be easier to catch a cow than catch THAT.'

Ethie snarled like a dog and flung the halter over the gate. 'You catch her if you want to go to the station.'

'ETHELDRA.' Her mother's voice boomed like a foghorn when there was a crisis. Even the chickens froze, and the two farm dogs slunk away and lay shivering against a wall. Sally only called her oldest daughter by her full name – Etheldra – if she was extremely displeased. 'Get a hold of yourself,' she thundered, 'your father is ILL, and we have to get Kate to school. Pick up that halter.'

Begrudgingly Ethie did as she was told, her face dark as a Victoria plum.

'I can catch Polly,' said Kate.

'Not in your uniform please,' objected Sally, her voice back to normal.

'I won't get it dirty, Mummy. It'll be all right.'

Kate took the halter from Ethie's angry red fist.

'Don't worry, Ethie, I've caught Polly lots of times,' she said, picking up a fallen apple from the garden.

When Polly saw Kate coming into the field she turned into a different pony. She trotted over to Kate, making whickering noises in greeting, then she took the apple and stood placidly while Kate slipped the halter over her head.

'Oh, well done. That's my girl,' said Sally, but Ethie

refused to look pleased. Her temper had set in for the day, like a weather front. She glowered and muttered as they led Polly over to the cart. The three of them harnessed her up between them, buckling straps and organising the cart in silence. Only Kate talked, non-stop, to the pony, and Polly flicked her ears back to listen. Kate ran her hand down the pony's sleek forelegs and inspected the neat little hooves.

'Kate, your UNIFORM,' protested Sally. 'It's already covered in hairs, and you can't start school smelling like a horse.'

Kate giggled, and Ethie's frown wavered for a second as she caught her sister's mischievous eyes.

'Don't START,' said Ethie, rolling her eyes and tutting.

Kate had lifted up Polly's near foreleg. 'She's got a shoe loose.'

'Oh lor,' said Sally. 'How bad is it?'

'One of the nails is up.' Kate fiddled with the metal shoe. 'She ought not to go on it, Mummy.'

'We can't bother about it now,' said Sally, 'just hope for the best.' She handed Ethie a watch on a chain. 'It's nearly half past nine. You'll have to drive hard to get there. But be careful, Ethie, don't get reckless, especially in Monterose with all those motorcars they've got now.

And just remember, Polly might be frightened by the trains. Get there early and move her away before it arrives.'

Kate turned to say goodbye to her mother, looked searchingly into her eyes, and there was a moment when both of them almost cried.

'Don't you worry – Daddy will get better,' said Sally. 'You just keep your chin up, Kate.'

'Will you COME ON, Kate.' Ethie was up in the cart, the reins in her hand, a tall whip propped in its slot beside her. The sun beat down on her face, her pimples itched annoyingly and her hair stuck to the back of her neck. She felt as if an over-tuned engine was hammering away inside her, and that she, not Polly, was the one being driven.

Impatient to start, Polly set off at a furious trot, the high wheels of the cart bumping over the stony driveway. Kate sat facing backwards, drinking in her last look at Hilbegut Farm, waving as her mother got smaller and smaller. The two stone lions stared sightlessly after them as they sped into the distance towards Monterose.

Freddie was earning lots of money. He was amazed to see the St Christopher's girls turning up at the station in their grey and scarlet uniforms, arriving in a variety of motorcars and horse-drawn carts. He ran to carry their luggage, mostly brown leather suitcases with names on the lid and hard knobs at each corner which bruised his shins mercilessly. The girls intrigued him. Neat plaits and clean pink faces, so different from the ratty-tatty bunch he saw at school. Their voices were different too. Ringing and confident. Except for a few who looked apprehensive and timid, and one who was sobbing relentlessly.

They were arriving early, so Freddie had plenty of opportunities, even a queue waiting for him. Time after time he carried cases over the cream and brown foot-bridge with girls who smelled of mothballs and soap, padding beside him in polished shoes. One tiny blonde girl was terrified of walking over the bridge where she could see the gleaming railway below through cracks between the boards. Her distraught mother was trying to drag her.

'I'll take her,' said Freddie, sensing the child's genuine terror. Remembering the times he had coaxed Annie a step at a time, he used those tactics now, holding the child's icy little hands and making her look at his eyes as he talked her over the bridge. Then he squatted down and looked into her face. 'When you come back,' he said, 'I'll be here again to help you, you needn't be afraid. My name's Freddie. All right?' The child nodded gratefully, her big eyes shining under the new oversized hat.

'You're a very special young man.' Her mother, draped in fox furs and an immaculate cream suit, looked at Freddie approvingly. She opened her heavy pigskin handbag, took out a coin that flashed in the sun, and pressed it into his hand. A florin! Two whole shillings. He'd never had one before.

'Thank you.'

'My pleasure. And the name is Joan Jarvis.'

The platform was now crowded with children and their parents. The man in the signal box pulled a lever with both hands, and the red and white signal clunked down. A train whistle screeched through the cutting and from the top of the bridge Freddie could see puffs of steam rising from the hills. Charlie pounded over the bridge, a rolled-up green flag in his hand.

'Be glad to see this lot off,' he winked at Freddie. 'Spoilt little madams, ain't 'em?'

Freddie leaned on the bridge to wait for the train, while he tied the precious florin into his hanky, which was now so full of money it weighed his pocket down like a stone. He relished the anticipation of counting it and hiding it under the floorboards.

Then he heard a terrible sound.

The clatter of hooves on the road, the banging of wheels. And screaming. Everyone seemed to be screaming.

'Look out. Stand back.'

'Out of the way.'

'Stop that pony.'

Freddie bounded down the stairs two at a time and out of the station gate, the nerves twanging in his stomach. It was Annie's story, for real. A horse and cart bolting through a crowded street, people screaming, barrows overturning.

It was quick, and yet the moments seemed ponderously slow to Freddie. With his hand over his mouth, he watched in horror as a pony came galloping wildly, sweat flying from its flanks, foam and blood around its mouth. The cart was bouncing and zig-zagging, and driving it was a girl with dripping wet hair and a face contorted with rage. She wasn't trying to stop the pony, she was thrashing the reins up and down. Words of fury spouted from her mouth as if she was a gargoyle.

Clinging with both hands to the sides of the cart was a girl in a scarlet and grey uniform, her plaits flying.

'Stop! Stop!' people were shouting.

'Whoa now. Whoa Polly.' Ethie hauled on the reins

and Polly slid to a halt, her flanks heaving. Ethie turned and shouted. 'Get out. Now. The train's coming.'

Freddie strode forward to help, and as he did so the train surged noisily into the station. He saw the younger girl trying to stand up from where she'd been clinging. Then the pony saw the train. Terrified, she wheeled around in a panic, the cart was hurled onto its side and both girls were flung into the air.

Ethie landed on the grass bank and quickly rolled over and sat up. But the girl in the St Christopher's uniform landed on the road with a sickening crack, and lay still.

A man in a cap moved forward to calm the plunging pony who was trying to drag the twisted wreckage of the cart. The train hissed as it pulled into the station, and a terrible silence descended over the scene.

Freddie reached the girl in a few strides. He picked up her hat from the road and knelt down beside her. She was motionless, her eyes tightly closed, her face peaceful. He remembered Granny Barcussy, how she had looked when he'd found her dead, how her shining aura had gone. This beautiful young girl wasn't dead, he knew that. She was in a cocoon of golden light, and only Freddie could see it.

But she was badly hurt, and deeply unconscious.

Blood was oozing in a dark pool across the road, soaking into the dust around her head. Freddie touched her arm and she felt hot and limp. He was aware of the people crowding round her, someone shouting and shouting for a doctor. He looked into the shocked eyes of the girl who had been driving the pony, and her skin was deathly white and blotchy, her lips still with terror.

'She's not dead,' said Freddie.

He glanced at the girl's suitcase lying nearby, and read the name embossed in white letters on the lid.

MISS ORIOLE KATE LOXLEY

HILBEGUT FARM

Hilbegut Farm! The stone lions. The girl on the Shire horse. It was her. Oriole Kate Loxley.

Chapter Nine

THE BONDING

The ten-thirty train steamed out of Monterose station with its precious cargo of children leaning out of the windows, waving to their parents. The atmosphere simmered with emotion, as parents craned on the edge of the platform to catch a last glimpse of the departing train. Hearing a shout, they turned to see Charlie thundering down the steps.

'Is there a doctor here? Or a Red Cross nurse?' he shouted. 'There's been a terrible accident – a little girl. Is there anyone who can help?'

The lady with the fox furs stepped forward.

'I'm Joan Jarvis and I was a Red Cross nurse,' she

said. 'And I have a motorcar here if she needs to go to hospital.'

'Come quickly, then. Quickly.'

A crowd had gathered around Kate, and Freddie was in the middle of it. In the moments before help arrived, he knelt close to Kate, hoping that somehow his presence might comfort her. He didn't know many prayers, so he made one up, saying it over and over in his mind. And he memorised every detail of Kate's face. To him she looked like a beautiful rose petal that had fallen there, her skin translucent, her lips a peachy pink, her eyelashes dark curling silks. She had high cheekbones, a softly rounded chin, and her nose, Freddie thought, was aristocratic, her nostrils like two perfect little shells. On her left temple was a small mole, and on her neck a tiny pink scar like a crescent moon.

Freddie had never been that close to a beautiful girl. Oblivious to everyone around him he committed her face to memory so that he could keep her image with him forever. It seemed like the longest and most fruitful moment of his life.

Clasping her hand between his two rough palms, he sensed the subtle vibration that was uniquely hers, singing to him like the harmonics from a bell, those rhythmic sound waves that rippled out and out until they were gone but not lost. He hoped his own hands were transferring a stream of his energy and strength into her. This mysterious healing force was something Freddie had experienced himself, from his mother's hand touching him when he was ill or hurt.

Watching Kate, through those eternal moments, he felt he was floating beside her, in a place of shining light, a sanctuary where there was no pain, no fear but only peace.

The noise of voices and running feet brought Freddie out of his trance unpleasantly like gravel spattering into his mind. Still holding Kate's hand, he kept his gaze focused on her face, watching her skin becoming paler and paler, the stillness deepening. He felt he was watching an angel, an angel slowly turning to stone.

'Move aside. Move back. Give her some air.' Charlie's voice was loud and rasp-like. 'This lady's a Red Cross nurse. Come on. Move back PLEASE.'

Freddie looked up then, into the coal-dark eyes of Ethie who was kneeling on the other side of Kate, and he saw straight into her frightened soul where guilt, frustration and terror were huddled together.

'Now then. I'm Joan. Let's have a look at the poor girl.'

The fox-fur lady was puffing and blowing from her

run across the footbridge. She took off her hat, and the fox furs fell to the ground in a slinky russet-coloured heap.

'Here, kneel on this, madam.' Charlie took off his coat and put it on the ground for her.

'Joan,' she said firmly. 'And put the coat over her, she's getting cold. Let go of her hands now, please.' She turned to Freddie. 'Ah – you again – you stay here, will you? I might need your help.'

'I'm Kate's sister,' said Ethie loudly. 'That boy's nothing to do with her,' and she narrowed her eyes at Freddie.

'Are you, dear? Now don't you worry. It always looks worse than it is,' said Joan. She smiled kindly at Ethie and gave her a little pat on the shoulder, a gesture which became a potent spark of love, igniting Ethie into an explosion of sobbing.

'Can someone look after her, please?' Joan appealed, and a buxom woman in a brown and white gingham dress stepped forward and led the sobbing Ethie away. She sat her down on the grassy bank and let her cry, holding her in both arms.

Ethie's sobs were peripheral to what was happening to Kate. Joan had checked her pulse and breathing, and was gently stroking her face.

'What's her name?' she asked Freddie.

'Miss Oriole Kate Loxley,' he said. 'From Hilbegut Farm – but I think they call her Kate, her sister did.'

'Come on, Kate.' Joan was gently tapping the child's cheek which was now ivory pale. 'She's deeply unconscious.'

'Cracked 'er 'ead,' said someone. ''Ell of a crack it were.'

'She must not be moved,' Joan said. 'She might have broken her neck, or her back. We must get her to hospital.'

Freddie was horrified. He began to go pale himself at the thought of the serious injuries Kate might have. He felt nauseous and giddy.

'You stay calm, lad,' said Joan, noting his white face. 'You're doing really well, Freddie. Are you her brother?'

'No.'

'Just take some deep breaths.'

Freddie sat back, determined he wasn't going to pass out, and he didn't. The feeling passed. He felt detached from Kate now, the image of her forever imprinted on his soul. There seemed to be little he could do to help her, except sit there and pray his prayer.

The shrill jangle of a bell announced the arrival of an old Model T ambulance with a red cross painted on it.

Everyone moved aside to allow it free passage down the street. In a daze, Freddie watched the driver and his crew of one nurse in a starched white hat. They brought a stretcher and carefully manoeuvred Kate onto it, immobilising her neck with big pads of brown leather. She didn't stir at all.

'Like the Sleeping Beauty, ain't she?' said Charlie who still had his rolled-up green flag in one hand.

'Someone should go with her,' said Joan, looking at Freddie.

'Her sister,' he said.

'She's in a bit of a state. Of course she is.' The motherly woman in brown gingham brought Ethie over to the ambulance. 'I'm Gladys,' she said, 'I'll go along with both of them. Someone's got to see to the pony. She's worried about it.'

And Freddie heard himself saying, 'I'll do that. I know where Hilbegut Farm is. I can lead the pony home.'

'She's called Polly,' said Ethie.

'I'll go ahead of you in my motorcar, and explain everything,' Joan offered. 'I know the way.'

Joan brushed herself down, and Freddie gingerly picked up the fox fur and handed it to her. They both stared after the ambulance as it revved and roared up the station road with Kate inside, its bell ringing urgently.

Freddie felt as if his whole life had been turned upside down and shaken violently, displacing his usual codes of behaviour.

'You're a very helpful young man, Freddie,' said Joan. 'I wish you were my son.'

With those encouraging words ringing in his ears, Freddie then found himself being given Polly's reins to hold. He'd never led a horse in his life but he tried to act as if he was used to it. Polly had been caught and disentangled from the cart, she'd had a rest and was munching grass from the bank.

'Take her gently,' advised the man who had caught her. 'She's very shaken, and a bit lame. It was a disgraceful way to treat a pony. I shall be lodging a complaint to that girl's parents. Headstrong young hussy.'

'What about the cart?' asked Freddie, eyeing the wreckage lying on the side of the road. One wheel had come off and was propped against a wall. 'I could get the wheelwright to fix it.'

'We'll do that,' said the man. 'You go on, 'tis a long walk to Hilbegut.'

Freddie set out awkwardly, surprised to find Polly walking meekly beside him. He remembered how Kate had been talking to the Shire horse, so he thought he would try it. What should he say? He wasn't used to talking non-stop the way Kate did, and he felt embarrassed. So he waited until they were out in the country and then started on 'Innisfree' and a few other poems he knew. Polly seemed to enjoy them. She flicked her ears and gave him a gentle nudge with her soft nose. He walked with his hand on the crest of her mane, scratching her gently, and he began to enjoy her company.

It was six miles to the village of Hilbegut, through beautiful countryside that Freddie knew well. Across the Levels, over the river bridge and through the peat-cutting fields where the 'ruckles' of cut peat stood in the hazy sun like a prehistoric village. Then through the withies, tall forests of willow stems shimmering red and gold, reflecting in the water. A pair of bitterns fishing, and vast flocks of lapwing with their strange wobbly flight that made their wings twinkle against the sky. The September meadows were full of the seed heads of knapweed, sorrel and thistle.

After the years in town, cooped up in the bakery, stuck all day in school, the walk into his old haunts was an unexpected delight for Freddie. He saw people working in the fields, cutting peat or bundling willow and it felt good to nod and touch his cap as he passed by, feeling proud to be leading Polly. He stopped by a stone water trough to let her have a drink, amused by the way she stuck her face in and sucked noisily at the water, then shook herself all over sending bright drops flying out.

'You're a nice pony, Polly,' he said. 'In fact you're lovely. I didn't know how lovely a horse could be.'

He leaned on her for a moment, his arm across her warm back, and wondered what it would be like to ride. Better not push his luck, he thought, especially after what Polly had been through that morning. A sense of togetherness settled into Freddie's heart as he plodded on with Polly. He liked the quiet way she walked beside him; it had an ambience of trust and acceptance. Freddie felt he had been walking alone all his life through lanes and fields and streets, and now he was no longer alone. It wasn't just Polly's company. It was Kate. He carried her now, in his soul. They had shared that shining sanctuary of peace, for a moment when time had stood still, and even though Kate was unconscious, he felt that she knew. They had bonded in spirit. Freddie was concerned for her, but he wasn't worried. He knew in his prophetic mind that she was going to recover.

The distant chimes of the Hilbegut Court clock interrupted his thinking. Twelve o'clock. Lunchtime at school. He must be home at the usual time. He planned to say nothing to his parents about his secret day, unless they asked, and then he would tell the truth. The time was coming when he would have to detach from them, stand up for himself. He was nearly fourteen, old enough to work, and he didn't want to be a baker.

The chimneys of Hilbegut Farm were coming into view now, and Polly had lifted her head, pricked her ears and was stepping out with new energy. Freddie walked with that thought going like a chant in time with his footsteps: 'Won't be a baker. I won't be a baker. I won't . . .'

The stone lions stared beyond him into the distance as he passed through the gate. After many secret visits in his childhood, he knew them well. They were old, and slightly different, covered in cream and soot-black lichens, both were snarling into the landscape, so alive that Freddie imagined them shaking the rain from their curly manes filling the air with droplets made fiery by the sun.

Passing through the gateway was a different sensation, as if the lions guarded a world from which he had been banned. Now Polly was taking him through, eagerly, and he felt a sense of gratitude, as if he had broken a seal, a way into fields of gold.

★   ★   ★

Ethie sat miserably in the hospital waiting-room on a brown leather chair. She felt grubby and unfeminine in her farm gear, her hair matted and dirty, her skin so prickly that she longed to run to the river and plunge her head into cool water. She wanted to strip naked, hurl her farm clothes into a dustbin, and wash and wash until the sweat and the pimples and the guilt had gone. The river would sweep her far out to sea, under the waves like a water baby, and transform her into a beautiful being whose captivating charm would guarantee eternal forgiveness.

Her parents would never forgive her for what she had done to Kate, and to Polly. She hadn't done it by mistake. She'd done it with a hatred, so strong it had driven her mercilessly like a demon on her shoulders. Ethie felt suicidal, and she didn't know how to deal with it.

She'd wanted to sit with Kate, be there when she opened her eyes, and say sorry, and Kate would forgive her like she always did. But the nurses had refused, stiffly, and Kate had been wheeled away on a squeaking trolley into the mysterious disinfected interior. Hours passed while the hospital clanked and rustled around her and every time the door opened Ethie jumped nervously, but nurses and other patients came and went, taking no notice of her.

133

At last her mother arrived with Joan, and Joan looked at Ethie kindly.

'Any news?' she asked.

'No. They won't tell me anything,' said Ethie.

'And are you feeling better, my dear?'

Ethie looked at Joan gratefully. No one usually called her 'my dear'. But she'd cried all her tears. She looked apprehensively at her mother, reading the darkness in her eyes as anger.

'I couldn't help it,' she said. 'We just got there and Polly was startled by the train. She . . .'

Sally gave Ethie a hug, patting her back reassuringly. 'Don't you distress yourself, Ethie. We'll talk about it tomorrow when you've had a bath and a rest. We just have to keep calm now and everything will be all right.'

Her kind words soothed her troubled daughter like hot cocoa.

'Kate's going to be all fine, you'll see,' said Joan.

The door opened again and a doctor in a white coat came in with a nurse fluttering beside him.

'Are you Mrs Loxley?' he asked.

'I am.' Sally's eyes flickered with anxiety.

'Your daughter is basically all right,' he said. 'She's conscious now. She's got a cut at the back of her head which we've stitched and bandaged. We've checked her thoroughly and everything is fine. She needs rest, that's all, to get over the concussion.'

Sally collapsed into a chair. 'Oh – thank God. Thank God,' she wept, and seemed incapable of saying anything else until she'd composed herself.

'You can see her in just a few minutes,' said the doctor. 'The nurse will fetch you.'

Sally nodded, her eyes misty. 'Our beautiful Kate,' she whispered. 'I couldn't bear to lose her. She's such a – a light – a shining light.'

'Freddie was right, wasn't he?' said Joan. 'And he's such an extraordinary young man.'

And Ethie glowered, thinking again of how she might float away in the river and become a beautiful sea nymph.

Kate lay quietly in the starched white bed, her eyes roaming around the unfamiliar hospital ward, her head tightly bandaged and her dark plaits, still with the red ribbons, over her shoulders. She was glad to be lying so comfortably, against a stack of pillows, and glad to be opposite a window which looked out on a clump of elm trees and the rooftops of Monterose. Hundreds of sparrows fussed on the roof tiles, and she could hear them chirruping, reminding her of the farmyard at home.

Her school uniform was neatly folded on the chair

next to her bed, and someone had put a jug of water and a glass on the table for her. She was fascinated by the nurses who glided to and fro like sailing boats. To find that someone so strict and efficient was also kind and cheerful was inspiring to Kate. Once she felt well enough to talk she asked so many questions that eventually the ward sister told her to be quiet and rest.

'She's a chatterbox,' she heard her saying.

'Where have I heard that before?' Sally came into the ward and straight to Kate's bed. Tears poured down her cheeks.

'Don't cry, Mummy. I'm all right.'

'I know. Silly, aren't I? These are good tears, Kate. Oh, I'm so, so thankful you're all right.'

'What about Daddy?' asked Kate.

'He's not very well, dear. He's got to stay in bed for two weeks. Doctor's given him some medicine – let's hope it works. Hope and pray.'

'And Ethie? Was Ethie hurt like me?'

'No, she wasn't,' said Sally carefully. 'But she's deeply upset, and sorry too.'

Kate was quiet. It wasn't the first time she'd puzzled and soul-searched over Ethie's behaviour. She decided not to say anything further, sensing that her mother had enough to deal with.

'I want to be a nurse, Mummy,' she said seriously, and then another question surfaced. 'What about Polly? Poor Polly, she was exhausted. She was sweating and she lost a shoe, and Ethie made her – made her gallop on the road when she didn't want to . . .'

Seeing her daughter close to tears Sally just hugged her quietly, rocking her a little.

'You stay calm, dear. Polly is fine. A nice young man brought her home, walked all the way with her. Freddie, he said his name was.'

'Oh.' Kate's eyes widened. 'I know him.'

'No, you don't. He's a big boy, not anyone from school that you know.'

'Oh, but I do,' said Kate. 'He was with me when I was lying in the road.'

'But how would you know that, Kate? You were out cold for two hours.'

'I saw him, Mummy. I did. He was with me, and he held my hand between his hands, and he had the bluest of blue eyes,' insisted Kate, 'and he . . .'

'He what?'

'Don't think I'm being silly, Mummy, but – he was like a guardian angel in ordinary clothes, a brown coat and a cap, and he made me better.'

Chapter Ten

THE LONELINESS
OF BEING DIFFERENT

Freddie lay awake that night, his face turned towards the sky. The harvest moon whitewashed the flaking paint on the open window, and lit up the treasures he kept there, his collection of bird's feathers, a chunk of alabaster, his tins and matchboxes, and Granny Barcussy's nature book. The night air smelled of cider and soot. As always, Freddie was listening to the owls in the distant countryside, his mind filtering out the sounds of the town. The owls made him feel at home again, where he felt he belonged.

But he did pay attention if a motorcar drove past the

bakery, sometimes even getting out of bed to watch the beam of headlights cutting through the darkness.

Engines fascinated him and he studied them at every opportunity. Today he'd had his first ever ride in one. Joan had driven him back from Hilbegut in her majestic Model T Ford, with its polished burgundy bonnet and silvery headlamps. She'd let him crank it for her, to start it, and he'd felt a buzz all up his spine when the engine responded, first with a splutter, then settling into a business-like rhythm.

'When you're old enough, you can have a go,' Joan promised, and Freddie was in awe of her as she confidently handled the huge metal beast, her bony arms steering it wildly through the lanes. He'd never been so fast in his life. Seeing hedges and trees whizzing past was strange and different, feeling the wind on his cheeks, and his legs vibrating as the car hurtled along the stony road.

He sat next to Kate's mother in the back, but they didn't talk. Sally clutched her hat with one hand and the back of Joan's seat with the other, sitting straight and alert as if she was driving herself. When they swept to a halt outside Monterose Hospital, Sally turned and looked at him.

'Thank you,' she said, 'for bringing Polly home. I don't know who you are – but I'm very grateful.'

Aware that he was playing truant from school, Freddie chose not to tell her he was Freddie Barcussy from the bakery. He just said, 'Kate is going to get better, I know it.'

'How do you know that?'

'I just do.' Freddie looked directly into Sally's surprised eyes and said no more. He thanked Joan for the ride, allowed himself one glance at the hospital where Kate was, and sprinted home through the wide streets of Monterose, reaching the bakery at his usual time of ten past four.

Sad that he couldn't tell his parents about this secret day, he'd gone to bed with his mind on fire.

The sound of the Model T Ford had set up home in his mind, a sound that was both satisfying and disturbing, like a new voice on earth.

The wooden clock in his bedroom seemed to tick faster and faster, and at two o'clock in the morning he got up, lit a candle and counted the clump of money tied in his hanky. It included the precious florin Joan had given him and he spent some time examining it in the candlelight. There were a few sixpences too, and in total he had earned ten shillings and ninepence. Breathing hard with excitement he prised open the floorboard under his bed and added the money to his hoard which was tied in a grey woollen sock, now so heavy that it had to be picked up with both hands.

Nothing had happened for years, and then so much had been packed into one day. His first experience of leading a pony, his nostalgic walk back to Hilbegut, the stone lions, the motorcar. All these events were stacked precariously in his mind and right in the middle was a window of honey-coloured light where he kept the memory of Kate.

Freddie sat on his bed in the candlelight and thought about her. The more he stared at the flame, the brighter it shone, growing tall with an edge of sapphire blue. Deep in its orange heart was an inviting archway. In his imagination he stepped through it, the flame was behind him, and he stood alone in a world of dazzling light. It was unlike any place he knew and yet he felt instantly at home there. The light energised and refreshed him, and in the bright core of the blaze was the face of an angel. He tried to see the wings, but the shifting patterns of iridescence were too swift. The eyes of the angel were all the colours of water, their expression imbued with wisdom and patience.

A voice called to him out of the light, its resonance infusing every shimmering strand like the wind blowing through wheat fields. He listened, and let the voice echo through him, through his hair, his skin, and the tips of his fingers.

'Many years will pass. Be patient. Be true to yourself. And, when the golden bird returns, you will meet her again.'

Drawing a breath from the night air, he returned with a jolt to his candlelit bedroom.

The words soaked into him, but Freddie had no idea what they meant. A golden bird? What golden bird? Mentally he ticked the ones he knew – a yellow hammer, a goldfinch, a canary. None of them fitted. He reached for Granny Barcussy's nature book which he kept by the bed. It was navy blue with the title embossed in gold letters, and inside was a cornucopia of painted illustrations and descriptions. Now he could feel her next to him, eagerly turning the pages in the dim candlelight, turning them faster and faster until a golden bird was there on the page, eating rowan berries from a branch. A golden oriole! He had it. Oriole Kate. She was named after a golden bird, and according to the text it was a rare visitor, and that described Kate perfectly, he thought, satisfied.

He'd never seen Kate properly, never looked into her eyes. He wanted to go down to the hospital with a bunch of roses. Red roses he'd give her. He drifted to sleep, threading the angel's words into the fabric of his life.

In the morning he awoke disturbed by a sense of foreboding. Mechanically he got up and helped Levi with the bread. They worked silently together putting batch after batch of risen loaves into the ovens, cottage loaves and tin loaves, French bread and the heavy lardy cake. He looked just once into his father's eyes as he packed the bicycle basket.

'You do your best at school today,' said Levi.

'Yes, Dad.'

'Don't go telling no lies.'

'No, Dad.'

'You know what I mean, Freddie. If you can't tell the truth, then keep quiet.'

Levi's drooping eyes looked at Freddie for a long moment, a moment he was to remember for the rest of his life.

'And look after your mother.'

'Yes, Dad.'

Freddie cycled off on the cumbersome bicycle into the misty morning. He didn't feel like going to school after yesterday's excitement. School seemed totally irrelevant. He didn't want to go, ever again.

★   ★   ★

144

Everyone in Monterose was gossiping about the accident at the station, and people came to look at the broken cart which was still lying there next morning with 'Gilbert Loxley, Farmers, Hilbegut Farm' painted proudly on the side of the cart.

'A disgrace, that's what it is.'

'It was the older daughter. Etheldra Loxley. She drove that poor pony like a mad woman. And her little sister in the back. Shame on her.'

'Could have killed someone.'

The gossip went on circulating until it reached the bakery.

Annie was coping happily with the queue. She loved being in the shop with the warm fragrance of freshly baked loaves. She enjoyed taking them down from the shelf and wrapping them in clean paper, then taking the money and chatting pleasantly. It was her ideal life. She didn't have to go out. Levi was there, and he was proud of what he had achieved, the bakery business was thriving. Freddie was nearly fourteen. Once he left school the business would do even better. Annie was satisfied that her son's life was mapped out for him.

Until it all changed.

'I saw your Freddie was there yesterday, at the

145

station,' said a woman in a brown and white gingham dress.

Annie frowned at her. 'What do you mean, Gladys? Freddie is at school that time of the morning.'

'He wasn't yesterday.'

'What?'

'Didn't you know?' Gladys had a piercing voice that filled the shop. 'Your Freddie was there. I saw him myself. And he was a good lad too.'

'What time was this?' Annie asked, and the sudden sharpness in her voice brought Levi out from the bakery, brushing the flour from his hands.

'Half past ten.'

'Half past TEN?' said Annie in astonishment. 'Freddie should have been in school.'

'Oh – well.' Gladys winked. She stood there with her hand on the loaf she had chosen, the rest of the queue listening. 'You know what these lads are. Boys will be boys, won't 'em?'

'And what was he doing? Are you sure it was Freddie?'

''Course it were. I know Freddie, he brings the bread round,' said Gladys, relishing the story. 'Well, I looked after the older girl, she was in a proper state, and Freddie was with the little 'un who got hurt so bad. And then he offered to lead the pony home, all the way to Hilbegut. Good of him.'

'WHAT?'

'And I'll bet he enjoyed his lift back in Joan Jarvis's posh new motorcar!'

Levi spoke then and the whole shop fell silent.

'Are you telling me that our Freddie was down there? And that he took some pony out to Hilbegut?'

'That's right, Sir.' Gladys looked staunchly at him over her brown and white gingham bust.

Levi's face went purple.

'Right.' With his big hands trembling he took off his baker's apron and hat and turned to Annie. 'You mind the shop. I'm going up the school, right now.'

The queue parted like the Red Sea to let Levi pass through, the whites of his eyes gleaming angrily. He took two strides into the street, and crashed to the ground, groaned and lay still, his huge body stretched out on the cobbles.

'Levi!' Annie screamed. She rushed outside and crumpled beside him. She cradled his dear face in her arms, and sat there rocking for long hopeless minutes. The morning sky darkened while they searched for his pulse and strained to hear him breathing, but Levi's mighty chest was still, his face frozen in anger.

''Tis too late. He's dead,' said Annie quietly, and she watched the last sparks of his life drift past her and disappear.

'You'll HAVE to go out now, Mother,' said Alice firmly.

'You'll have to get over it,' agreed Betty.

Annie sat miserably between her two daughters on the morning of Levi's funeral. Her heart was full of heat and teardrops, her grey hair a storm of impossible curls, her face swollen with grief. She was silent now, rocking slightly, her hand picking threads out of the black shawl around her shoulders. She'd repeated and repeated her words: 'I can't,' but no one would listen, and there was nothing left to say. Only Freddie understood her fear. She looked at him now, sitting in the window, his long legs folded awkwardly, his eyes staring into the garden. He would take care of her, she was sure. He'd leave school and run the bakery. They'd manage.

Betty and Alice had always collaborated in forecasting gloom. They'd been away from home for years, and Freddie had hardly seen them in his life. Annie knew he found them intimidating, especially today. Both were dressed in the blackest of black outfits, identical hats with black net veils covering their faces, trendy tight-fitting black skirts and jackets, and grim expressions to match. Annie felt she no longer knew who they were. To her, Betty and Alice were a long ago memory of happy children.

She looked at her elder son, George, who was hunched on a chair, so like Levi, inarticulate but wise. He'd arrived on a throbbing motorbike, and she could see that Freddie was fascinated by it, more interested in the bike than in his brother who was fifteen years his senior.

Annie had wanted to blame Freddie for Levi's sudden death, but she chose to keep quiet. A death was trouble enough. She understood Freddie's aversion to school. Surely he'd suffered enough, she reasoned, and in the months and years to come she would need him. Without Freddie, Annie saw herself ending up in the asylum. She even felt threatened by her two daughters, Alice the manager and Betty the echo. There was something ominous about the way they wanted to manage her, the cast-iron conviction they had about her agoraphobia. Levi had tolerated it, Freddie understood, but Alice and Betty wanted to deny its existence.

The slow clop-clopping of the horse-drawn hearse brought a respectful silence to the street. Neighbours stood outside their doors, workmen downed tools and took off their caps, playing children stood silently, their backs against the wall.

'It's coming,' said Freddie from his seat by the window.

Together they filed outside in their black clothes, with Annie wedged firmly between Alice and Betty.

It was the second funeral Freddie had experienced in his life. At Granny Barcussy's funeral he had walked, white-faced and distraught beside his father, and Annie had stayed at home, peering out at the sad procession. At the graveside Freddie had broken down and sobbed uncontrollably, and Levi had picked him up and held him like a baby. The smell of his coat and the feel of his big hands patting him had comforted Freddie.

Now he was nearly a man, and no one would comfort him at his father's graveside. He would have to stand there, stiff and expressionless like Alice and Betty.

When he saw the two black horses turn into the street he had a terrible feeling of deep, deep cold. The power of death to suddenly strip the vigour out of the whole street was almost disabling.

He stood at the door, next to George who towered over him with his face set rigid. Freddie wanted something from the stranger who was his brother, warmth or eye contact or a touch on his arm, but there was none. He wanted to walk backwards in front of Annie, helping her as he had always done, but Alice and Betty had her in an iron grip, their fingers clamped onto her black shawl.

Loneliness engulfed Freddie, and it was the loneliness of being different. This was his family, but he wasn't remotely like any of them, nor did he want to be. What he wanted most in that moment was to run away, to arrive at his father's funeral from a different direction and watch it as a lone observer. He wanted to experience the funeral with the sky and the wind and the twisting flight of gathering swallows. He wanted to sit on the floor of the church and feel the music rumble through stone, and watch the faces of coloured glass and stone, watch and read their expression and feel their empathy. And he wanted to share his father's journey into the unknown, into the silent land.

So he walked alone at the back of the black procession on its way to the cemetery, falling further and further behind, and he looked down from a great height and saw himself detaching, step by step, from the silver cords that bound the generations. He was alone. He saw his family drifting away from him on a river of forgetfulness, and he was glad to walk alone, his feet governed by the tolling of the church bell, his eyes gazing at a sparrow hawk hovering in the distance.

The silence of the funeral seemed to have a shape, an elongated elliptical space that extended ahead of the cortège and for some distance behind, the shape excluding the normal life of the street. Freddie kept within its boundary, close enough, but apart. George didn't turn to see where he was, and Alice and Betty minced along – almost carrying Annie, the backs of their three heads bobbing in the wake of the hearse as it halted outside Monterose church. A group of people who had known Levi were at the entrance, hats in hand, and the vicar loomed like a heron inspecting an estuary.

Once, Annie had sent Freddie to Sunday school, and the teacher had refused to have him there again. 'All he does is walk around and stare at the statues and the windows,' she'd complained. 'He won't sit down with the others.' Freddie had longed to go in there again but he'd never had time off from school, the bakery, the railway, and Annie's endless errands.

He hung back as the coffin was unloaded – to the tolling of the bell, the jingle of the horses' harness, and the shuffle of footsteps. The way the coffin was carried high on the shoulders of the pallbearers gave him a strange feeling of finality. His father's body was inside.

There was no going back. It was grim, and it was glorious. The majesty of the church was there for Levi, the stained glass and the brass eagle, the tapestries and the music. After all Levi's work in the corn mill, his arthritis, his uncontrollable tempers, the broken china, the crying, the po-faced storytelling, the years in the bakery. After all that he was paraded into this magnificent building.

Freddie was last to go into the church, and he noticed that Gladys was there, looking at him with a blend of concern and disapproval. Ignoring her, he lifted his eyes to appraise the wood carvings in the roof, and to gaze at his favourite window which had a saint with a halo underneath a tree of the richest emerald greens, a white curly lamb at his feet, a scarlet cloak and a golden sword at his belt.

'You should sit with your family. Up there,' Gladys whispered loudly, but no one looked round. Freddie ignored her, and walked to the back of the church where he sat down on the stone step leading into the bell tower. From there he could see the entire church, his father's coffin and the backs of heads. The vicar's voice droned, the congregation stood up to sing, but Freddie closed his eyes, touched the stone floor with his hands, and went into a trance.

Through his sensitive fingers he could feel the earth

below the church. It had energy like an arrow of light fired into the rocks, a sound that resonated for miles and miles through the land, through churches and castles and monuments far away. And he could feel water down there, the secret wells and springs winding, branching like arteries of silver through the dark of the earth.

The drone of the funeral service cushioned his senses like moss. Freddie stayed in his blessed trance, and then he saw something so amazing that he wanted to leap to his feet. Shining in the gloom of the church was an angel of light stretching from floor to ceiling. Its wings were rays of gold fanning out from wall to wall. Its skirt was a cone of radiance covering the whole congregation. The face was so bright that the features were invisible, only a feeling of omnipotent mysterious love emanated through the angel's resplendent being. Under its brightness, the people sat like dominoes, wooden and unresponsive.

Freddie held his breath. He longed to shout out in a loud voice, a voice louder than him. But all his young life he'd been told: No. You mustn't. You shouldn't. Don't you dare.

The shades came down, the angel vanished, and the words of his father's favourite hymn reclaimed his consciousness:

'Rock of ages cleft for me,
Let me hide myself in thee.'

Freddie thought about the words: 'Let me hide myself.' Wasn't that what he'd been doing all his life? Hiding himself. Hiding his soul. And why? Because of Harry Price. Because of Levi smashing china over the accusation of his son telling lies. It hadn't been lies.

As the hymn progressed into the final verse, Freddie felt rebellious. Sad as he was to lose his father, Levi's death had liberated him. He was nearly a man now, his voice was deepening and he longed to use it, to feel its new full rumbling power in the echoing church. He hadn't joined in the singing, but now he stood up and waited for the silence that would follow the hymn.

Empowered by his solitary stance and his golden vision, Freddie took a deep breath and felt his voice rise up from the bowels of the earth. He didn't need to shout. The voice was effortlessly resonant.

'I saw an angel,' he declared. 'A golden angel shining over all of you, here in this church.'

The heads turned, the mouths dropped open, a hundred accusing eyes stared down the church at Freddie. Even Levi's coffin seemed to tremble, the feathers of

155

the brass eagle bristled, and someone's hymnbook crashed to the floor like a shot pigeon.

Once he started, Freddie couldn't stop.

'I'm not a liar,' he said quietly.

The 'shades of the prison-house' began to crack around him, letting in chinks of light, bright glimpses of the kind of life that freedom could bring.

'And,' he added, his voice gathering strength as he let go of his final issue, 'I am NOT going to be a baker.'

He'd said it. The shades of the prison-house collapsed into rubble, and through the rising dust, George crossed the church like a leopard, seized Freddie by the collar and frog-marched him outside.

Out in the sunshine he slammed Freddie against the blue-lias stones of the porch.

'Don't you bring shame on the Barcussy family.' The words came spitting and sputtering from between George's big yellowy teeth, and with each word he shoved Freddie harder into the wall. 'I am the head of the family now. You'll do as you're told – BOY.'

Shaken, Freddie looked into George's furious eyes, and saw that Levi was right inside him, looking out.

Chapter Eleven

HE WHO DARES

On the morning of Freddie's sixteenth birthday, he got up in the dark as usual, climbed into his clothes and lit a candle. He held it up to the window to observe the way it glistened on the fern-like patterns of ice on the inside of the glass. With his fingernail he scraped out a peep hole and peered outside at the moonlight shining on frosted branches and rooftops. His heart was thumping with excitement. Today was the day. He must keep his nerves steady, act as if everything was normal. He'd worked it all out beforehand, choosing a time when George had gone to the pub. First he'd smuggled an empty flour sack upstairs and hidden it.

George wasn't good at early starts. He slept heavily, often after a night out drinking, leaving the early morning bread-making to Annie and Freddie. This morning Freddie had made sure he was up first.

He slid the flour sack from under his mattress, snagging it on the rusted metal springs which groaned and twanged in the silent house. Gingerly he lifted the floorboards and a musty mouldy smell was released into his room. Reaching inside he withdrew his bundles of coins, all twenty-six of them, tied into old socks, hankies and bits of rag, glad that he'd tied them tightly to stop the coins jingling. Over the years he'd counted and recorded each bundle on a strip of cardboard, and he knew approximately how much he had. Enough for what he was going to do. The only things he'd bought for himself were a pencil, a drawing book and a penknife.

Freddie paused to listen. Only one lot of snoring, and it was Annie. He didn't know if George was awake or not, so he waited, the raised floorboard propped in his hand. George was too close, just next door in the back room overlooking the garden. Reassured by the silence Freddie stuffed the bundles of money into the flour sack and gathered the top with a piece of string. He lowered the floorboard back into its slot.

Heaving the sack with both hands, he struggled down the steep stairs, bumping it on every step. He was breathing hard and the tips of his fingers ached with frost. The candle was left flickering in its metal holder at the top of the stairs.

'What the hell do you think you're doing?' George's voice rumbled out of the dark, and the sofa springs twanged and creaked. Freddie could see the shadow of him rising, throwing his blanket aside. A sour stench of alcohol filled the room, a bottle glinted on the floor.

Freddie hadn't expected George to be downstairs on the sofa, and awake. What could he say? Tell George how sick he felt at the way he was spending the bakery's hard-earned profit on booze? Tell him to mind his own business? He set his mouth in a stubborn line and locked his mind into the power of silence. Moving calmly, as if he had all the time in the world, he fetched the candle down the stairs and put it on the scullery table.

George was standing at the bottom of the stairs, yawning, and looking at the sack of money.

'What you got in there, baby brother?' He gave the sack a kick with his toe and Freddie noted he didn't have his boots on. That gave him a chance. He thought quickly, unravelling his carefully laid plans. His intentions had been to put the money sack into the front box of the bicycle, camouflage it with loaves of bread and appear to set off on his rounds as normal. That wouldn't work now.

'I said – what's in that sack?' hissed George putting his beer-soaked face close to Freddie's cheeks. His breath steamed in the candlelight. 'Answer me, baby brother.'

He pushed Freddie against the wall and a picture fell down with a crash. It was a sepia photograph of Levi which Annie was proud of, and now the whites of his eyes gleamed up at them through cracked glass. Freddie ignored George and calmly picked up the picture, propping it on the scullery table. He could feel the anger in George's clenched fists, and he just looked at him steadily. George had tried many times to get him to fight, but Freddie wouldn't. He'd stand there, silent and still, and something in his gaze always stopped George in his tracks, a becalming blend of obstinacy and peace, something George didn't have. Freddie knew it confused him, and that he would cover the confusion with a volley of verbal abuse.

George bent down and fumbled with the neck of the sack. He had clumsy hands like Levi, and in the ice-cold air his fingers were too stiff to untie the string, so he patted the Hessian sides. It jingled a little, and a puff of flour dust rose into the candlelight.

'Ah!' George's eyes sparked with suspicion. 'That'd feel like money. You got a sack of money, baby brother? Where d'you get that from? Been stealing it, have you? Stealing the takings. Pilfering. What you gonna do with it, baby brother? Run away to London?'

'I earned it,' said Freddie quietly. 'Every penny. Carrying luggage at the station. I've saved it up for three years. It's mine. And I'm doing what I like with it, George.'

He looked George squarely in the eyes. Creaking, shuffling sounds of Annie getting up came from the stairs. Both men looked up at the faint strip of light under her door.

'Now,' thought Freddie. 'Do it now.' With his freezing hands he grabbed the sack and heaved it into the bicycle, seized his coat and flung it on top. Puffing and wheezing from the effort, he shoved the back door open, and grappled the heavy bike outside.

'Good riddance,' shouted George, standing on the mat in his socks.

Freddie mounted the bike and pedalled into the darkness, the handlebars swinging awkwardly with the weight of his sack of money. With no lights front or back, he was glad of the moon's brilliance which cast a lattice of shadows across the street. Everything looked black or silver, the frozen puddles on the rough road had yellowish curls and flaked white edges to their mirror-like surface. The church clock struck five, its chimes slicing through the sub-zero air. It was a Monday in February, Freddie's sixteenth birthday, and his plan had gone badly wrong. Instead of working in the warm bakery, he was out in the hoar frost. It wouldn't be light for two hours, and he'd got nowhere to go.

The frost burned his ears and crystallised under his collar, between the buttons of his jacket and up his sleeves, which were too short for him. It grazed the back of his throat and etched its sharpness deep into his lungs. He paused in the market square to blow on his hands, which were now completely numb and locked onto the handlebars. Obviously he couldn't stay out there for two hours. He had to find a warm refuge for himself, his bike and his bag of money.

No lights shone from any of the houses or shops, and the square which was so busy during the day was deserted except for a bunch of rats scuttling along the base of the church wall. Freddie inspected the church porch. It was clammy and unfriendly. He thought about the station waiting-room which usually had a welcoming fire, and decided to go there.

The old bread bike had no brakes and with the heavy

bag of money in the front it careered down the station hill like a toboggan. Freddie stuck his long legs out straight, his hobnailed boots striking sparks along the road, making a lot of noise, and he arrived breathless at the station railings. He felt like laughing out loud. No one was around as he wheeled the bike onto the platform, and the moonlight gleamed on the rails. He turned the brass knob of the waiting-room door and, to his great joy, it was unlocked. The smell of coal and leather lingered in the air and it felt warm as he pushed the bike inside and stood there in heavy darkness. A faint red glow came from the embers of the fireplace.

Freddie carried the clanking coal bucket outside and helped himself to some chunks of the silvery coal stacked in the yard. Then he re-lit the fire and sat toasting his face and hands against its cheerful flame. The first train was not until eight o'clock, so he had plenty of time to luxuriate by the roaring fire, guard his bag of money, and reassemble his daring plan.

Annie was distraught when she discovered Freddie had gone. She ranted at George as they made the bread together.

'How could you let 'im go out in the frost and the dark like that, George? What were you thinking?'

'I couldn't stop him,' protested George as he stoked the coke oven vigorously.

'He's not strong, our Freddie, he suffers with bronchitis,' said Annie. 'He's not like you, George. He never had what you had, a healthy childhood and good food. He grew up in the wartime and he suffered – oh you should've seen his little feet. Covered in blisters, all septic they were, from wearing clogs. You never had to do that, did you?'

'No,' agreed George shortly, 'but you'd no business having another baby at your age, Mother, and with the war coming.'

Annie bristled. 'Don't you dare tell me that. We didn't know the war was coming. And Freddie was born easy. He's a lovely boy, lovely, been so good to me he has. You were always jealous of him, George, don't ask me why. And the girls – they never wanted to be bothered with Freddie, had their heads full of fancy hats and silly dancing. My Freddie, he's done more for me than any of you lot.' She pounded a batch of dough, flapping it over on the floured tabletop and digging her knuckles into it. All the time she was watching the door and listening for Freddie to return.

'He wouldn't have gone out like that – in the DARK – without breakfast, George. What did you say to him?'

'Nothing much. Just asked him about the sack of money he had. He woke me up, banging it down the stairs. What was he doing with a hoard like that, smuggling it out at that time of the morning? Looks suspicious to me. Very suspicious.' George plunged his hands into a bowl of water, took the bar of Sunlight soap and started washing the coal dust from his arms. 'There's something odd about that boy, Mother. You can't see it.'

Annie's cheeks flushed with frustration. 'Freddie is not odd,' she said, frowning at George. 'You've never taken the trouble to get to know him. He's clever, and he's artistic.'

'Artistic!' George's voice went up an octave. 'What good is that?'

'Who are you to judge? Freddie's been miserable in this bakery, I know that. It's not what he wants. He wants to be a mechanic. And surely you could have helped him? Fine brother you've been, and now look at you – boozing and wasting your money. Shame on you.'

George shrugged.

'And don't you shrug your shoulders at me.' Annie was getting more and more upset. She felt like a kettle about to boil over with two years of unexpressed grief at losing Levi. Two years of extreme anxiety when Freddie had quietly gone on helping her the way he always had. Suddenly she felt engulfed by remorse. She'd never even told Freddie how much she appreciated him, she'd never said thank you to him, and today it was his birthday. She looked at his present sitting on the dresser, wrapped in brown paper. It was a pair of gloves she'd knitted him. How badly he would need them now, out there somewhere in the deathly cold. Annie began to tremble with anxiety.

'Don't treat me like a child, Mother. I'm a man now,' said George, and then he added something that demolished the remains of Annie's self-control. 'I expect he's run away to London. You'll probably never see him again.'

Annie collapsed into a chair with a howl of anguish. She put her head in her hands and the tears erupted from her hot face, the sobs deep, deep down in her body. Her crying was loud and harrowing in the bakery, as if her sorrow was going everywhere, across the table, into the neat trays of uncooked loaves and buns, into the waiting ovens and the listening stones of the cottage walls.

George was shocked. He'd never seen his mother cry, even when Levi had died. She'd always been rock solid and in control. And now she was crying – over Freddie!

He walked over to her, and put his hand on her humped shoulders.

'There – don't cry. I didn't mean to . . .'

'Yes you did,' accused Annie and her eyes burned up at him like two cracks of sapphire. 'Freddie's left because of you. You've treated him bad – BAD. And he won't come back when you're here, George. You've made him hate you. I wouldn't treat a dog like you've treated him.'

George picked up a tray of loaves and started to slide them into the oven, and Annie cried even louder.

'LEAVE THE BREAD,' she shouted. 'It's me you should care about, and your brother.' She pushed her chair back and stood up, facing George with her chin and her ample bust lifted imperiously, her eyes steady again and in control. 'I think you'd better leave, George. You get on that smelly motorbike and go home, back to Yeovil, and don't come here again until you can look me in the eye and apologise. From the heart. Go on. Just GO.'

'And who's going to deliver this bread?' George raised his eyebrows and went on stacking the oven.

'Just GO,' said Annie. 'I don't care about the bread. I don't care if it's burnt to a cinder. I care about my Freddie.'

'You've got flour in your hair,' said George lightly. But when he saw the ultimatum in Annie's eyes, he brushed the flour from his own hands, hung up the cloth he was holding, and took his coat from the back of the door.

'All right. I'll go. But don't come running to me next time you want help.'

Annie stood at the window like a stone statue, her hands at her sides, her eyes watching the February sunrise over Monterose, the red sky brightening over crystallised rooftops, glinting on icicles which hung in long strips from the eaves, and she watched the steam from the first early trains come curling through the town. She drew the curtains and looked out at the back garden where the moon was sinking into the west, its marble face tinged with rosy pink.

She went upstairs and stood in Freddie's bedroom. Mechanically she made his bed and sat down on it, staring bleakly around at the whitewashed walls. The picture of Granny Barcussy looked knowingly at her. Annie had never liked Levi's mother. She'd been too bubbly for Annie's way of being; she'd found it hard to tolerate her enthusiasm for life and the bewitching effect she had on Freddie.

George's words rang in her head, but she couldn't

believe Freddie had run away to London. He'd be back in a few hours, she was sure, her frightened mind refusing to even consider what she would do if he never came back. Annie picked up Freddie's precious drawing book and turned the pages, marvelling at his detailed pictures of birds. There were owls and herons, and one of a hawk hovering high in the air above a speeding train. There were cows and horses, drawn from all angles, always moving. The book was nearly full, and towards the end Freddie had drawn motorbikes, cars and steam engines in meticulous detail. Annie frowned, and turned back again to the first page. There was a message hidden in the sequence of pictures, some clue about Freddie's secret life, something she'd been missing. Looking deeper into the pictures, Annie saw that on every page was the face of a beautiful young girl, the girl on the Shire horse. Freddie had cleverly hidden her in his pictures. She would be sitting under a tree, or standing on a bridge or looking down from the clouds, always with her hair blowing in the wind. Freddie had never told his mother who she was, but Annie felt she was alive, looking at her from the pages of his drawing book.

She closed the book, smoothed it and put it back on his bedside table. New and startling thoughts came into her mind. Freddie was sixteen. He would want a life of his own, a wife maybe. How would she live without him? To Annie those thoughts were like a firebox. Open the lid and tongues of flame would come writhing out. She smelled burning, slammed the box shut and refused to look at the smoke seeping through the cracks, refused to acknowledge that one day the box would no longer contain that smouldering fire. She sat rocking herself on the edge of Freddie's bed. It was nine o'clock and the smell of burning was real.

'The bread!' Annie gasped and struggled down the narrow staircase as fast as she could in her creaking slippers. The bakery was full of acrid smoke. She flung the door open and let it escape into the street. Then she opened the ovens and took out tray after tray of loaves and buns, all burned black and smoking.

'Oh, what have I done?' she wailed, slamming around with trays of charcoaled remains, brittle black shells of what should have been lovely sweet smelling buns. These were so dangerously hot that she hurled the trays outside into the back garden and left them. She began talking to herself, 'You keep calm now. Just keep calm, get on and clear up the mess.'

By now, Freddie should have been out on his rounds with fresh loaves in the front of the bike. She would be stacking the shelves and getting the shop ready to open. Customers were already walking up the street, muffled in furry hats and scarves, willow baskets over one arm, breath steaming in the morning air. As usual, the first customer was Gladys. She knocked on the window and peered in.

'Are you all right, Annie?'

Annie hesitated. She wanted to hide for the rest of the day. She didn't want to face those expectant customers and admit she'd burned the bread. She sighed resignedly.

'No peace for the wicked,' she said, and, shamefaced, she let Gladys in.

'Pooh. What a smeech!' Gladys came in with her reassuring busybody manner. 'What 'ave 'e done?'

'Burnt the bread.'

'Where's Freddie?'

'Out on the bike.'

Gladys eyed her knowingly. 'Come on. I'll help you,' she said, and without waiting to be invited she took off her chocolate-brown hat, coat and gloves, rolled up her sleeves and set about scraping charcoal out of the ovens. 'I'll do this. You make some more dough. Put a notice in the window saying NO BREAD UNTIL MIDDAY.'

Annie looked at her gratefully. Trembling inside,

she made herself get on with it. The two women scrubbed and scraped and by lunchtime a new batch of bread was in the oven. But there was no sign of Freddie.

Annie gave Gladys a generous basket of free bread and a warm thank you. Inside she wished she was like Gladys, always cheerful and out there helping people.

'So where's Freddie?' Gladys asked, putting her coat on to leave. 'It's nearly two o'clock.'

'He'll be back later,' said Annie, avoiding the concerned eyes.

'Hmmm.' Gladys gave her a shrewd stare and left, waddling down the street with her basket. The winter sun shone hazily, and a song thrush sang for a short interval, but the frost had hardly melted. By three o'clock Annie had sold the limited stock of bread to disgruntled customers. She closed the shop and stood in the doorway, her hands wrapped around a mug of tea, her eyes looking up and down the street, watching for Freddie to appear amongst the jumble of horse-drawn carts and motorcars. She could feel the cold closing in, coming down with the night. Too upset to eat, she dragged a chair to the window and sat, endlessly, hopelessly watching, a hollow loneliness in her heart.

'Abandoned, that's what I am,' she thought, 'abandoned and unwanted.'

As twilight fell, she lit the two gas lamps and a few candles, her hands shaking with gathering fear. Freddie was not coming back. Her worst nightmare was coming true. She would be alone, housebound, with no one to help her. A prisoner, that's what she would be. Despair and fear of insanity were already claiming her. She imagined the asylum with its miserable corridors and clanking, cream-painted beds, the wailing of madness around her, the unsmiling faces of doctors. A world without kindness, without love.

Annie remained sitting in the window, immersed in gloomy predictions. What had happened to all the love and the hard work she'd put into her life? Was it out there, somewhere roving around, wasted like time and spent like money? What would God do with her now?

'How can you do this to me, Freddie?' she whispered. 'Wasn't I a good mother?'

The tears were brewing again. She watched two bright headlights coming slowly up the street, a big motor vehicle with its wheels bouncing over the potholes. She heard the gears grind, the brakes squeak, and the lorry shuddered to a halt, to her alarm, right outside the bakery door. She watched, horrified, as the driver got out and slammed the door shut. A tall figure walked towards the door. She saw his face in the lamplight, a face glowing red and a smile bigger than itself.

'Freddie!' she screamed. 'My Freddie!'

She threw her arms around him and gazed up at his face, noticing for the first time that he was much taller than her, and his eyes were sparkling with secrets waiting to be told.

'I can't believe it's you. You're not cold.' Annie touched his coat and smelled a new smell on him. Oil.

''Course it's me, Mother,' he beamed. 'And – I bought a lorry.'

'You did WHAT?'

Freddie could feel the shock waves emanating from his Mother. He sat down at the kitchen table, took his cap off and pushed his hair back from his brow. His face ached with unaccustomed smiling.

'Well – first, I didn't intend to go out like that, in the dark, mother. But George wasn't too happy about my bag of money.'

'He's gone home.'

'For good?'

'We'll see,' said Annie, non-committedly. She looked out the window at the shadowy bulk of the lorry standing there in the dusk.

'It's a Scammell,' said Freddie. 'I was lucky to get it.'

'Ah. You were.' Annie was still trying to take it in. 'Did you have enough money?'

'Yes, and some left over for petrol.'

'I know. You've been saving for a long time.' Annie's eyes smiled at Freddie, and her mouth moved just a little. She knew about his secret hoard under the floorboard. Sometimes she'd stealthily opened it up and added a few pennies or a shilling when Freddie was out, so she smiled to herself. Then something else occurred to her. 'But you can't drive.'

Freddie grinned. 'I thought about that. I'm sixteen and the law says that when you're sixteen you can drive. But I didn't know how, so I asked Joan Jarvis to give me a lesson, and she did.'

'You did WHAT?' Annie said again, dropping the wooden spoon she'd been holding. 'You asked JOAN JARVIS of all people?'

'There's nothing wrong with her, Mother. Ages ago she offered to give me a driving lesson, so I took her up on it. I knocked on her door and asked her. Before I bought the lorry. She let me drive her Model T all up over the Polden Hills, and I soon got the hang of it.'

Annie snorted. She didn't approve of Joan Jarvis.

175

From what she'd heard, Joan Jarvis was a scarlet woman who wore lipstick and silly hats and raced about in her Model T Ford, scattering chickens and upsetting horses. But Annie couldn't be cross with Freddie. She was flabbergasted at what he'd done, and she'd never seen him look as red-faced and confident as he did now. It was almost as if he'd been recreated in one day. The pale, exhausted little boy had gone and a vibrant young man sat there in his place, but still with that caring, quizzical intensity in his eyes.

'And – what are you going to do with this lorry?' she asked.

'I intend to start a haulage business,' said Freddie. 'And – I've got two jobs already, for tomorrow morning. I went to see the stonemason – Herbie – he's a friend of mine, and he needs a load of stone brought down from the quarry. Then I went to the wheelwright place, and he wants me to deliver a stack of wheels he's been making. There's plenty of work and not enough lorries to do it. I reckon this one will have paid for itself in a month or so.'

There was a silence between them. Freddie thought his mother might have said, 'Well done' or something like that, but such platitudes were not in Annie's mind-set.

She frowned. 'But Freddie – what about the bakery?'

'I was coming to that,' he said, 'and don't worry, I'll help you in the mornings for as long as I can, Mother – but . . .'

'But what?'

Freddie breathed in slowly through his nose. Then, looking directly into Annie's anxious eyes he said the words he'd waited so long to utter. 'I do appreciate what you and Dad did for me, but I don't want to spend my life in the bakery.'

Annie nodded bleakly, 'I know.'

'I don't want you to feel hurt,' said Freddie.

'Doesn't look as if I've got much choice does it?'

Annie lapsed into a bitter silence.

'I'll help you out, for now,' promised Freddie, 'but not forever, Mother. I've got plans.'

'Plans?' She looked at him sharply and he could feel the atmosphere between them changing. 'What plans?'

The way he hesitated to answer threw Annie into one of her panics.

'No. You can't leave me,' she cried and her whole body began to shake violently. 'Please. Please don't leave me. I can't go out. How will I manage? They'll take me to the asylum, they'll say I'm a mad woman.'

Freddie felt the weight of her need. He'd wanted to assert himself, but Annie's nerves seemed to overpower both of them. In the silence of his soul, he vowed that he'd find a way to break free, no matter what.

Chapter Twelve

FOREVER BLOWING BUBBLES

Polly was used to trains by now. She stood placidly as Kate tied her to the station railings alongside a row of other horses and carts which had brought goods to be loaded onto the freight train. There were baskets of racing pigeons stacked in fours, the birds peeping out and muttering in their iridescent throats; sacks of early potatoes; cartons of ripe strawberries; bundles of willow baskets and boxes of terracotta flowerpots; stacks of fencing posts and rolls of wire. Several lorries were parked there, one unloading bundles of leather shoes, boots and sandals.

Kate took a hay net from the cart and tied it to the

railings for Polly. 'Good girl,' she said, rubbing the pony's neck just behind her ears. 'You did bring us here nicely, didn't you? Now you have a rest and eat up this lovely hay. I'll get you a drink.' Polly gave Kate an affectionate push with her head.

'For goodness' sake, Kate, stop fussing. We've got to unload,' complained Ethie.

'There's plenty of time.' Kate wouldn't be hurried. She took Polly's bucket from the cart, carried it over to the water trough, filled it and brought it back. She put it down, glad to see the thirsty pony plunge her lips into it and drink noisily. 'Good girl, Polly,' she said again, and then, to Ethie's annoyance Kate began to sing.

'I'm forever blowing bubbles
Pretty bubbles in the air . . .'

Her lovely voice mingled pleasantly with the shouts of men unloading goods and the whirr of trolley wheels being hauled onto the platform. A man who was whistling took up the tune Kate was singing, doffed his cap and winked as he walked by trundling one of the heavy iron and timber station trolleys with its T-shaped handle and rusting wheels. Kate ran after him, calling out in her bright voice, 'I say – I say, can we share your trolley, please? There's none left.'

The man turned and looked at the beautiful young woman. She wore a red dress with a swingy skirt, made of a heavy cottony fabric with tiny black and pink rosebuds. It had short puff sleeves showing off her rounded sunburnt arms, and the bodice had strips of black lace gathered in ruffles over her bust.

'Do anything for you, darling!' he leered, dropping the metal handle of the trolley.

'KATE!' shouted Ethie. She rolled her eyes and marched up to the man. 'We can manage, thank you. Go on your way, please.'

'Suit yourself, missus.' He looked Ethie up and down with a very different expression. She cut an intimidating figure in a plain navy dress with big shoulder pads and a droopy black hat casting a shadow over her face. He turned his back and walked off with his trolley, rollicking his hips rebelliously.

'Do you HAVE to flirt with anything in trousers?' said Ethie, glowering at her younger sister.

Kate refused to be ruffled. 'Oh, he's just a lad,' she said pleasantly. She thought Ethie was behaving like an old hen, but she didn't say so. 'Let's not spoil this lovely morning.' She went on singing, and started unpacking boxes of cheese from the cart, her hair falling over her shoulders.

'I'll go and fetch a trolley,' said Ethie. 'We only need one for the big truckle.'

She stalked off and returned a few minutes later wheeling a hand trolley. 'This will do,' she said, 'and Charlie says the freight train is late. He says the signals are stuck on the other side of the tunnel. It's going to be half an hour late.'

'Why don't you do the shopping?' suggested Kate, taking the willow basket out of the cart. 'I know you like shopping. I'll stay here with Polly, and I can unload.'

'What about the big truckle of cheese?' said Ethie.

'Oh, someone will help me I'm sure. Go on, you go.'

Kate knew Ethie loved shopping. She handed her the basket, and was glad to see her sister walking away into the town. Still singing, she briskly unpacked the boxes of cheese and stacked them onto the trolley. In the middle of the cart was an enormous truckle of farm-house cheddar, well matured, and wrapped tightly in a cloth. It had a very special destination, clearly printed on a brown label.

Confident that someone would come along and help her lift it out, Kate sat on the open back of the cart, swinging her legs and lifting her face to feel the hot May sunshine on her skin. The station yard was full of spar-rows, hundreds of them hopping and pecking and having dust baths at the sides of the road. Blackbirds and thrushes were singing and in the distance a cuckoo was cuckooing. Kate watched a big Scammell lorry rum-bling down to the station. It had nothing on the back so she assumed it was coming to collect something to be unloaded from the freight train. She watched it drive slowly to the far side of the yard and park.

As soon as the news circulated about the train being late, people started to gather in small groups, talking and laughing as they waited. Someone produced a har-monica and began to play vigorously and before long a man with a fiddle had joined in, and people were starting to clap and sing. Kate couldn't resist going over there, and soon her feet were tapping, her eyes sparkling.

'You look as if you'd like to dance.' The man to whom she'd spoken earlier was there, standing in front of Kate with a twinkle in his eye. 'Has your mother gone shopping?'

Kate laughed at him. 'Oh that's not my mother. She's my big sister – Ethie.'

'Bit of a dragon, is she?'

'No,' said Kate mischievously. 'I'm the family

dragon.' She laughed again and caught the eye of another girl who was standing there twirling her skirt in time to the music. 'Come on, let's dance!'

The next minute, she and the other girl were dancing wildly in the street, kicking their legs and clapping, their hair whirling around and both of them giggling. The men stood around whooping and whistling. Kate was enjoying herself. She loved to dance, it felt good and right on such a beautiful May morning when the bank opposite the station was covered in wild flowers, moon daisies, corncockle, buttercups and cowslips, with butterflies dancing and fluttering all over them. The whole world seemed full of music and exuberance.

Freddie got out of the lorry and stretched. A board was propped outside the entrance to the station announcing that the train was late. He was glad. He'd been hard at work since 5 a.m., first in the bakery, then out in his lorry delivering timber to the wheelwrights. He'd come to the station to collect some bales of fabric for the tailor's shop and six brand new wheelbarrows for the builder's merchant.

Glad of the break, he took off his jacket and strode across to his favourite place on the sunny bank facing the station. Bleached by the sun, the hot grass was spangled with flowers, and the glistening wings of honey-bees. Butterflies danced through the shimmering sunlight, and Freddie studied them with pleasure. One pitched on his finger, spread its wings and settled there. It was a peacock. The breeze ruffled the gingery down on its body, and rich patterns of blue and red glowed on its wings. The antenna had tiny grey and white stripes, its slender legs were hunched as it clung to his finger, looking at him with wise black eyes. The contact with its fragile beauty touched some forgotten place in Freddie's soul. Working long hard hours through the golden summer days gave him fewer and fewer spaces to dream. Engines chugged in his mind; his clothes smelled of oil; his shoulders carried heavy sacks; his drawing book lay untouched in his bedroom.

Three years had passed since he'd bought the Scammell lorry. His bank account was growing, and so was his confidence. At first he'd practised driving, espe-cially the reversing, until he could manoeuvre the lorry in and out of the tightest spaces, necessary as some of the villages had streets so narrow that the lorry almost touched the walls of cottages as he drove through. He knew the engine like an old friend, listening to it and interpreting its every need and mood. The strength of it was exhilarating to Freddie, and sometimes when it roared up a steep hill with a load of stone he would lean forward, hold his breath, and then laugh out loud when he made it to the top.

Freddie had never had friends like those he had made now, other men he could talk to, tell yarns and share laughter together. For the first time in his life, he felt respected and welcome. His best friend was Herbie, the stonemason. Herbie often invited Freddie to go to the pub with him, but Freddie always refused. He hated the smell of beer and the clink of glass, and the women with red lipstick who 'made eyes' at him.

The only shadow in Freddie's life was his mother's increasing unhappiness, her anxieties and needs which piled into his mind as soon as he got home. Juggling the bakery and the haulage business wasn't going to work forever, he knew, but he carried on helping with the bread to placate Annie.

He looked at the butterfly still resting on his hand. His skin was cracked and sore, his knuckles red from constant scrubbing, for each night he had to remove every trace of the ingrained engine oil so that he could make bread. He had a rash on the backs of his hands and wrists, and he often hid them away in his pockets when he was talking to people. Yet this butterfly didn't care how rough his skin was, it had chosen to pitch there

and stay with him. And as he gazed at it, he heard
singing, a clear, pure, happy voice that was somehow
familiar.

> *'I'm forever blowing bubbles,*
> *Pretty bubbles in the air,*
> *They fly so high, nearly touch the sky . . .'*

Freddie turned his head very slowly, so as not to alarm
the butterfly, and scanned the busy station yard, peering
past the parked motor vehicles to where the horses were
tied up along the railings. He saw the girl who was
singing. She sat on the back of an open pony cart, in a
red dress, swinging her legs.

The butterfly flitted away, and Freddie stood up as if
in a dream. He brushed the grass from his clothes and
walked over there in long deliberate strides, his jacket
slung over one shoulder. The blood in his veins ran hot
and fast, like mulled wine, and a haze of sweat glistened
on his brow. He didn't know what he was going to say,
only that he had to go to her. The walk felt strange as
if a golden string was pulling him towards her, winding
a loop of gold around the two of them.

As soon as he recognised Polly, and saw the flaked
old lettering on the cart, he knew his dream was coming

true. She was watching him walking towards her, and as he came into her presence, Freddie couldn't help staring. The little girl whose face he had carried in his mind for years had blossomed into a vibrant young woman with plump, firm breasts, a curvy waist and shapely legs swinging in a carefree way. Her beautiful face with its shell-like nostrils and rose-petal skin was the one he had memorised, but when he saw the life that flashed from her eyes he almost gasped. Tight-lipped, he stood in front of her, and he couldn't think of anything acceptable to say.

But Kate made it easy for him.

'Hello,' she said warmly, and beamed as if she'd been waiting for him. 'Have you come to help me? How kind of you.'

Freddie looked deep into her eyes and saw that they were not dark as he'd thought but a warm bright amber. There was no fear, no suspicion and no anger in there, only a breath-taking sense of purity and love, and it filled him with the sudden glory of new life, open and trusting like the butterfly.

'So – what do you need help with?' he asked awkwardly.

Kate jumped down from the cart with a flounce of red skirts and lace. She was shorter than him, about up to his shoulder, and now she smiled at his concerned face. 'I need to unload this truckle of cheese,' she said, 'and take it onto the platform with the rest of the stuff.'

'I can lift that,' said Freddie.

'Oh, can you? That's marvellous,' she cried. 'It's terribly heavy.'

Freddie leaned into the cart and slid the truckle of cheese towards him. He couldn't help noticing the label.

'That's a long journey for a piece of cheese,' he remarked.

Kate laughed. 'Oh, it's going to my uncle's farm in Gloucestershire,' she said. 'He's got a thousand-acre farm on the banks of the Severn Estuary. It's lovely. I've been there for a holiday, and you have to go in a BOAT.' She announced the word boat in a dramatic whisper, her eyes widening as if a boat was the most exciting thing on earth.

'A boat?'

'Yes, a ferry boat. It goes from Aust Ferry, over the wide brown river. People take motorbikes on it. They wheel them on over a big ramp and then they pull the ramp up and the boat goes chugging out into the swirling river. Oh, it's so exciting. And the wind blows up the river and gives you roses in your cheeks, and you can smell the SEA. Ooh, I love the salty sea, don't you?'

'Well – I've never seen the sea,' said Freddie, captivated by the way Kate talked with such fluency.

'Haven't you? Oh I expect you will one day – and you'll love it. It SPARKLES like DIAMONDS.'

'Sparkles like diamonds!' repeated Freddie, and he found himself smiling at the thought. 'I'd like to see that.'

He lifted the truckle of cheese onto his shoulder, and crooked his arm around it.

'You are strong,' said Kate. She took the trolley and walked beside him, talking all the time in her chirruping voice. 'Perhaps you can help me unload something from the train as well. If you wouldn't mind. It's a huge salmon and it's in a box filled with ice.'

'A salmon!'

'Yes. My Uncle Don has got a set of putchers on the River Severn. It's tidal, you see. And the fish swim up with the tide and they get stuck in the putchers which are like long pointed baskets and when the tide goes down you can paddle out there and get them. Every year my mother makes a massive cheese and we swap it for a salmon. We send the cheese up on the train and they send the salmon down in a box. Have you ever tasted salmon? It's PINK inside and it's delicious with a pat of butter and a sprinkle of fresh parsley.'

Freddie carried the truckle of cheese to the far end of the platform with Kate bustling beside him, talking non-stop. The train was now due in ten minutes. Ten blissful minutes, he thought, to sit in the May sunshine with the girl he secretly loved. Why hide it? Why not tell her? he thought impulsively, and immediately a word shone large and bright in his head. 'WAIT.'

He put the huge cheese down on a brown bench, and made an attempt at a joke. 'The mice will be after me now,' he said brushing his shoulder, 'I smell of cheese.'

'So do I!' said Kate and went off into a volley of laughter, her eyes gleaming. It was such a bubbly, inviting laugh that Freddie found himself laughing too.

'You're like my granny,' he said.

'Well, thanks very much. There's a nice compliment!' Kate went into another peal of laughter that rang all over the station.

'Sorry,' said Freddie, but the word didn't feel right. Kate was so full of joy and confidence that an abject apology slunk past her and escaped into the gutter.

A small silence followed, like an undiscovered jewel, both of them looking attentively at each other's faces.

'I should have asked your name,' said Kate warmly.

'Freddie Barcussy, and I know your name,' he said. 'Oriole Kate Loxley.'

She looked surprised. 'How did you know? Not many people know my first name.'

'I saw it once, on your suitcase,' said Freddie, 'when you were a little girl. I was there when you had the accident, and I stayed with you when you were lying unconscious in the road.'

Kate gasped. For the first time she looked serious, and he saw her eyes settle into stillness, like a rippling pool becoming a tranquil mirror.

'It was you!' she said. 'Fancy you remembering that.'

'You had plaits, with red ribbons,' said Freddie.

Kate looked at him searchingly.

'I remember – I dreamed you were an angel,' she said.

'Angels don't smell of cheese,' said Freddie, and was rewarded with another peal of laughter.

'The train's coming.' Shouts and movement stirred all along the platform as the freight train came puffing slowly in, and squealed to a halt. Immediately, two of the station workers in dark blue sooty clothes jumped down onto the rails and walked along tapping the metal wheels, a routine inspection. The ramps were lowered onto the platform and the unloading and loading began.

'Big box here for Loxley, Hilbegut Farm,' shouted Charlie.

'I'll help you, Kate,' said Freddie. 'I can collect my load in a minute.'

He took the cold wooden box in both hands.

'You mustn't tip it over,' laughed Kate. 'You'll bruise its nose.'

'What's in there then, Kate?' asked Charlie who obviously knew her.

'A SALMON!' she whispered dramatically.

'Cor. Can I come to dinner then?' he joked.

'I'll ask my mother,' said Kate mischievously. 'And if she says no, I'll bring you down a slice – with a knife and fork.'

Freddie was fascinated by the camaraderie she seemed to have with everyone on the station. He felt proud to be carrying the salmon in its box, proud to be walking beside her down the platform. She swanned along beside him, pausing once to make a fuss of a collie dog that ran to her squirming and wagging its tail.

'No, you can't have that,' she said as it sniffed hopefully at the salmon. 'That's not for dogs.'

'So now I smell of fish as well,' said Freddie, smiling at her. She smiled back and his heart almost stopped when her eyes looked up at him. He pointed at his Scammell lorry. 'That's my lorry over there. I've got a haulage business.'

'What – your own?' she asked.

'That's right,' said Freddie.

'It's a beauty!' She paused to admire the lorry. 'I'll tell everyone, if you like, and get some business for you, Freddie. Where are you based?'

'Barcussy's Bakery – top of the hill. My mother runs it, and I help her, since Dad died. I saved up for years to buy the lorry, and the day I was sixteen I took it all to the bank, and bought the lorry.'

'Well, good for you, and good luck!' said Kate brightly, and Polly raised her head from the hay net and whinnied at the sound of her voice. 'Here we are, this is our cart.'

Freddie slid the box into the back and went to stroke the pony's head.

'Hello, Polly. Remember me?'

'She likes you,' said Kate, seeing Polly give Freddie a push with her soft nose.

'I like her. I took her home, that day,' said Freddie, 'and it was the first time I'd ever led a pony. She's lovely.'

'Ethie's coming,' said Kate, and her expression changed a little. 'She's my sister. So we'd better say goodbye now, Freddie.'

Ethie was still some distance away, the laden basket on her stout arm.

Freddie felt himself go cold all over. He didn't want his time with Kate to end so soon. There was so much he hadn't asked her, so much he hadn't said.

'Well – not goodbye, Kate. I hope I'll see you again,' he said, and looked deeply into her brown eyes as she stood gazing up at him.

'Thank you, Freddie, for your help. I couldn't have managed without you,' Kate said warmly, and hesitated as if a thought from very deep within was surfacing. 'And thank you – for staying with me and holding my hand that day.'

She stood on tiptoe and kissed him in the hollow of his cheek, very softly, like the butterfly. He smelled her hair, and a whiff of lavender from her clothes, and her skirt brushed against his knees. Freddie was so stunned that he felt he could float away in a beautiful bubble. His body felt weightless and his mind bathed in her sweetness.

Ethie was bearing down on them with her basket.

'Cheerio for now – Oriole Kate.' Freddie doffed his cap, took a last look into her eyes, and strode off without looking back, the feel of her kiss embossed on his cheek forever.

Chapter Thirteen

THE 'BEE-LOUD GLADE'

'He's only a lorry driver, Kate,' said Ethie spitefully, 'I don't see why you've got to have the best picnic set for HIM.'

She slammed the light brown pigskin case on the kitchen table after Kate had persuaded her to reach it down from the top shelf.

'Thank you.' Kate smiled disarmingly at her sister. 'Wait 'til you've got a young man, Ethie. You won't care what job he does as long as he's kind and handsome like Freddie.'

'Well, I shan't fuss over any boy like you do.'

'You'll never get a husband with that attitude, my

girl,' said her mother, who was busy wringing sheets through an old wooden mangle, the water streaming out across the flagstone floor and into the yard.

'Who said anything about husbands?' retorted Ethie. 'I shall find a husband when I'm good and ready, and he won't be a lorry driver.'

'Nothing so common.' Sally winked at Kate and the two of them laughed.

Ethie's expression darkened with jealousy. 'Don't you laugh at me, Kate, just 'cause you're such a flirt, twirling your silly dress around and showing your legs. At least I've got some decency. If you get married before me I'll – I'll never speak to you again.'

'She's jealous. Don't take any notice,' said Sally as Ethie slammed out of the kitchen and marched across the farmyard sending the chickens scattering. 'I don't know what gets into her. You go and have a lovely picnic with Freddie, with my blessing, Kate. You deserve a day off – and so does he, I should think. You be happy while you can.'

Kate opened the picnic set which had a set of green Bakelite plates, four round mugs and a set of cutlery neatly fixed into the lid with thick leather straps and brass buckles. She sang as she made the cucumber sandwiches, cut some slices from the big pink ham which stood on a marble slab in the larder, and packed it all into the little green dishes. She cut a hunk of cheddar from the truckle, and picked some ripe tomatoes from the plant outside the sunny kitchen. A large saucepan stood on the range full of boiled milk. The cream had risen to the top and Kate took a spoon and skimmed off some of the rich yellow crust and put it in a jar. She added fresh scones and a small pot of homemade straw-berry jam.

'There. Doesn't that look sumptuous?'

'Mmm – I might change my mind and come with you,' teased Sally, and Kate laughed.

'Don't you dare!' she cried, rolling up the tartan picnic rug.

Sally looked at her shrewdly, thinking her vivacious daughter was too alluring for her age, especially in the new slinky dress which she'd made herself from a satiny cream fabric. It clung provocatively to her curvy body, and the neckline allowed a glimpse of her ample cleavage. As usual, Kate had trimmed it with red ribbons threaded around the sleeves and waist, tied with little bows. And she had a flashy pair of red shoes which Sally had bought for her June birthday.

'Seriously, dear – you will be careful, won't you?' she said. 'You know what I mean, Kate.'

'Of course. Don't you worry at all, Mother. I can look after myself.' Kate smiled reassuringly, and added, 'It's Ethie you need to worry about, not me.'

Sally nodded, staring out of the window at the sunlit yard where Ethie was heaving a straw bale into Daisy's stable. Then she saw a cloud of dust moving along the lane in the distance.

'Here comes Freddie. Bring him in for a cup of tea, if he wants it.'

Kate was already taking the picnic case and rug outside to the cart, which stood at the door with Polly harnessed into it. She was pawing the ground and tossing her head at bothersome flies. The cart was covered in sparrows busy pecking out grain from its cracks and corners. They flew up and settled inside the dome of honeysuckle that hung over the porch.

'Poor Polly. I should have tied you in the shade,' said Kate, giving the pony a cuddle. She picked some elder leaves and sprigs of lavender and stuck them in the pony's bridle. 'There, that'll keep the flies away. Now you be a good girl. We're going up the hills and there'll be a nice cool breeze for you there – and we're going through the shady woods. You'll love it, Polly.'

★   ★   ★

Freddie was nervous as he slowed the lorry and approached Hilbegut Farm with care, knowing there were always ducks or sheep pottering about. It felt strange, having what Kate called 'a day off'. He couldn't remember the last time he'd had a whole day without working, and he felt oddly furtive about it, especially as Annie had said proudly, 'I never had a day off in my life, and neither did your father, or his father before him.' Then she'd added, 'I don't know how I'm going to manage all day on my own, I hope I don't have to go out.'

The guilt felt heavy like a yoke across his shoulders, but a tingle was in his soul. A whole day out with Kate was more than he could have dreamed about. Freddie felt apprehensive too. A picnic, she'd said, and her eyes had lit up like stars, so he'd agreed to go. He didn't know what a picnic was, so he'd asked Herbie.

Herbie had snorted. 'Picnics!' he'd said. 'I think picnics are an abomination.'

'Why? What do you do on a picnic?'

'You have to eat your dinner sitting on some outlandish place by the river or up some hillside. It's always too flaming hot and you end up getting stung by a wasp or getting ants in your pants.'

Herbie had laughed his wheezy laugh then and

disappeared into his dust-covered workshop. 'Oh yes – picnics are an abomination.'

So Freddie was even more apprehensive. He hoped he wouldn't have to dance. Kate had told him she loved dancing, and it worried Freddie. He'd never danced in his life and didn't know how. He parked the Scammell lorry and rather awkwardly picked up the bouquet of six red roses. Annie had made it for him, cutting them from the garden and making a posy with some green leaves and a few white and purple Sweet Williams round the outside. She'd grumbled all the time, but Freddie could tell she was enjoying it as he watched her fold a cone of bread paper around the posy and tie it with a strip of ribbon.

He walked across to the cart holding the posy behind his back. Kate turned, and when he saw her radiant smile he felt welcome, and he felt life and energy flood into him.

'You're holding something, Freddie!' she cried and he whipped the bouquet out and gave it to her.

'Here you are. I brought you some roses.'

'Oooh – Freddie!' Kate buried her face in the bouquet and breathed its fragrance. Then she looked up straight into his eyes. 'That's beautiful. Oh, aren't they beautiful? Thank you!'

Soon they were heading across the peat moors towards the blue-green ridge of the Polden Hills, with Polly trotting smartly along the narrow lane bordered by deep ditches and pollarded willows. Kate held the reins attentively and Freddie felt redundant, as if he suddenly didn't know what to do with his hands. He wasn't used to being a passenger, and he could scarcely believe that he was sitting next to the beautiful girl who had chosen to go on a picnic with him. They weren't going fast, yet he felt he was flying through the diamond summer, the grass and the willow leaves sparkling and the sun flashing over the brown water.

Kate began to sing, and Polly flicked her ears back to listen, and her hoof beats clip-clopped to the music. When she started on 'Danny Boy', Freddie found himself joining in, surprised by the new depth and texture of his voice, and surprised at the joy it gave him and the feeling of camaraderie with Kate.

But when they reached the woods at the foot of the hills, a different feeling lulled them into silence. Polly slowed to a walk as they entered the luminous green flickering twilight, the beeches, limes and oaks towering like the pillars of a temple. Cool and smelling sweetly of leaves and moss, the woods whispered around them, Polly's hoof beats were muffled and the wheels of the

Sheila Jeffries

cart crackled softly on the pink brown layer of calyx fallen from buds and blossom.

'Stop,' said Freddie suddenly.

Kate glanced at him, her startled eyes bright in the shadowy wood. She pulled Polly's reins gently and the pony stopped and stood motionless, listening, the cart creaking a little as the wheels became still.

'What is it?' Kate asked in a whisper.

'Listen!' said Freddie in an electrifying tone.

Kate froze and they were totally still together. They were in a wide glade surrounded by trees, the ground thickly covered in the stripy leaves and black seed-heads of dead bluebells. The sound of the glade filtered into Freddie's consciousness, stirring a distant memory. Above the clink of Polly's harness and the occasional chuck-chuck of the woodpeckers, was a humming, droning sound, at first high among the leaves, then close, then distant again. He looked deep into the woodland flora and saw the sunlight glisten on the zig-zagging bodies of dozens of bees. Honeybees, bumbles and tiny hoverflies, and the bright gold of a queen hornet buzzing through the nettles and campion.

He looked at Kate and her face was like that of a startled child, listening to the unexpected symphony of silence.

'The bees,' whispered Freddie. 'Can you hear them?'

She nodded, her mouth open in surprise, and the sunlight glinted through the trees onto her cream silk dress and the gloss of her dark hair.

'Magic,' she whispered.

They listened together.

'It's the bee-loud glade,' whispered Freddie. 'From Innisfree.'

'What?'

'It's a poem I used to like.'

'Ooh – tell me. I want to hear it.'

Freddie hesitated, embarrassed. And as soon as the embarrassment came, the magic disappeared and the bees melted away into the emerald light.

'Why are we whispering?' whispered Kate and her eyes danced with amusement. Polly gave a reverberating whinny, her harness jingled and the cart trembled and creaked. Kate broke into one of her peals of laughter. She picked up the reins again and Polly moved on, up the sloping lane through the shady wood.

'You're going to tell me that poem, when we're having our picnic,' Kate said bossily. 'I shan't let you have one of my cucumber sandwiches until you've told me.'

The spell was broken, but Freddie felt as if she had

opened a door to a part of his mind that had lain forgotten for years. Hearing the bees, then the sound of
Kate's bell-like laughter ringing through the woods, he
felt a sense of restored happiness, a wild precious
freedom he'd only experienced with Granny Barcussy.

Kate pulled Polly to a halt again.

'We must walk with her from here, Freddie,' she
said. 'It's too steep for her to pull us as well.'

They plodded one on each side of Polly as the gra-
dient increased and the ground wound upwards into the
hills. At every bend the view across the Somerset Levels
grew bluer and more panoramic, the tall trees gave way
to dense hazel copses, gnarled hawthorn bushes and field
maples festooned with bunches of pale green winged
seeds. Freddie was quiet, feeling he wanted to drink
deeply of the beauty around him, and Kate chattered
like a bubbling stream. Only when he linked his index
finger with hers in Polly's hot mane did she become
quiet. The touch was charged with a gentle energy like
the tip of a candle flame which had the potential to
ignite into a hungry fire.

Finally they reached the top of the Poldens, the lane
undulating into the distance. Kate steered Polly through
a gap in the hedge. She unhitched her from the cart and
tied her under the shade of an oak tree.

'Now for the best bit,' she said, her eyes shining. 'Let's walk up the ridge and see the view. Then we'll choose a place for our picnic.'

Before them stretched a ridge of hill against the sky. Freddie and Kate walked up towards it, winding their way through enormous anthills, patches of wild thyme, and domes of yellow trefoil.

'Tom Thumbs,' said Kate, picking one of the tiny pea-like flowers, '– and ORCHIDS! Look Freddie – orchids. They smell divine.'

'Butterfly orchids,' said Freddie. 'That's what those white ones are – and look, here's a bee orchid.' He bent to touch the complex flower which had a petal resembling a small bumblebee.

Kate looked at him in surprise.

'Fancy you knowing that, Freddie.'

'I grew up in the country, not far from here,' he said. 'And I had a granny who taught me a lot about nature, and what she didn't teach me, I learned from watching. I know all these butterflies.'

'I thought you only loved engines,' said Kate. 'You never told me.'

'Well,' Freddie considered what he wanted to say, and decided against it. He didn't want to risk upsetting her.

She looked up at him with a searching, caring gaze. 'Oh dear,' she said. 'I've done all the talking, haven't I? I know I'm a chatterbox but I do want to know about your life, and your hopes and dreams, Freddie – oh, don't look so serious! Come on, I'll race you up to the ridge.' She kicked off her red shoes and ran, grinning wickedly back at him, her hair and dress flying.

Freddie watched the two red shoes land far apart in the grass, then he ran after her in long strides, the money jingling in his pockets. He felt like an old man who wasn't used to running, and he felt like a young man who hadn't discovered himself. As soon as Kate heard his big creaky shoes thudding after her and his pockets jingling, she started to giggle.

It was like running up to the sky, being an aeroplane that could reach the ridge and take off into the air. At the top Kate stretched her arms, twirled around and stood barefoot, waiting for him.

'I love it up here,' she cried. 'Look at this view.'

The vast landscape stunned them both into silence, even distracting Freddie from wanting to stare at Kate who looked so free and alive standing beside him with her bare toes in the wiry grass.

'That's Glastonbury Tor,' she said pointing to a steep

green mound with a tower at the top. 'And the Mendips. Don't they look blue? Turquoise blue like a peacock.'

The Levels stretched below them like a chessboard of black peat fields and hay meadows of buttercup and sorrel, the rhynes shining silver, on and on into the distance where a tiny steam train was puffing its way along the track from Glastonbury to Burnham-on-Sea.

'What are those hills down there?' asked Freddie, pointing south.

'The Quantocks,' said Kate. 'And Exmoor beyond. Then you can nearly see the sea at Burnham, the Bristol Channel and sometimes you can see into WALES and see the MOUNTAINS.'

Freddie kept quiet. He'd never seen the sea, or a mountain. Kate knew a lot more than he did about their own land. Did it matter? No, he reasoned. He loved Kate, and he hoped that one day she would love him, but while that love was growing he felt he had to be quiet and respectful. He'd heard other men boasting and laughing about what they had done with girls. It sickened Freddie, and so did the girls he saw wearing lipstick and strutting around in silly clothes, or dressing up in breeches and boots, riding motorbikes, smoking fags. Kate was like a secret jewel he had discovered, he was going to keep her close to his heart, and under wraps.

It occurred to him that he hadn't given her a compliment yet, so he opted for a safe one. 'That's a beautiful dress you're wearing.'

'I'm glad you like it. I made it myself,' explained Kate, sitting down on the soft grass and leaning back on both arms. She looked at him expectantly. 'Now – I want to hear that poem.'

'Do you? What do you want to hear that for?'

'Please,' she pleaded.

So Freddie recited 'The Lake Isle of Innisfree', his quiet voice shaking a little with emotion, especially when he came to the last verse.

'I can see it means a lot to you,' said Kate. 'I'm not very good at poetry so can you explain it to me?'

'Well – I'll try to.' Freddie stared out across the Levels, gathering words from corners of his childhood, the beechnuts, the gleaned barley grains, the broken china. 'When I was a boy I never had time to play. We were poor. I had to walk a mile to school and a mile home in a pair of wooden clogs, and when I got home I had to run errands for my mother – she couldn't go out, see? And I was always hungry, I used to live on beechnuts and hazelnuts, like a squirrel I was.'

Kate's eyes were wide and solemn, her mouth open as she listened to his story, so different from her own.

'Then, when the war ended, Dad bought the bakery in Monterose. He wanted me to be a baker, see? He thought that would be a fine life for me. But – I didn't want it, and I had to do it, Kate. Can you understand that?' He paused, reassured by the way she was listening so attentively. 'Then for the rest of my life I had to get up at five in the morning, every morning, help make the bread, then load it into the bike and do the delivery round, all that before school – oh and I used to go down the station to carry luggage – so that poem, where it says "I shall have some peace there," and "live alone in the bee-loud glade", it used to give me peace, just saying it, or thinking it. When we moved to Monterose, I missed the countryside, but no one ever knew that. I never told anyone. But that last verse, about "standing on the pavements grey" and "feeling it in the deep earth's core" – I understood that feeling so well . . .'

'Oh Freddie.' Kate reached out and touched the back of his wrist, looking into his face with compassion. 'Go on.'

''Tis a miserable story,' Freddie said, suddenly afraid that he had caused a cloud to drift over their summer picnic. 'You don't want to hear all that.'

'I do,' said Kate, and her eyes never left his face.

'Well – I'm coming to a better bit now.' Freddie remembered the storytelling tradition in his family, the exaggerations, the silences, and the laughter. He wanted to do that for Kate, turn his miserable tale into something entertaining and positive. 'I'll tell you how I got that lorry. Well, one frosty night in the middle of February – hard as diamonds the frost was – I gets up, quiet as a mouse . . .'

Kate sat spellbound, not moving a muscle as she listened to his story, holding her breath in the silences. She let go of Freddie's wrist so that he could gesticulate with his long fingers, his eyes beginning to twinkle, his voice still slow and quiet. Then he came to the part where he had escaped down the steep dark street on his bike.

'The bike had no brakes, see? So I went whizzing down there, in the pitch dark, with my legs stuck out straight and sparks flying from my boots . . .'

He was rewarded with a scream of laughter. Kate doubled over, clutching her stomach with one hand and wiping her eyes with the other. She laughed and laughed as if she would never stop, and Freddie managed to stay po-faced.

'Well 'tis true,' he said, and that set her off again. Secretly pleased, he continued his story, restraining himself from smiles as he related how he had paid his money into the bank.

'As soon as the doors opened, I went in with my flour sack, dragging it along the floor. Then I stood at the counter taking out the old socks full of money and some of them blue and mouldy, and the hankies, all dusty they were and bursting with coins. And the bank clerk, he didn't like it. He looked me up and down as if I was a tramp, and he said, "You can't bring that dirty old stuff in here." So I looked him in the eye and said – quite politely – "Excuse me Sir, but I can, I'm sixteen and this is legal tender," and he didn't like it, but he had to count it all. Took him three quarters of an hour jingling and cussing, and there was a queue behind me right out the door, and they were all grumbling. But I had the last laugh. I came out of there with my money in crisp new bank notes, then I went flying down to the motor yard on me bread bike, and I had that Scammell lorry.'

He paused to take a breath, and saw that Kate was wanting to say something.

'What a WONDERFUL story, Freddie,' she said passionately, 'so funny, and inspiring. Tell me again. I loved it.'

'Well 'tis true. True as I'm sitting here,' said Freddie, and his smile stretched right to the edges of his face.

'I love to see you smile,' said Kate and she kissed him impulsively on his smiling cheek.

Startled and moved by her response, Freddie slipped his arm around her shoulders, feeling the silky dress and her warmth underneath, and she put her hand on his shoulder. For a moment they were both still, feeling each other's heartbeat, and Freddie buried his chin in the soft lustre of her dark hair. The moment filled with light and stretched into infinity as if it had registered in some ethereal archive.

He held her in a shell-like hug, afraid of his own strength and of the sudden rush of energy through his body. His pulse wanted to race like a wild horse, yet his mind stayed calm, his inner voice telling him to slow down and savour the intoxicating feel of her satin dress, the way her dark curls were hot from the sunshine as they slipped over his bare arm.

'This is only the beginning,' he heard himself whisper, but he held back from speaking the words that echoed in his heart, words that Granny Barcussy had fed into his soul. 'When you love, you must love wisely and slowly.' Nothing in his life had felt so exquisitely precious as the warm bright silk of Kate in his arms.

A flock of small birds came bobbing and bouncing out of the woods, their voices tinkling like bells, and the grass around them came alive with fluttering wings.

'Goldfinches,' whispered Freddie.

But Kate was listening to something else.

'I can hear your tummy rumbling,' she said, laughing, and sat up. The goldfinches vanished with a burr of wings. 'I think it's time for our DELICIOUS picnic.'

Chapter Fourteen

THE STONE GATEPOST

Freddie stood in the stonemason's yard, staring in disbelief at a load of stone which had appeared there. It wasn't stacked neatly as Herbie would have liked, but tipped in a jumble of old saddle stones, and blocks of golden sandstone, some still joined together with mortar. The stones gave Freddie a strange feeling, as if they had voices and stories to tell, stories locked into the grains of sand and crystal. He looked at the wheel marks in the mud and saw the large hoof prints of a Shire horse, as if the heavy load had been delivered by horse and cart, probably early in the morning before it got too hot. Seeing the hoof prints increased his inexplicable sense of doom.

Right in the middle of the heap were two round domes of stone carved with curly patterns and covered in moss and lichen. Carvings! With a terrible sense that he was going to discover some unforeseen tragedy, Freddie climbed over the blocks to investigate. Gingerly he cleared a space around one of the domes until he could see a face glaring out at him with blind stone eyes and snarling lips. Shocked, he sat down on a chunk of sandstone, reached out his hands and touched the stone lion's curly head. It was warm from the August sunshine, but under its chin it was cold as a tomb. Silently he uncovered both the carvings and sat studying them, not wanting to believe the thought that hammered insistently at his mind.

'Mornin', Freddie!' Herbie came padding into the yard in his leather apron and dust-covered overalls. ''Tis hot,' he remarked, taking his cap off to let the top of his bald head dry in the sun.

'Mornin',' said Freddie.

'You're looking uncommonly serious,' observed Herbie. 'Has your mother been at you again?'

'No,' said Freddie. He looked at Herbie's challenging grey eyes. 'Where did this lot come from, Herb?'

'Hilbegut.'

Something swept over Freddie like a gust of hot air,

charged with emotion. He rubbed the backs of his hands over his eyes, brushing away the tears that prickled in there.

The stone lions from Hilbegut Farm.

Something had happened to Kate.

'Haven't you heard?' said Herbie. 'The Squire of Hilbegut died weeks ago. And he didn't have an heir. So his place is just left empty, that great big place with the turrets. And all his tenants in the farms and cottages have got to move. Tragic, ain't it? Those poor families. Got nowhere to go.'

'So who's done this?' asked Freddie. 'These two stone lions were on the gateposts to Hilbegut Farm.'

Herbie's prominent eyebrows drew together in a frown, and he shook his head. 'Can't say I know that,' he said, 'I only knows what I hears, see? Maybe 'tis gossip, but they say his sister and her family have come over from Canada, and they don't care nothing about the place. They're stripping out the carvings and the stone and anything they can sell. They just want the money, see. Then they'll go off back to Canada and leave Hilbegut to go to rack and ruin. That's all I know, and 'tis none of my business.'

Freddie began to shake inside. He made an instant decision. He would unload the stone he'd brought down from the quarry for Herbie, then drive out to Hilbegut and find out for himself. But first . . .

'What about the stone lions?' he asked.

'Oh – I've not really looked at them properly yet,' said Herbie, 'but they'll fetch a lot of money. Rich folks with money to burn buy that sort of stuff.'

'I'd like to buy them,' said Freddie.

'You couldn't afford them, Freddie. Come on. What d'you want 'em for anyway? Stick one on the front of your lorry!' Herbie gave one of his wheezy laughs that went on and on until it ended in a coughing fit.

Freddie thought about his savings. He'd done well with the haulage business and was planning to buy a second lorry. To blow it all on two stone lions would be foolish.

Herbie was leaning forward, his eyes looking curiously into Freddie's soul. 'So tell me – why do you want them?'

'I'm interested in carving. I've watched you a lot,' said Freddie. 'I'd like to do it myself.'

''Tis hard,' said Herbie, 'a hard, dusty old job. Makes me cough. And look at me hands. You don't want to do that, Freddie. You stick to your lorry, if you take my advice. Anyway, I doubt whether you could do a decent stone carving; it's not as easy as you think.'

'I could,' said Freddie with unexpected passion. 'I know I could.'

'So what do you want to carve?'

'An angel.'

'That's about the hardest thing you could choose.'

'I know I could,' insisted Freddie, thinking of Kate's beautiful bewitching young face. 'I can see it in my mind exactly.'

Herbie's eyes looked thoughtful under the bushy brows. He began moving the blocks of stone around as if searching, and heaved out a big lump of sandstone from the Hilbegut gateposts.

'I'll tell you what, Freddie. This here, this is Bath stone, and it's easy to carve. If you like, I'll give you this block, and I'll bet you can't carve an angel out of that 'cause I couldn't.'

Freddie's eyes lit up. The angel inside the stone shone out at him. He could see its curved wings, its praying hands and flowing hair, and the tranquillity of its gaze.

'How much d'you bet then, Herbie?'

'A pound.'

'Right. You're on.'

The two men shook hands, their eyes glinting at each other. Together they heaved the block of Bath stone into the back of Freddie's lorry.

221

'You got any tools?' asked Herbie.

'A few.'

'Chisels?'

'No.'

'I'd better lend you some.' Herbie rummaged in his workshop and came out with a wooden box full of chisels. 'I don't want 'em back, Freddie. I got plenty.'

'Thanks,' said Freddie. He itched to take the chisel out and begin to carve the angel still shining in his mind. He had another job to do, hauling timber, and then he would go to Hilbegut.

'For goodness' sake, Kate, stop that crying,' said Sally briskly. She stood very upright, dressed in her best navy blue dress and hat, the breeze ruffling a few wisps of grey hair that had escaped from her tightly coiled bun. 'We've got to make the best of it.'

'I'm trying to stop,' said Kate.

'That's my girl.' Bertie gave his daughter a fatherly pat on her proud young shoulders.

'I'm not crying,' gloated Ethie. But she was. Inside her mind, a weather front was coiling itself into a hurricane with storm force winds and rain, just waiting to come sweeping across her new life.

Together the Loxley family stood on the jetty,

watching the ferry boat chugging towards them with its load of passengers. The brown waters of the Severn Estuary swirled with fierce energy, the tide sweeping the boat sideways as it reached the middle of the river. And Bertie said what he always said when they were in the queue at Aust Ferry.

'Fastest tide in the world, they say, except for one in South Africa,' he said. 'I'll warn you girls now. Never, ever go swimming in the Severn. If the mud doesn't get you, the tide will.'

'Look at that boat,' cried Ethie. 'It's having a real fight to get out of the current.'

'Now it has,' said Sally, seeing the boat turn and head for the jetty, sending a wide creamy brown wave fanning across the calmer water. 'Come on now, Kate, you usually enjoy the trip.'

Kate nodded. Her throat felt dry and sore from unaccustomed crying. She couldn't believe they were leaving Hilbegut. Everything there was so dear to her. The swing in the barn door, the happy chickens, the sweet-smelling haystacks and the shady elm trees. The beautiful avenue of copper beeches where she'd skipped and played on her trips to deliver milk to the Squire. The home paddock where white Aylesbury ducks, geese, sheep and chickens pottered happily under the branches of the walnut tree. Her lovely bedroom with its window peering out under a brow of thatch where swallows and sparrows nested under the eaves.

She'd been used to leaving home and going to boarding school, but home had always been there for her to come back to. Now, unexpectedly and with merciless speed, it was gone. Her father was suddenly jobless, homeless and in poor health, her mother stoically trying to hold them all together. The only person who seemed intact was Ethie. But Ethie, Kate thought, hadn't got a boyfriend to leave behind.

Kate was breaking her heart over every single duck, chicken and cow. All had gone to auction, except for Polly and Daisy who were loaned to the farm next door until they could be transported to Gloucestershire. Bertie had insisted on the four of them travelling together in a friend's motorcar, and Kate had been terribly sick all the way to the ferry, giving Ethie another opportunity to say scathingly, 'For goodness' sake, Kate, can't you stop being sick?' It was either 'stop crying' or 'stop being sick' or 'stop mooning over that BOY.'

Nobody knew how Kate felt about Freddie. Since the day on the hills she'd respected the depth of his artistic soul, the determined pragmatism that had driven him to save his money and build a business, and her admiration for him had grown. She'd found herself longing to be looking into his eyes. They reminded her of the sea, so blue and sparkling, but so deep and so full of immense perception. Freddie hadn't had an education like she'd had, yet she felt he knew so much more, and when he looked at her she felt a steadiness and a kindliness, a feeling of guardianship, as if Freddie was a harbour and she a boat coming home from a storm.

Kate was seventeen, and she loved to flirt and laugh with the local lads on the farm, but she had boundaries. Her sexuality felt to her like a secret jewel she must not wear. She made sure that no man touched her, and if they tried she would deflect them in a firm but humorous way, and she felt confident of her ability to do that. It was something Ethie didn't understand. Ethie ragged her constantly, berating her for being a flirt and a shameless hussy. Kate rarely reacted. She felt sorry for Ethie who seemed cursed with unpleasantness both in her dour appearance and her mood.

Freddie had only held her for a few moments, but Kate had heard his deep slow heartbeat, and smelled the tweed of his jacket, and sensed the gentleness of his big hands on her back, holding her as if she were a fragile shell. She'd felt a tiny movement as his fingers explored the curls at the ends of her hair, and that had been strangely electrifying, as if her hair itself was sensitive, as if he was touching her whole being. Wary of the intensity, she had pulled away. Now she wished with all her heart that she'd kissed him.

The throbbing engine of the incoming ferry boat had a finality about it, yet on previous trips it had excited her and set her dancing around on the quay. Something else was pulling at her mind. Kate didn't want to be a cheese-maker and a farm girl. She wanted to be a nurse. Sally had taken her one day to Yeovil Hospital to enquire about training, and the matron had liked her and said to come back when she was seventeen.

The boat was pulling in to the jetty, with much hauling of ropes and shouting.

'Stand back. Stand back. Let 'em off,' shouted the pier attendant, as the ramp was lowered and the first passengers disembarked. Next came the motorbikes and bicycles.

'They say that one day they'll build a boat that will carry motorcars,' said Bertie, 'think of that. A great heavy motorcar being driven onto a boat. But that's years ahead – years ahead.'

'You say that every time we come here, Daddy,' Ethie said and strode ahead of them onto the boat. 'We can get on now.'

'Come on, Kate.' Sally saw her daughter hanging back, white-faced, and she was sad. She'd never known Kate so uncannily silent. 'Come on, dear,' she encouraged. 'We've got to make the best of it. You stick with your family, girl. Come on – chin up.'

'You'll feel better when we get settled in,' said Bertie. 'And it won't be easy for Don and his family, having us lot. We're lucky to have a place to go. Don will be waiting for us over there at Beechley, in his motorcar.'

'At least it's a farm,' said Ethie, making a rare attempt to be cheerful. 'At least we haven't got to live in a town.'

Kate squared her shoulders and stepped onto the boat. She went to stand by herself at the back, leaning on the rail so that she could take a last gaze at the land she was leaving. And she thought about the secret letter she'd left tucked into a crack in the wall by the front door. He had to find it, he just had to. Freddie would think she had just abandoned him.

The sky was plum dark over Monterose as Freddie unloaded the last pine plank into the furniture-maker's warehouse. Coppery lightning was playing in the distance, illuminating clouds and hilltops. It hadn't rained for weeks, the earth was cracked, and a haze of dust hung in the air above the streets.

'Cuppa tea, Freddie?'

'No thanks, Bill. I've got to go somewhere else before dark,' said Freddie. He took out his wallet and added the two crumpled pound notes that Bill had paid him. It was four o'clock on a Saturday, and he had a few hours of daylight left. Part of him wanted to go home and start carving the block of stone, but going to Hilbegut seemed more important. He'd been due to see Kate tomorrow, after she'd been to church and had lunch with her family, then she had a few hours before milking time. Since the picnic they'd been meeting most Sundays, spending the time strolling in the lanes around Hilbegut, or sitting by the river. Precious hours for both of them. In the busy lives they had, work came first.

Annie hadn't met Kate yet, but Freddie had tried to tell her about their friendship. Her reaction had been ominous.

'You're both too young to be courting,' she'd warned.

'We're not courting,' said Freddie, annoyed.

'Well, what do you call it then?'

'We're just friends.'

'You should be helping me on a Sunday, not running round with the likes of her.'

Freddie had felt his face go hot with anger at hearing Kate described in such a way. Still haunted by the memory of Levi's rages, he deliberately distanced himself from his mother's inflammatory remarks with a brief silence and a calm, unruffled reply.

'Kate is a decent girl; you'd like her. She's from a good family, farmers they are, out at Hilbegut.'

'Oh them. That Loxley family, is it?'

'Yes.'

'You don't want to get mixed up with them. They're POSH,' Annie said bitterly. 'Sent those girls to boarding school. They aren't our kind of folk, Freddie. That Sally Loxley. I KNOW HER. Went to school with her. Sally Delby she was then. And when she was growing up, she was a flirt. Wild and shameless, that's what she was – and when she married Bertie Loxley, then she turned into such a snob. She . . .'

'Calm down, Mother. I'll be back to help you later.' Freddie had said no more, but left Annie grumbling to herself in the kitchen, and headed out resolutely to see Kate.

That was a fortnight ago. He thought about the last time he'd seen Kate. She hadn't been any different. Or had she? He remembered a couple of times when a shadow had crept into her eyes, but when he'd asked her if anything was wrong she'd changed the subject in her cheery way.

As he set off for Hilbegut through the dark afternoon, Freddie felt increasingly anxious, and guilty too about leaving his mother alone with a thunderstorm brewing. Annie was frightened of thunder. She would be sitting under the table, Freddie thought, as he steered the lorry out across the Levels. The fields looked sombre, the cattle huddled into corners and the breeze was turning up the leaves of the silver poplars, their white undersides like shoals of fish underwater.

The roads across the Levels were dead straight with grass verges sloping steeply down to deep rhynes. Freddie concentrated on keeping the lorry on the narrow, uneven track. One wheel on the grass verge and the lorry would roll into the ditch. The lightning was distracting, and above the noise of his engine, he heard thunder. Hailstones bounced on the road in front of him and pinged on the bonnet of the lorry as he drove into the storm that had broken over Hilbegut. Blinded by the violent hail, Freddie was forced to stop in the middle of the Levels, and, fearing the engine would overheat, he turned it off and sat there in the cab next to an old crack willow which stood alone on the green Levels.

Within minutes the ground was white all over with

a layer of crunchy hailstones, and lightning was dancing over the fields as if the thunderclouds had come right down to touch the earth. Freddie had never felt afraid of storms, in fact he'd rather enjoyed them, but out in the open, he knew there was a danger of being struck. If that happened, the petrol tank would explode in a fireball and he would die. All his life Annie had relentlessly instilled her fears into his young mind and he felt engulfed by the accumulated mass of terror, the sting of each hailstone was like a word she had spoken, bombarding him with ice. He felt he had to hack his way through it to get to the bright flame that was Kate.

Freddie wrapped his arms over the steering wheel and put his head down on them, the sound of the hail roaring in his ears, the lorry shuddering with each roll of thunder and the branches of the crack willow bending and tossing outside. He closed his eyes and saw himself hunched there in the storm, like a pip inside an apple, protected in a hard shiny case. The cab of the lorry was shielding him, the hailstones battering at the glass, building peaks of ice up the windscreen, but he was inside, and once he had travelled into the centre of his mind, he felt calm. An old sweet scent from long ago filled the cab, a sharp tang of boot polish, the heavy sweetness of meadow hay.

'Start the engine.'

Freddie looked up into the eyes of his grandfather, the man he had seen under the lime tree in the wood. He was stunned. After all the years of unyielding toil he could still see spirit people. He wasn't dead inside. And they hadn't abandoned him.

He pulled the starter, and the engine hiccupped a few times, then fired, blowing smoke out of the exhaust. Freddie smeared the steamed-up windscreen and peered out. Now he could see the far edge of the storm like a slice of apple in the western sky. It was still hailing, but he drove forward slowly, the tyres crunching through slush. He didn't dare turn his head but he sensed his grandfather was still beside him along the treacherous road, over the river bridge, and up onto higher ground, the hailstones melting and pouring down the lanes in twisting rivulets of brown water. The hail changed to silver bristles of rain sweeping and swerving across the landscape, and when he reached the village of Hilbegut it was awash with flood-water. People were rushing about with brooms and buckets, the water lapping at their doorsteps.

Freddie drove slowly through, making a small bow-wave, and headed uphill towards the chimneys and turrets of Hilbegut Court. He paused outside the entrance to the avenue of copper beeches, and saw that the great wrought iron gates were closed, the lawn grass was long and unkempt, and a thousand jackdaws sat on the roof, beaks to the western sky, the brassy light glistening on their black feathers.

Turning in to Hilbegut Farm brought a familiar buzz of excitement in his body. He imagined Kate opening the door to him, her big bright eyes filling his soul. She always made him feel like the most important person on earth. When he'd spent a couple of hours with her, his face actually ached from unaccustomed smiling.

He knew that Kate's parents liked him. Sally and Bertie had made him welcome with cups of tea and scones fresh from the oven. Only Ethie had been offhand and resentful, and he'd been surprised to find Kate being so kind and understanding towards her prickly-natured sister. Today he felt sure they would welcome him and perhaps be glad of the help he and his lorry could offer if they were moving house.

The storm had slunk away towards Monterose and the late afternoon light glowed mellow on the farmhouse chimneys. But the stone lions were gone, the tall gateposts demolished, and in their place were two iron stakes and a pair of metal gates.

A dread, cold as the hailstones, entered Freddie's heart. He parked the lorry and got out, stretched, and picked his way through puddles to open the gates. A terrible sight confronted him. Barbed wire had been wound along the tops of the gates, and a padlock on a heavy chain held them firmly closed. Inside was a white notice with black letters: 'TRESPASSERS WILL BE PROSECUTED'.

Devastated, Freddie stood at the forbidding gates, looking in at the farmyard. Not a duck or a goose or a chicken, no sound of cows from the milking shed, no dogs barking. Only the swallows dived in and out of the barns. The swing hung, unused, in the barn doorway. And the windows of the farmhouse, which had always been bright with curtains and ornaments, had the wooden shutters closed, barred and padlocked. It made the friendly old house look blind and sad.

They couldn't have gone far, Freddie reasoned. Kate knew he lived at the bakery in Monterose, and surely she would contact him. He walked along the boundary wall round to the back, seeking a way in. The back gate was locked and wired and he peered through, noticing that the saddle stones which had lined the path had gone. He stood on a milk churn against the wall and climbed over, using the espalier pear tree as a ladder to climb down inside. He listened, and heard the garden dripping and the gurgle of water pouring over the sides of the rain butt. Even the sparrows seemed to have gone, and only a robin sang in the abandoned garden, the ground covered in lingering clusters of hailstones and mirror-like puddles.

One of the shutters was broken, and he squinted through into the interior of the kitchen. In the dim light he was surprised to see the kitchen table and chairs still there, the mat still on the flagstone floor in front of the stove. A shining trickle of water was creeping across the floor. He watched it gathering into a pool, and no one was there to sweep it out with the brooms that stood unused against the wall. The room which had been a hub of life with Sally and her two girls bottling fruit and making butter, a room which had rung with Kate's laughter, now looked colourless and tomb-like.

Freddie needed to think, so he sat on the swing in the barn door, feeling sure that no one was watching him, a grown man swinging like a child in a place where trespassers would be prosecuted. The words sounded dreadful to him, like 'hung, drawn and quartered', but he didn't care. He moved the swing to and fro, higher and higher, and he could feel Kate there with him, her red ribbon flying as she swung out of the barn and in again. The higher he swung the more he could see over the wall, and in the golden, storm-washed sky of late afternoon a tower of black smoke was rising. Freddie got off the swing and climbed the stone steps up the side of the barn to the open archway of the hayloft. From there he could see across the Levels to Monterose, the rhynes gleaming in the sunlight, the fields glinting with water. Freddie focused on the smoke billowing from a blazing fire in the middle of the Levels. A tree. It was a tree on fire. A cold realisation crept up Freddie's spine. The old crack willow where he had parked his lorry had been struck by lightning and was burning fiercely.

Stunned, he watched it, suddenly aware that his life had been saved. Why? he thought. Why me? Why does my life matter? The answers came as he thought of Kate, and he thought of the stone angel waiting to be carved from the block of Hilbegut stone. I'm not a lorry driver, he thought. I'm someone else, someone I haven't discovered.

A loneliness crept over him. Cold and tired, he headed back to climb over the wall and go home. Then something made him turn, as if a hand pushed him, and he walked round to the front of the house. He stood looking at the front door under its thatched porch, and a fragment of red caught his eye. A red ribbon, hanging from a crack in the wall.

Freddie reached up and pulled it gently, and found it attached to a white sealed envelope which slid out of the crack and into his hands.

Chapter Fifteen

THE WATER IS WIDE

'How much is this map?'

'Ninepence,' said the postmistress, peering at Freddie through the iron grille of her domain. 'And they're good ones. You won't find better. It's got all the roads, and the railways and even the hills and valleys in Great Britain.'

'What about the rivers?' Freddie asked.

'And the rivers. They're shown in blue squiggly lines,' she said, hanging on to the tightly folded map.

'I'll take it, please.' Freddie delved into his pocket and produced a sixpence and three pennies. He wasn't used to shopping, and it had taken him about ten minutes to decide to buy the map which he wasn't allowed to look at first. Ninepence seemed expensive for a bit of paper.

'Going travelling, are you?' The postmistress raised her eyebrows, teasing him as she took the money and slid the map over the counter. 'Now, is there anything else? We've got a long queue behind you.'

Freddie hesitated.

'Well – a box of writing paper and envelopes please – and a book of stamps.'

'Ah!' she grinned knowingly. 'Got a young lady to write to, have we?'

Freddie could hear some girls giggling in the queue behind him, and he felt his neck going red as he stood there, his trousers too short and covered in dust and oil.

'That'll be another shilling.'

He had a shilling but chose to rummage in his pockets again, the postmistress rolling her eyes as he slowly counted out twelve pennies. Then he paused to put the map into his inner jacket pocket, and turned to pad thoughtfully out of the post office, his eyes staring at a kestrel hovering in the sky outside. He didn't want to look at anyone. The pain of losing Kate stung in his throat and he wanted to go home, spread the map out on the scullery table, and see where she had gone to live.

'Hello, Freddie!' Joan Jarvis was at the back of the queue, dressed up in her fox furs, a brand new willow basket squeaking on her arm.

'Oh – hello, Mrs Jarvis,' said Freddie, respectfully. He looked down at the hand she had put on his arm and saw long red painted nails. Bird's claws, he thought with a shudder.

'Joan,' she insisted. 'How's business?'

'Pretty good. Busy.'

'I hear you'll be getting a second lorry soon,' said Joan brightly. 'You are doing well.'

Freddie knew that Joan liked and admired him. She'd often stopped to talk to him in her encouraging way, but right now he didn't feel like talking, especially as her voice carried all over the shop and out into the street.

'You remember Susan, my daughter.'

Freddie glanced at the slim girl with bobbed blonde hair who looked as if she didn't want to be there.

'This is Freddie Barcussy, Susan. You know – he used to help you over the bridge. Oh, you were silly.'

'Hello.' Freddie looked briefly at Susan. She didn't interest him, but he remembered the frightened little girl she had been, and thought she still looked frightened, of her mother, he guessed. 'I won't shake hands,' he said, 'I'm covered in stone dust.'

239

'Stone dust? What have you been doing?' asked Joan.

'I'm having a go at a bit of stone carving,' said Freddie.

Joan looked at him with keen interest, and to Freddie's relief the queue moved forward. 'I shall come and see what you've made one day.' Joan looked back at him perkily like a bird on the lawn. 'Bye now.'

'Bye.'

He walked home without looking at anyone, carrying the box of writing paper. The bakery was busy with customers, Annie in the shop and Gladys making scones in the back. Freddie escaped upstairs and spread the map on the table in his bedroom window. He found Monterose, and followed the road with his pencil stub, along the ridge of the Poldens where he and Kate had picnicked, on through Glastonbury and Wells, then over the Mendips. Kate had vividly described the River Severn to him, but when he found Aust Ferry and saw how wide it was, Freddie's heart sank. He'd visualised an ordinary river, a bit wider than the Cary or the Brue, not such an expanse of water coloured blue like the sea. He took his ruler, looked at the scale of the map, and measured, once, then again in disbelief. The Severn was a mile wide at Aust Ferry. Freddie had never even seen

the sea, and he couldn't imagine a mile of water. All
that space, hills and valleys and a wide, wide river sep-
arating him from Kate.

Kate's letter was in his inner pocket next to his heart.
Extracting it from the silky lining of his jacket he read
it again.

Dear Freddie,
I will always treasure the time I have spent with you,
such a happy time, and I thank you for sharing it with
me.

Sadly, I must tell you that we are leaving Hilbegut.
The Squire has died, and his family from Canada are
ruthlessly reclaiming his estate, and we were given two
weeks' notice to leave. I didn't want to go, of course, but
I must support our family, Mother and Dad and Ethie.
We are all broken-hearted, but we must make the best
of it. Luckily we have somewhere to go. We shall be
living with Dad's brother, Uncle Don, at Asan Farm on
the banks of the Severn River. He's said we can live in
the gatehouse cottage. It's derelict but we can make it nice
and we shall all help with the farm. Polly and Daisy are
still in Hilbegut, on the next-door farm, and they are
being looked after there until we can find a way to trans-
port them to Gloucestershire.

*I still want to be a nurse, and perhaps one day I can,
but for now I must stay and help the family.*

*I'll never, ever forget you Freddie, and I hope with all
my heart that we will one day meet again.*

All my love,

Kate xx

PS. Write to me!

A small sepia photograph on a square of cream cardboard was enclosed. It was a portrait of Kate's face, a
serious image of a young woman with bright caring
eyes. Freddie placed it on the map, in Gloucestershire,
and was suddenly overwhelmed by the enormity of the
space between them. His heart was no longer in his
haulage business. He felt unsettled and disconnected
from everyone; he needed time alone to think about his
life, and how to disentangle himself from his present
commitments. The biggest of these was his bond with
his mother. He loved her, yet she drained his energy
and his time. Since Levi's death he'd felt sorry for her,
and her agoraphobia had intensified. She was totally
dependent on Freddie, and on Gladys who she now
employed for a few hours a day.

When he had finished his haulage job, Freddie felt an
old familiar feeling – he couldn't stay at home. He filled

the lorry with petrol and headed for the Polden Hills in the balmy afternoon, driving past orchards where the trees were laden to the ground with ripening apples and the hawthorns heavy with berries. He drove slowly along the hilltop until he reached the gap in the hedge where Kate had taken him for the picnic. He parked the lorry tight against the hedge and walked up to the ridge of hill, aware that the grassland around him was now bobbing with seed heads, the orchids had died, the thyme had turned brown, and the trefoil was covered in tiny black pods of seed. Summer was over. And so was his life, Freddie thought gloomily.

He sat down in the spot where they'd had the picnic, and touched the earth where Kate had been sitting. It was warm and crisp like fresh bread, but there was an emptiness, a hollow place in his soul where Kate should have been. His eyes roamed the landscape, scanning that empty strip of silver sky between the Mendips and the Quantocks. Far away he could see the islands of the Bristol Channel floating in some shimmering misty place, and beyond was a whisper of an outline of high and distant hills. Was he seeing over that mile-wide estuary into Gloucestershire where Kate was now? It comforted Freddie to think that he could come up here and gaze directly towards her.

Surely it was possible to send his thoughts whizzing over there on some ethereal network. He remembered the vision he'd had at his father's funeral. Sitting on the steps at the back of the church he'd seen a beam of gold deep down in the earth and stretching for miles and miles, following the curve of the earth. Granny Barcussy knew some amazing things, and once she'd told him about the Aborigines who lived in Australia, and how they communicated with distant tribes by using the song lines. It wasn't logical, but in his prophetic soul, Freddie understood it. He wished he had a drum to beat out a message that would carry across the water to that distant shore. All he had was his voice. He looked around, checking that he was alone on the ridge, and he was.

He started to sing, huskily at first, furtively, then confidently as he remembered some of the songs Kate liked. 'Danny Boy' – he could sing that – and the words mirrored his feelings exactly, so he sang that first. Then he remembered 'The water is wide, I cannot cross over'. He sang until the tears started trickling down his cheeks and drying on his skin in the afternoon sun. Then he strolled along the ridge, whistling the nostalgic tunes, and the sadness began to disperse as if the music was sweeping it away. It was a time for courage, he thought, for making the best of it, as Kate had said. He must focus on building his business, making enough money to afford a home fit for Kate. And there was no reason why he shouldn't go to Gloucestershire and see her, he thought, especially if he had a motorbike.

Kate sat on the top bar of the high wooden gate, her arms round the neck of a sleek chestnut horse. The feel of its warm silky coat, the softness of its muzzle and the kindly dark eyes were cheering her up. There were other horses in the field, but this one, a thoroughbred, had made a beeline for Kate as if it knew she needed a friend.

Bertie knew his daughter very well, and he had deliberately sent Kate out on her own, 'to check the sheep' he'd said, knowing that the route to the sheep pastures would take Kate past the racing stables, and she would be sure to find a horse to cuddle. So while Ethie and Sally organised the new cheese-making enterprise, Kate had gone off by herself, dressed in her farming gear of breeches, long boots and a red shirt. She'd enjoyed the walk through the sheep fields on the wide flat banks of the Severn Estuary, the fresh salty air and the light on the water, the surge of the incoming tide as it covered the expanses of sand and spilled into mirror-like pools where thousands of seabirds bobbed and fished, their cream

Sheila Jeffries

heads and silvery feathers shining in the morning sun. This landscape was so different from Hilbegut. The tidal river was dominant and powerful, eating away at the sheep fields, making low turfy cliffs and inlets. In the distance were the high wooded hills of the Forest of Dean.

Kate had walked a mile along the green banks, carefully looking at the grazing sheep and the fat summer lambs, seeing no signs of illness or trouble. She had sat on the turfy cliff edge, swinging her boots and enjoying the fresh wind on her cheeks, and watched a line of barges chugging up the river. Laden with massive mahogany logs from the rainforest, they turned into the canal entrance to wait at the lock gates and then unload their cargo at the timber mill.

Parallel to the sheep pastures, on slightly higher ground, was the land belonging to the racing stables, a circuit of it expensively fenced with post and rails to make a 'gallop'. Kate hadn't had much experience of racehorses and she was eager to see them. The horse she was petting suddenly raised its head and whinnied loudly. Along the lane came a man riding an elegant dappled grey racehorse and leading a second one, a glossy bay with a black mane and tail.

'Hello there.' He paused, surprised to see the dark-haired, dark-eyed girl sitting on the gate. Kate flashed a

246

smile at him, and he smiled back. He had very white teeth and black merry eyes.

'Hello.' Kate jumped down from the gate and went to stroke the two tall horses who arched their necks graciously and blew in her hair. 'Are they racehorses?'

'Yes – both, in training for Cheltenham.'

'They're so beautiful,' breathed Kate. 'Are they yours?'

'Yes. Bred them both, I did,' he said proudly, smoothing the neck of the grey horse who stood staring thoughtfully into the distance. 'I'm Ian Tillerman. And you are?'

'Kate Loxley.'

'Ah – a Loxley.'

'I'm Don Loxley's niece.'

'Just on holiday, are you?'

'No. We've come here to live at Asan Farm with my uncle. Mother, Dad, Ethie and me, from Hilbegut in Somerset.'

Ian Tillerman's eyes brightened with interest. He looked intently at Kate who, he thought, exuded confidence and sparkle as she stood looking up at him.

'Want a ride?' he said impulsively. 'Can you ride?'

'Ooh yes. I love riding.' Kate beamed. 'But I've never ridden a real racehorse. I'd love to.'

Ian Tillerman kicked his feet free of the stirrups and

jumped down. He stood gazing at Kate for a moment. 'Are you used to galloping? These horses are fast, believe me.'

'Yes,' said Kate firmly, even though her nerves were on fire with excitement.

'You ride the bay. She's called Little Foxy, and she's a good girl. She's fine as long as she doesn't see a motorbike. Just let her have her head. We'll do two circuits of the track,' he said. 'Keep her level with me, then I'll know you're all right.'

He gave Kate a leg up onto the horse, a bit too vigorously, so that she nearly shot over the other side.

'Whoops. Steady on!' she laughed loudly and Little Foxy flicked her ears back to listen to this new rider on her back, a girl with a bird-like voice and kind hands that smoothed the crest of her neck. Kate adjusted the stirrups, and took the reins.

'I can see you'll be fine,' said Ian Tillerman. He vaulted onto the grey horse and they set off at a sedate walk, through the gap in the hedge and into the gallop circuit. Kate was thrilled. Little Foxy was quivering with excitement, knowing she was going to gallop like a wild horse. She began to dance sideways, her muscles rippling in the sunlight. Ian Tillerman glanced at Kate and raised his black eyebrows. 'Ready?'

'You bet,' she said, and before he could say anything else she had let Little Foxy go and was galloping ahead of him, her hair streaming back as she crouched low over the horse's neck, her knees gripping the leather saddle, her heels well down. He tore after her, his heart pounding when he saw the risk he'd taken so impulsively, letting a perfect stranger, a girl, ride his expensive, corned-up racehorse. Supposing she couldn't cope and had a terrible accident? It would be his fault, and Don Loxley would never forgive him, and neither would his father.

But Kate was exuberant, loving the feel of the powerful horse, the wind whipping her cheeks to flame, the ground speeding past. She flashed a smile at Ian Tillerman as he thundered up beside her, and urged Little Foxy even faster, the two horses flying over the turf, their nostrils flared, and hooves kicking up lumps of mud. Beside them in the wide river, the fast running tide glittered as it raced up the estuary under a wild and shining sky.

Freddie drove his lorry slowly down the wooded hill into Yeovil, past the hospital and on through the streets of terraced houses, looking for George's motorbike. When he saw it propped in the front garden of a red brick house, he parked at the kerb, got out and walked through the overgrown garden. He knocked at the door with his fist and waited, glimpsing a movement through the front window. George was at home, watching him behind mustard-coloured curtains. Freddie knocked again, louder, and eventually George came to the door. The way he opened it a crack and peered out reminded Freddie momentarily of Annie, the same fear in the same eyes.

'Oh, 'tis Freddie.' George opened the door fully. He looked rough and unshaven, his clothes smelled fusty, and he wore battered leather slippers with a hole through which a calloused and grubby toe protruded. 'You better come in,' he said, and led the way over bare floorboards into a room with mould up the walls and stacks of yellowing newspapers. One was spread on the floor with some oily black bits of an engine on it.

'That your lorry?' George pointed to the dirty window where the bulk of the Scammell lorry glowed red.

'Yes,' said Freddie shortly.

'Bet you haven't paid for it.'

Freddie ignored the jibe and sat down on a rickety kitchen chair.

'I've come to see you about Mother,' he said.

'What about her?' George sat back and folded his arms across his chest in a defensive stance.

Freddie was silent. He tried to get eye contact but George wouldn't look at him, and everything Freddie had planned to say was suddenly useless. So he stayed quiet and waited, thinking he had to approach George from a different angle.

'So what about Mother, then? Not ill, is she?' George asked, and Freddie could see that his silence was unnerving. He maintained it until George's questions started to disintegrate into stumbling attempts to recon- struct the armour he'd always worn in front of his brother.

'We're brothers, George,' said Freddie very quietly, 'and I'd like us to be friends.'

'Ah.' Finally George met the steady blue gaze of Freddie's eyes. They were full of light and a deep mys- terious peacefulness that George didn't have. He didn't feel good about the way he'd treated Freddie. Right from the start he'd either ignored or teased him, jealous of the way his mother had been so besotted by the waif- like blond child who had grown into this quiet, confident young man who was offering him friendship. George crumbled. His big hands shook and his eyes glistened. He took a fag from a squashed packet and lit it, offering one to Freddie.

'No thanks.'

''Tis hard,' said George. 'I miss the old man. And 'tis lonely here, see? I do care about Mother. It's just – well, 'tis hard, a hard life I got. I'll tell 'e, Freddie . . .'

Freddie kept quiet and listened attentively. George was talking to him for the first time, telling him about his job at Petter Engines, sharing his dream of having his own garage, the pains in his legs and shoulders, and how he hated living alone. And right at the end of the tale he said sadly, 'I were all right, see, 'til she went off.'

'She?'

'Freda. My lady love. Oh, I loved her. Lovely girl, lovely she was. A singer and a pianist. Play anything she could – make that piano dance, she did. I give her everything, Freddie, everything, and she just upped and left me for some fancy boy from London. Nothing I could do. Nothing. You wait 'til you're in love, Freddie. Then you'll know.'

His voice broke into fragments, and Freddie went on listening as George talked about his pain. His aura was clearing as if the talking was a polluted liquid draining from a barrel, and all the time Freddie could see Levi standing next to him, radiant and shining as he'd never been in life. He had his arm around George's shoulders, and he looked just once at Freddie, put his finger to his lips and shook his head.

Freddie nodded. Keep quiet, Levi was telling him.

George heaved himself out of the low leather chair, his knees cracking. 'I better make you a cuppa tea,' he said, 'or I got cocoa. Do 'e want that?'

'Tea please,' Freddie smiled, thinking it was the first time in his life that George had offered him anything. They stood looking at each other and he could feel the change, the melting of the barriers, the new friendship floating through in wisps. He'd come to talk about Annie, but instead he'd been silent and it had worked.

'Want a ride in my lorry?' he suggested. 'It's a Scammell.'

'Could do,' said George with the ghost of a twinkle. 'I suppose you'll be wanting a go on my motorbike.'

'I was hoping you'd say that.'

Chapter Sixteen

LITTLE BLUE LETTERS

'Cor, that's a beauty.' The postman leaned over his bicycle to admire the salmon in Ethie's bucket, its tail flopped over the edge. 'Ten pounder that 'un, I reckon.'

Ethie put the bucket down, rubbing her arm which was aching from lugging the heavy fish up the lane to Asan Farm. Collecting salmon from the putchers at low tide was her favourite job. She'd had to persuade her father that she was responsible enough to do it, and Uncle Don had taught her well how to read the tides and how to tread carefully over the shifting sands of the estuary. It gave her time alone close to the power of the river she loved. Going home with a huge fish gave her a new feeling in her life, a sense of being welcome. She almost felt grateful to the rainbow-skinned fish which had lost its life so that she, Ethie, could feel wanted and successful.

'Shall I take the letters?' she asked. 'It'll save you going down the lane.'

The postman rummaged in the box on the front of his bicycle. 'There's two for Mr D. Loxley, one for Mr B. Loxley – and this little blue one, for Oriole Kate Loxley. Lovely handwriting that. Real copperplate. Beautiful.'

'Thank you.'

'Don't put 'em in the bucket with the fish,' teased the postman, but Ethie didn't smile at him. 'Where's your young sister today then?'

'She's working,' said Ethie shortly. 'At the Tillerman's racing stables.'

'Lovely girl, your sister. Lovely girl. Always got a smile.'

The darkness crept back over Ethie's morning. The way the postman looked her up and down, the way he expected a smile, annoyed Ethie intensely. Then he had followed it with the usual warm accolades for Kate, and the remark had sucked the glory out of Ethie's journey home with the salmon.

'Good morning.' With a curt nod she picked up the

bucket and walked on briskly, the letters in her jacket pocket. The postman shrugged and pedalled off on his bicycle, whistling a rebellious refrain.

When he had gone into the distance, Ethie stopped and took out the little blue letter with the copperplate writing. She knew it was from Freddie. Every Tuesday it came, and Kate's eyes would light up as she sat there reading it and smiling, her dark eyes full of joy.

Ethie stood in the middle of the lane considering her options. Tear the letter into hundreds of pieces and sprinkle them into the hedge? Bury it under a cowpat? Burn it? Or should she open it first? The letter felt velvet-smooth in her hands and it had a feel of Freddie's peacefulness which Ethie secretly admired. Spoiling the beautiful writing would only compound her crime. Ethie smiled to herself and tucked Freddie's letter into her inner pocket. She planned to take it home and hide it in a place where Kate would never find it.

Jubilant, she walked on, carrying the bucket with the fish iridescent in the sunshine. From now on, she resolved, she would meet the postman every Tuesday.

The stone angel was slowly emerging from the block of Hilbegut stone. Freddie had chipped away at it in the mellow September evenings, sometimes working on into the twilight. He'd shaped the curving wings and the head of the angel in between. Now he was chiselling out the deep clefts between the wings and the body, so absorbed in the task that he didn't notice anything around him, even the comings and goings of birds. So he was surprised to look up and see Annie standing there watching him in her flowery apron, her head on one side and a puzzled frown over her eyes.

'How much longer are you going to be out here?' she asked.

'As long as I can.' Freddie brushed the dust from the carving.

'What about the bread?'

'I'll do that when it's dark. I've got to do this in daylight.'

'This is starting to look like a stonemason's yard,' said Annie, pointing at the blocks of stone Freddie had stashed against the wall. 'What are you going to do with all those?'

'Make things.'

'Make a mess, more like. Look at all this dust.'

Freddie went on chiselling silently.

'And when you're not out here, you're upstairs writing letters to that Loxley girl,' complained Annie.

Freddie slowly put his tools down, dipped his hands

in a bucket of water and dried them on a cloth. He looked at his mother's eyes in the soft blue twilight and saw past the anger and into the pain.

'You want me at home, don't you?' he asked.

Annie nodded.

'Then it's time we had a talk,' said Freddie. He put an arm around his mother's shoulders, led her inside and sat her down at the scullery table. He looked at her quietly, thinking that this armour-plated woman, who had both protected and intimidated him in his childhood, was getting smaller and smaller. It wasn't just the physical weight she was losing. It was a dying flame. Since Levi's death, Annie's inner light had burned down like a candle flame reaching the end of the wick, turning slowly to a smoking bead of fire.

'What is there to talk about?' she asked, a sharp blade of anxiety in her voice.

'Well, there's Kate,' said Freddie, and even saying her name brought a glow to his heart. 'The fact is, Mother, whether you like it or not, I love Kate Loxley and I intend to marry her.'

'Marry her?' Annie went stiff. She stared into Freddie's eyes and saw that he meant it. Her life stretched out before her like a wintry road leading into a dark forest where finally she must face her demons alone.

259

'Now you listen to me,' began Freddie, and his eyes flared blue with wordless passion, compelling her to listen. 'It's not going to happen straight away. But you've got to prepare yourself, Mother, find a way of managing your life without me. If you do it one step at a time, you can, and I'll help you, but I'm not going to be here forever.'

Annie was twisting her ring round and round her finger. She wanted to be glad that her youngest son had found a future wife, she wanted to say how proud she was of Freddie. But layers of extreme fear had constructed a chrysalis around what was really in her heart.

'I hope that brazen young hussy deserves you,' she said, and immediately felt the sting of guilt, especially when Freddie's face registered the hurt. She marvelled that even though his face went a deep red, his eyes stayed calm, and he didn't get up and smash china like Levi would have done. She wanted to say sorry but the apology was buried too deep in her psyche.

'You don't mean that,' Freddie said, watching the conflict crawl through her eyes.

Annie reached for his hand and held it tightly between her swollen fingers. Her throat felt paralysed.

''Tis no good. I can't go out. I just can't,' she

whispered, and Freddie sat looking at her, letting the silence settle between them. Once again nothing had been resolved. They had taken the same old journey and arrived at the same old barrier, and once again his plans to go and see Kate had to be put on hold. He'd seen a motorbike he wanted to buy, and he'd told Kate about it in his letter. A motorbike would enable him to go across on the ferry, and inside he was buzzing with excitement at the thought. He could stay the night at Asan Farm, and have salmon for supper, Kate had promised in her letter. He must go before the autumn weather set in. It was now nearly October, and, once the rains started, the Levels were flooded through the winter. Monterose was cut off, standing like an island in the flooded fields. A motorbike would have no chance.

Freddie was pondering how to explain this to his mother. If he told her about his proposed trip she would close down like a roller blind, and her attitude to Kate would darken. But now she said something surprising.

'You'll have to buy her a ring,' she said, her eyes brightening a little.

'A ring. What – a wedding ring?'

'No. An engagement ring.'

Annie went to the dresser and opened the secret

drawer at the back. She took out a scuffed navy blue box, brought it to the table and opened it. Inside was an ornate gold ring set with a dark sapphire.

'That was my engagement ring,' she said. 'Your father gave it me. It's like a promise, an engagement ring. I don't wear it now, 'tis too good to wear, but sometimes I take it out and look at it.'

Freddie nodded. 'I'm saving up for one,' he said. 'But I've got to get the motorbike first.'

'A motorbike!' Annie looked horrified. 'You can't ride a *motorbike* in the *winter*! Why, you'll catch pneumonia, Freddie, believe me, with your bad chest. Don't do such a stupid thing. I'll worry myself sick about you. I worry enough as it is.'

Freddie wished he hadn't mentioned it, just as he'd thought Annie was coming round to the idea of him marrying Kate.

'That's two shocks in one day,' she complained. 'How can I sleep in my bed at night?'

'Whether you like it or not, Mother, you'd better start getting used to it,' said Freddie steadily. 'And the stone carving. It's what I've always wanted to do. I'm carving an angel, and when its finished I shall give it to Kate. Then I'll make you something. How about an owl?'

'I don't like owls,' said Annie. 'They give me the creeps.'

'You're not really going to do this, Kate?' asked Ethie as the two girls swanned up the main street of Lynesend.

'I've made my mind up.'

'But what will Freddie say?' teased Ethie, a touch maliciously.

Kate tossed her head. 'He's not going to see me, is he?' She pushed open the door of the new Ladies' Hairdressing Salon and went in with her usual radiant smile. 'Wait until you see mine, Ethie, then you can decide whether to have yours done. Come on, it's the latest fashion. We've got to move with the times. And just think, Ethie, we won't have to go through all that agony every week, combing it out and disentangling it, and we won't have it blowing in our faces. It's so windy up here.'

Half an hour later both girls emerged with their hair cut short in a fashionable bob, Kate beaming and Ethie scowling as she caught sight of her reflection in shop windows.

'Wheee! I feel LIBERATED!' cried Kate and she flung her arms in the air and danced in the street, swishing her skirt and laughing.

'For goodness' sake, Kate!' Ethie rolled her eyes. She

had to admit Kate did look good with her glossy hair short and curling cheekily onto her rosy face. Whatever Kate did, she looked marvellous. It wasn't fair. Ethie touched the back of her neck and it felt cold and bristly. She was sure the new hairdo accentuated her pimples and made her face look fat.

'Come on. We're going to buy some STOCKINGS.' Kate dragged her into a draper's shop and bought them each a pair of silk stockings. 'Now we can go dancing,' she said, her eyes alight as they left the shop and found themselves opposite the town hall where a poster proclaimed 'Saturday Night Dance'.

'I can't dance,' said Ethie. 'You know that, Kate.'

'You can. You learned it at school like I did, Ethie. Come on, it's time you had some FUN.'

'Dancing isn't fun. Dancing is torture.'

Kate stood and looked at her sister in concern. Ethie looked like a guilty dog who had stolen a chicken carcass. Her mouth drooped and her pale blue eyes were furtive and full of pain.

'What is wrong, Ethie?' she asked, holding out both her hands to her sister. She wanted to understand what it was that made Ethie perpetually unhappy. 'Are you homesick?'

Ethie's eyes prickled. She couldn't accept Kate's

warm kindness. She thought of the stolen letters and suddenly wanted to blurt it all out, there in the street, but she couldn't.

'It's nothing,' she mumbled.

'Is it time of the month again?'

'NO.'

'What is it then?'

'Nothing. Just leave me alone, Kate. And I am not going dancing with you.'

Kate took her sister's arm determinedly. 'Would you like to come and see the horses with me?' she asked. 'You'd love Little Foxy, she's so friendly. Ian might invite you to ride.'

Ethie looked tempted. 'Oh, all right, if you insist,' she sighed.

The walk back to Asan Farm took the girls along the towpath between the railway line and the canal, then past the Tillerman's Racing Stables where Kate worked every morning. She did everything from mucking out stables, cleaning tack, grooming and feeding the beautiful horses. It was hard work, but the highlight of the morning was going out on Little Foxy for the gallop. Ian Tillerman always wanted her alongside him, the stable boys behind them on the other four horses. Kate had made friends with everyone, quickly laughing away the initial smirks, joking and teasing as they worked. She enjoyed it and liked having money to spend.

She took Ethie to see Little Foxy. The mare arched her sleek neck over the stable door, her ears pricked and eyes shining as she greeted the two girls.

'She's lovely,' said Ethie, reaching up to stroke her along the crest of her mane. 'I'll bet she's a lovely ride.'

'She's wonderful. Light as air,' said Kate. 'But she is a bit nervous. She's petrified of tractors and motorcars, and motorbikes. We have to be careful she doesn't meet any on that narrow road.'

The two girls stood petting the beautiful horse, and Ian Tillerman soon appeared, carrying a saddle on his hip, his brow furrowed.

'Oh, it's KATE.' His frown changed to a smile of recognition. 'I didn't recognise you with . . . with . . .'

'The new hairdo!' Kate beamed coquettishly and patted her newly bobbed hair. Ian reached out a suntanned hand and moved a curl gently away from her cheek.

'Hmm. I quite like it. Very trendy – and cheeky too,' he appraised, then he glanced at Ethie and frowned again.

'My sister, Ethie,' said Kate.

'How do you do.' Ethie shook hands stiffly, trying not to stare at the leathery hunk of a man. Ian Tillerman was her ideal image of the kind of man she wanted.

Broad tweedy shoulders, long confident legs, white teeth and dark, attentive eyes. But as usual his eyes looked her over quickly, distastefully she thought, and turned back to gaze raptly at Kate.

'We want to go dancing,' Kate was saying brightly. 'So we had our hair bobbed. It's liberating!'

'I'll take you dancing,' said Ian. 'I'll pick you both up at seven tonight, and take you home afterwards.'

'Oooh. Yes, we'd love that. Wouldn't we, Ethie?'

Ethie scowled down at her neat navy shoes.

'No thanks,' she said abruptly. 'I've got to be up early to collect the salmon from the putts.'

She didn't look at Ian Tillerman again. Sensing the look of relief on his face was enough, she didn't want to see it any more than she wanted him to see the sudden fury in her eyes. It wasn't fair. Her plan to hurt Kate by stealing Freddie's letters was backfiring. Now, she thought, Kate was flirting with the man she wanted, and Ethie could see that Ian Tillerman was already besotted.

It was late October and the trees were aflame with autumn colours, an Indian summer blessed with misty mornings, and afternoons drowsy with the perfume of cider and wood smoke. At sunset, the white tendrils of mist crept low over the Levels, leaving the town of

Monterose isolated like an island of rosy light, the church clock glinting, the bakery windows golden.

A beam of sun flared through the garden gate into the yard, lighting the delicate face of the stone angel. It glistened with moisture from the final wash-down Freddie had given it. Now he walked round it, looking at it from every angle, his mind ringing with a blend of excitement and satisfaction.

It was finished. Freddie thought it was the best thing he had ever made. He'd seen the angel waiting inside the block of stone, and his hands had brought her alive. She had Kate's beautiful face, and Kate's flowing hair. She had praying hands and outstretched curving wings. He didn't need to show her to anyone. It was enough to have brought her into being with the combined skill of his artistic soul and his careful hands. Everything else he had done in his life was suddenly meaningless, as if this *was* his life, his reason for living.

Standing in the twilight with one bright star in the smooth sheen of the western sky, Freddie sensed he was not alone. A circle of radiance hung around the stone angel, like an aurora, gently shifting, settling into shapes that he recognised, faces looking in at him: Granny Barcussy, Levi, his grandfather, and there were others, a crowd of shining faces looking at his angel.

Freddie nodded at them, dried his hands on a cloth, and stooped to pick up his scattered tools and put them in their wooden box.

Annie was asleep in the armchair, her knitting on the floor beside her. Freddie helped himself to a bowl of soup from the pot, cut a hunk of cheddar and broke a crusty end from the loaf on the table. He ate his supper, staring out at the silhouette of the angel in the garden, until it was too dark to see her. Then he closed the heavy curtains, locked the door and sat looking at his mother's sleeping face, thinking it had brought him down to earth with an uncomfortable thud. She was so tired lately that he had to wake her up to send her to bed. It wasn't the work in the bakery that tired her, it was her nerves. Something had to be done.

In the lonely weeks since Kate's departure he'd focused on the stone carving, and it had lifted him into a different dimension, and while he worked on the angel he was thinking about the other blocks of stone he had accumulated. He knew exactly what he was going to carve from each one, the images catalogued in his mind. Owls, squirrels, foxes, eagles, dolphins, he wanted to try them all, and right at the end of his list he planned to buy a substantial block of Bath stone and have a go at a lion.

Finishing the angel was like coming to the end of an

epic novel which had taken weeks to read. Without it, there was an awkward space in his mind, and the complications of his life came diving and swooping like returning swallows. He picked up Kate's last letter and read it, frowning. It was shorter than usual, and she hadn't said anything about his planned visit, which seemed strange. He'd written about the stone angel, and she hadn't mentioned that either. It wasn't like Kate. He was concerned about the job she had started. Riding racehorses seemed dangerous for a beautiful young woman like Kate. And Freddie didn't like the sound of Ian Tillerman one bit. A toff, that's what Ian Tillerman was, he decided.

But first something had to be done about his mother. Freddie sat thinking in the candlelight, and one person kept popping up in his mind. She'd always taken an interest in him, encouraged him with whatever he was doing, and, he thought suddenly, her husband was a doctor! Freddie put on his coat and cap, and stepped out into the moonlit street. With long, decisive strides he headed up the hill to the Old Coach House with the new electric lights shining from its windows. He opened the wrought iron gate, took a deep breath, and knocked on Joan Jarvis's door.

Chapter Seventeen

THE ROAD TO LYNESEND

Freddie pushed the heavy motorbike onto the waiting ferry boat, his stomach tight with nerves as he eyed the foaming clay-brown river water slopping at the edges of the ramp. He parked the bike and went to stand at the front of the broad boat which rocked and creaked on the tide.

'Last trip today,' shouted the ferryman. 'There's rough weather coming in.'

Freddie peeled off the woollen balaclava Annie had knitted him, and let the unfamiliar salty breeze stream through his hair. The weather was uncannily bright for late November, the hills a sharp blade of indigo, the last leaves of the elm trees along the shore a lurid yellow. The waters of the Severn Estuary glittered ferociously, the fast tide surging up the middle.

When he saw the sunlight on the water Freddie remembered Kate's vivid description of the sea. He took the black velvet box out of his inner pocket and opened it to steal a glimpse of the diamond ring he had bought for her. Exposing it to the salt wind and the light seemed a romantic thing to do and the strobes of crystal light from the diamond satisfied Freddie. Imagining her face when she saw it gave him immense pleasure. He'd spent all his money on it, after buying the motorbike, but Kate was worth every penny. It was odd that she hadn't responded to his letters telling her about the stone angel and the motorbike, but he'd decided to go anyway. Especially when Herbie had made him listen to the weather forecast on his crackly radio.

'You go now, lad – before those storms come in,' he'd warned. 'You don't want to be stuck on top of the Mendips in the snow, do you?'

Freddie had been in a dinghy a few times across the winter floods on the Levels, but to him this Severn ferry boat was awesome. The throb of its engine under his boots, the ageing, sea-soaked timber, the fat ropes, the rusting cabin. He was unprepared for the savage power of the tide, the way it swept the heavy boat sideways as if it were a bobbing walnut shell. Used to listening to the sound of an engine, he could hear this one labouring against the current and sense the tension of the boat's structure. Looking at the other passengers, he was reassured to see that nobody seemed worried. People were laughing and talking while he had been holding his breath.

Safe on the other side, he paused on the jetty to study his map and rearrange his clothing. He would have liked to sit and watch the flocks of geese dipping and swerving over the river, their barking cries like a cantata on the wind. But it was too cold to keep still. He pulled his mud-caked balaclava over his head, glad that it covered most of his face. His goggles were mud-spattered too, from the rough ride over the Mendips, through Bristol, and down to the estuary, and he thought his face would be covered in mud too. Kate would think that very funny, but he wouldn't mind. Just to hear her laugh again would feed his soul. He buttoned the thick leather jacket Herbie had lent him, cleaned the goggles and put them on, and set off, glad to feel in control again. The satisfying roar of his bike cut a path through the rain-swept silence as he headed for Lynesend.

Ahead of him the wooded hills of the Forest of Dean

were bulked against the sky, appearing and disappearing through the masses of low rain-bearing cloud. The north wind whooshed in his ears, barbs of sleet stung his cheeks. Soon his hands and feet were numb, his knees and elbows ached, and he could feel his cold lips cracking. Determined to reach Lynesend before the weather closed in, he pushed on, the motorbike bouncing and splashing over the puddled road. He thought longingly of Kate's family, the warm kitchen and the cups of cocoa Sally used to give him with a dollop of scalded cream on the top, and sometimes Kate would wink at him and add a dash of rum. The memory of her smile illuminated his journey along the shores of the Severn, and the feel of the little velvet box in his pocket kept him going. The anticipation of seeing her again burned in his heart like a lantern.

He turned east, following the road inland, the sleet flying sideways out of the dark sky. No one was on the road except him, no horses and carts, or motorcars, and the villages he rode through were deserted, the cottage chimneys smoking as if people were huddled inside sheltering from the icy weather. He paused once to look at a signpost and clean the mud from his goggles. His feet were two blocks of solid ice, his hands and wrists ached and the breath wheezed in his chest.

Annie had given him a small leather case with a tot of brandy in a silver bottle. Freddie disliked the medicinal taste of brandy but a good swig brought a welcome glow of heat into his throat. Exhausted, he pressed on, through the mud and the cold, and at last he came to the place Kate had described in her letter. A sign saying 'PRIVATE ROAD', and a narrow lane alongside the canal. Food, and shelter – and Kate – were not far away now.

Enormous barges were moored on the canal, laden with the biggest logs Freddie had ever seen. Fascinated, he lost concentration and when he looked back at the lane it had curved sharply to the left. He braked, skidded and revved the bike, just managing to steer it round the corner, and right in front of him two tall racehorses loomed out of the mist.

Annie bristled when she saw Joan Jarvis come mincing into the shop. At closing time she was tired from a day of worrying about Freddie. Why had he insisted on going off on that dreadful motorbike?

A new bakery had opened in Monterose and gradually Annie's regular customers were choosing to go there instead of climbing the hill to Barcussy's Bakery. The new bakery had a motor van for their delivery round, with smart lettering on the side. Annie knew she couldn't compete, especially without Freddie's input. Every day there was bread left on the shelves, wasted, and soon she could no longer afford to employ Gladys. She kept the shop open for mornings only, and spent her afternoons sleeping, knitting or pottering in the garden, battling the depression and the fear which had intensified since Levi's death. In the afternoons she needed to hide from the world.

So the last person she wanted to see was Joan with her nauseating fox fur dangling, her scarlet nails and her intimidating confidence.

'Yes. What would you like?' Annie asked, her eyes suspicious.

'I don't want any bread. I came to see the stone angel.' Joan smiled disarmingly right into Annie's defences.

'Wait a minute. I'll close the shop.' Annie locked the door and turned the sign to CLOSED. She led Joan through the scullery and into the garden.

'Oh, my dear! Look at your chrysanthemums.' Joan stopped by the flowerbed along the sunny wall. 'Aren't they beautiful? You must have green fingers.'

Annie thawed a little. 'People say I have.'

When Joan saw the stone angel she gasped and flung

her arms in the air, her painted mouth opened wide showing two yellowy front teeth crossed over each other.

'I can't believe it,' she said in a whisper, her eyes turning to look at Annie. 'Freddie did this?'

Annie smiled, puffed up with pride.

'Ah. He did. And he's never had no training. 'Tis just a gift.'

'It's beautiful.' Joan sidled round the stone angel, looking at it from all angles. 'Isn't she beautiful? Perfect, just perfect. And the patience! Freddie is a remarkable young man. You must be so proud, Annie – may I call you Annie?'

'Yes, of course. And yes, I am proud of Freddie.' Annie's eyes glistened. Hesitantly she glanced into Joan's eyes and found them unexpectedly warm and friendly.

'But isn't this exciting?' Joan placed a manicured hand on the stone angel's head. 'And the face! It's exquisite. Did he have a model for it?'

'He didn't say.' Annie didn't want to tell Joan about Kate Loxley.

Joan pursed her lips and stood gazing raptly at the stone angel as if it was a newborn baby. Annie watched her, suddenly aware of the bright aura of light that surrounded Joan. Seeing it brought Annie's own gift, long suppressed, to life, like a treasure discovered in an attic. She allowed it for a few guilty moments, then rearranged herself, smoothing her apron and twisting her wedding ring round and round her finger.

'Has anyone seen the angel yet?' Joan asked.

'No.'

'Then I'll tell you what I'm going to do, Annie, if you don't mind. I'm going to tell the vicar. He ought to see it, don't you think?'

'Could do.'

'Annie, he's looking for someone to do a statue of St Peter for the church porch. The church has some money set aside for it.' Joan's words jingled with such enthusiasm that Annie could hardly follow.

'And – is Freddie going to do more carvings? He's got all this stone.'

'Oh yes. He's got plenty of ideas.'

'Then I shall give him a commission.'

Annie looked bewildered. 'What's that?'

'A job. A stone carving job. I want two majestic eagles on our gateposts. My husband would love them. We'll pay him of course. Is Freddie here?'

'No. He's gone off today on his motorbike. I hate the thing.'

Joan hardly seemed to hear her. 'I'm going to see the

vicar right now,' she said, her eyes gleaming. She slid her hands into a pair of fox fur gloves, and smiled caringly at Annie. 'It's only down the road. Why don't you come with me?'

A suffocating silence crept over Annie. Instead of looking at Joan's bright encouraging eyes, she looked down at the floor, her eyes clouded with shame.

'I—' She was going to say 'can't' but the word froze in her throat. A person with Joan's energy and fire was not going to accept 'can't', that was obvious to Annie, so she said, 'I won't, not just now.'

Joan cocked her head sympathetically as if she sensed a problem. Annie could see the question hovering and she braced herself, but Joan just gave her a little pat on the shoulder.

'Perhaps another day,' she said. 'But I'll go anyway. Thank you, Annie, for showing me Freddie's work – and your lovely flowers. I'll come and see you tomorrow. Bye now.'

'Bye.'

Annie showed her out, and watched her skittering down the road towards the vicarage.

'She knows,' Annie thought desperately. 'She knows.'

★   ★   ★

Ian Tillerman looked down from the lofty height of his dappled grey racehorse at the mud-spattered stranger on his motorbike.

'Turn the engine off, will you please?' he shouted. 'Don't you know horses are frightened of motorbikes?'

Ian Tillerman's horse didn't look bothered by the motorbike, but the other horse, a bay, had wheeled around and bolted back down the road, its rider clinging on, its hooves clattering on the stony surface.

Freddie sighed and begrudgingly turned off the engine. Plastered in mud, he sat back astride the bike and tried to bend his frozen fingers. He realised he must have looked a sight in the black balaclava and goggles stuck to his face with mud. He eyed Ian Tillerman through the mud-splashed lenses and waited silently.

'I gotta go on my way,' said Freddie.

'Oh, no you don't.' Ian Tillerman got down from his horse and confronted Freddie, his face an ugly brick red. 'You've no business riding that damned motorbike down here. This is a private road. Can't you read?' He didn't wait for Freddie to reply but ranted on, flicking his whip as he talked. 'That's a valuable racehorse, can't you see that? She could break a leg galloping on the road like that. God knows what's going to happen, and if there's an accident I shall be suing you – whoever you are.' He moved closer, his arms looped through the reins of the grey horse who stood watching the bay one still galloping in the distance. He put his red face close to Freddie and sniffed like a dog. 'I thought so. Alcohol. You've been drinking. You've no business riding a motorbike in that state. Drunken bloody lout.'

Freddie was reminded of the times Levi had lost his temper. He knew it was no good trying to stop him, the explosion would go on until all the storm had been released. So Freddie hunkered down and let him rant, feeling nothing but contempt.

'Who the hell are you, anyway? Where've you come from? Eh? Answer me.'

'Now you listen to me,' said Freddie calmly, looking Ian Tillerman in the eye. 'I got a right and a reason to be here, and I don't have to tell you who I am. Who are you, anyway?'

'I'm Ian Tillerman. I own those racing stables, and this land.'

Freddie heard the name Ian Tillerman and no more after that. The rest of the diatribe hurtled past him as he remembered Kate's letters.

'And who is that on the other horse?' he asked.

'My fiancée,' said Ian Tillerman pushing his chest out

arrogantly. 'Not that it's any concern of yours. And if anything happens to my Kate – you – you and your noisy bloody motorbike will end up facing MY lawyers in court.'

The shock burned into Freddie's heart as if he'd been stung by a thousand wasps. His body wasn't ready for it and neither was his mind. His heart took the full force of it and began to beat furiously in his cold body; the small velvet box with Kate's ring shook in the secret silk of his pocket. Kate, his Kate. No wonder her letters had stopped. But why, why hadn't she told him?

On automatic pilot, Freddie revved the motorbike, swung it round and roared back towards the ferry, a new blast of rain spattering his hunched form as he headed into the wind.

The motorbike which had carried him steadily all the way suddenly behaved like a demon, wrenching and twisting his angry body, skidding and flying over the ruts and potholes. Freddie pushed it faster and faster, no longer caring, hardly seeing where he was going, the wind howling in his ears, a searing pain deep in his chest.

Two miles further on, the rough road turned sharp left over a bridge that spanned the canal. Freddie heard the fierce rasp of skidding wheels and the handlebars jammed sideways as the front wheel hit a stone post with a sickening crunch. He saw the canal water steaming, he saw leaves and clods of mud storming through the air, and then an almighty splash of briny water hit the side of his head, forcing itself straight through his balaclava. He landed spread-eagled on the squelching wet bank, turned his head and watched his motorbike sinking into the dark water, making a deep groaning bubbling sound that gradually settled into a silent lap-lapping of water. Gasping for breath, Freddie clawed at tufts of grass with his hands, then laid his cheek on the cold mud and plummeted down, down into an echoing coma.

Nobody came running. Except for a lone workman standing up on a barge in the distance, the place was deserted. The fuel from the submerged motorbike coiled into swirling rainbows on the still surface of the canal and a shaft of acid sunlight lit up the mud-covered body lying on the bank.

Kate sat back in the saddle and pulled steadily at Little Foxy's reins, talking to her constantly, trying to keep fear out of her voice. Ian had warned her that the young mare was frightened of motorbikes. But there hadn't been time to take evasive action. This motorbike with its mud-plastered rider had come at them on the bend just as they were returning from the gallop. The horses were tired and steaming in the cold air, and Kate had relaxed and let Little Foxy plod along on a loose rein. She'd been in the middle of telling Ian a joke about a chicken when they'd heard the motorbike, and Little Foxy had whipped around and bolted, her head and tail high, her eyes wild. Kate heard Ian's roar of rage and his voice shouting. She clung on, gradually regaining her grip, shortening the reins and trying to calm the panicking horse.

She steered Little Foxy through an open gateway into a ploughed field, knowing that the rough ground would slow her down, and it did. The mare soon came to a halt, her sides heaving. Kate got her feet free of the stirrups and swung herself down, quickly pulling the reins over Little Foxy's head so that she had control.

'Poor girl. It's all right. I'm here,' Kate said, her hand on the horse's neck. She was surprised to find her own legs shaking. The incident had unnerved her. Quivering all over, she leaned against Little Foxy who gave her a sympathetic nudge as if she understood. 'Well, look at us both, in such a state,' said Kate in her normal cheerful voice. 'Now we're going to turn around and walk quietly back – no more panicking.'

With her legs still trembling, Kate coaxed the horse out of the field and into the lane where they both stood listening. The sound of the motorbike was fading into the distance, and she waited until it had disappeared completely, leaving only the whine of the wind and the rain pattering. Kate took a deep breath. She wanted a little cry but didn't allow it. She was all right, it was just a memory that haunted her, of that day when she had been thrown from the cart at Monterose station. She found herself thinking of Freddie, wishing it was his thoughtful blue eyes welcoming her now, not Ian's demanding stare.

When Freddie's letters had stopped coming, Kate had covered her disappointment with lots of laughing and chatting. Ignoring Ethie's gleeful jibes had been hard, but she'd managed, and Sally had said, 'Freddie's a young man, Kate. He's not going to wait around for a girl who's far away. Forget about him. He'll soon find someone else – and so will you.' The brisk assumption had hurt Kate. For a while she kept writing to Freddie, hoping he would reply, but the weeks went by and no letters came. She was glad of her morning job with the horses, and flattered by Ian Tillerman's attention.

Little Foxy lifted her head and whinnied, and there was an answering whinny from Ian's horse as he came to meet them, also on foot. Kate wanted a hug, but instead she got a blast of anger from him as they reached each other.

'Damned infernal motorbikes,' he stormed, 'and you should have seen the state of him. Covered in mud and stinking of brandy. Bloody arrogant lout. I sent him packing. I told him he'd got no business down here. Bloody townies think they can go anywhere. No respect for horses. I mean, the way he came round that bend. Disgraceful hoodlum behaviour. And I told him if anything happened to that horse, I'd sue him. He soon turned tail and went, bloody lout. Good riddance too. By the way, are you all right?'

Kate opened her mouth to reply but Ian didn't wait for an answer. He checked Little Foxy over. 'Better get these horses back to the stables or they'll catch a chill. Can you stay and rub her down, please? Come on, we'll lead them back.'

He marched off briskly, leading his horse, and Kate followed, her eyes downcast. She didn't want to work late today. She wanted some lunch and a warm fire, and time to be with her family, and time to recover.

When Freddie didn't return that night, Annie wasn't too concerned. He'd told her he was spending the night with Kate's family and coming back the next day. So she kept herself busy, mixing dough and stoking coke ovens. She made Freddie's bed up with fresh sheets and cooked his favourite shepherd's pie to heat when he came home the next day.

But as she settled down with her knitting, a sense of isolation spread itself around Annie like a ripple from a stone dropped into a lake. On distant shores the waves broke like quiet folds of satin, so hushed that no one knew of the anguish that had started them.

Annie went to bed in the silent cottage, blew out her candle and lay listening for footsteps in the night street, or owls outside on the trees. She heard some drunken revelry from the pub, a man coughing and retching as he trudged past, the whirr of a bicycle and the click-click of a dog's paws as it trotted by. Then it was so quiet she sensed the tick of the church clock and the rhythmic swooshing of her heartbeat. She lay rigid on her back, her eyes hopelessly staring into the velvet darkness. Eventually she got out of bed, groped her way to the door where she unhooked Levi's old tartan dressing gown, took it back to bed and went to sleep cuddling it, comforted by the musty, malty smell of the corn mill.

It was still dark when she got up at 5 a.m. and put

the first batch of bread in to cook. She mixed lardy cake and rolls, cut the dough and left them to rise. She was short of yeast. Freddie would get it for her, and he'd said he would be back about midday. Annie was glad she had plenty to do and customers to chat to, but the morning seemed endless.

Once again Joan appeared, full of enthusiasm, just at closing time.

'I need a chat with you, Annie. Is Freddie back? No? Oh dear – but never mind, that can wait.'

'What can wait?' asked Annie. 'Slow down a bit, Joan, will you? I think your mind goes twice as fast as mine.'

Joan smiled. 'That's what my husband says. Now then, Annie, those beautiful flowers you grow – and I see you're good at arranging them too. How would you like to do the flowers for the church? They really need someone, and I'm no good at it.'

Annie frowned. She turned her back and busied herself brushing crumbs off the shelves. 'I've gotta get on.'

Joan stood there determinedly. 'I'd come with you and help,' she said. 'I can take you down now if you like. Annie?'

'I – I don't – walk too well,' Annie mumbled, and her heart started thumping. The skin on her face felt tight and hot, and she wanted to cry.

'Annie?' Joan was there instantly, her hand on Annie's tense shoulders, her eyes concerned. 'What is it? You're shaking. Here, sit down.'

She dragged a chair out but Annie wouldn't sit down.

'I can't tell you,' she said, gripping the counter.

'Oh, you can,' said Joan persuasively. 'You can tell me. I promise I won't gossip, Annie. It'll just be between the two of us. Come on. Let's sit down at your lovely table.'

Annie couldn't move. She hadn't had a friend since before the war. Levi and Freddie had been her whole world. It had to change. This woman with the scarlet nails and the fox furs whom she had totally misjudged was offering her a lifeline. She allowed herself to be led into the scullery where she sat at the table, her hands spread out on the friendly well-scrubbed wood.

'I can't – go out,' she whispered, and put her hands over her face to catch the tears which broke through the layers of shell she had inhabited over the years. At first she could only rock to and fro and say, ''Tis terrible – terrible. Nobody knows, only my Freddie.' She risked a glance at Joan, surprised to see how caringly and closely the woman was listening.

'What happens when you go out?' Joan asked gently.

'I'm all right in the garden, but soon as I go outside

that gate – I don't know why, but I'm so giddy, and I'm frightened of falling. I'm a big woman, I fall heavy. Oh 'tis terrible, the pavement goes all wavy like water, and the buildings look like they're falling down on me. I panic, see. And the panic is the worst thing. My heart races and I shake and I can't get my breath. I think I'm going to die. And – and . . .' Annie glanced up at Joan. 'You don't want to be listening to this.'

'Yes I do. I've plenty of time,' said Joan firmly. 'You tell me everything, and I mean – everything.'

Annie nodded. Her greatest fear waited at the end of her talking, like a boulder, wobbling, waiting to fall.

'I can only go out if my Freddie is with me. He's wonderful. Ever since he was little he's looked after me, he holds my hands and talks me through it. Many times he's got me home – and – and Levi never knew. I'm so ashamed of myself, Joan, so ashamed. I'm afraid I'll make a fool of myself, see? So now I don't even try to go out. God knows what would happen if I had to.' Annie looked at Joan again, noticing the confident warmth in her eyes that made the painful silences bearable, and then she finally let go of the boulder. 'And I shouldn't be telling you all this – I know your husband is a doctor and I'm so frightened they'll think I'm a mad woman and put me in the asylum.'

'My husband wouldn't,' Joan assured her, 'he's a really understanding doctor. I shan't tell him, Annie. But – let me think about this – it may be that I can help you.'

'You already have,' said Annie gratefully. 'I've got it off my chest.'

'But,' Joan wagged her finger, 'I can only help you if you really want to get over this.'

'I do.'

The two women smiled at each other and Joan raised a clenched fist, her eyes twinkling. 'Courage to change,' she said. 'That's what we need.'

When she had gone Annie felt better, more light-hearted. She even sang while she was making Freddie's meal. She looked at the clock. He should be home by now.

Annie sat in the window to watch for his motorbike coming up the street. For two hours she sat there through the sunset and into the twilight. She watched the lamplighter work his way along the street, and saw people hurrying home, bent against the North wind. She heard the six o'clock train puffing into the station.

But still Freddie didn't return.

By nine o'clock Annie was distraught. Wrapped in a

shawl she paced round and round the cottage, up and down the stairs, looking out of different windows, opening them and listening, watching the distant hills for a moving cone of light that might be a motorbike. All night she paced and she prayed and in the deathly hush of early morning she fell exhausted into the rocking chair and slept, clutching Levi's dressing gown up to her chin.

At first light she was awoken by a thunderous knocking on the door. Terrified, she heaved herself up and struggled across the flagstone floor. She opened the door just a crack and peered out.

George stood there in a heavy winter coat, his face unshaven, his hair wild, and a grim expression on his face.

''Tis bad news,' he said. 'I had a telephone call, from a hospital up in Gloucester.'

Chapter Eighteen

FLOATING

Freddie had never been so comfortable in his life. He was floating on a cushion of deliciously warm air and the light streaming over him was intensely yellow like marsh marigolds. He looked down at his body lying in the hospital bed, its face deathly white, its blistered hands limp on the grey blanket, its knees and feet making orderly bumps in the tightly tucked bed covers. He didn't want to go back into that body which was filled with pain and struggling to breathe.

Each time he looked down, his mind opened up a cavern of nightmares. Ian Tillerman's voice echoed in there, his eyes gleamed avariciously, he smelled of beer and horse manure and the stench engulfed Freddie like smoke from a wood fire, he had to breathe it and it stung and choked his lungs. Or he would see his motorbike sinking into the deep canal, bits of it shining and bubbling, the handlebars and the headlight were the last to be submerged as the iron grey water closed over that particular pain. A bloody lout, Ian Tillerman had called him. A bloody lout.

For hours he had lain there on the bank of the canal, face down in the mud, the cold earth and the cold sky clamping him like the jaws of winter. Then the floating had started, floating on a cloud made of ice, watching, unable to speak, as his body was dumped on a kha-ki-coloured stretcher and pushed into the back of an ambulance.

The voices of nurses and doctors had burbled like a distant stream, and he'd felt hands peeling off his muddy clothes. Through half-open eyelids, he glimpsed Herbie's leather jacket being dropped into a basket, and the pain of thinking he would have to buy him another one sent Freddie deeper into a comatose state, and with the sleep came a profound feeling of surrender as he let go and drifted into the shadows.

Over three days, the darkness of his floating place transmuted into deep colours, ultramarine and crimson, and in the crimson phase he became aware of smells. He lifted his arm and sniffed his skin, vaguely hoping for a reassuring whiff of oil and stone dust, but it reeked of Sunlight soap and Dettol. A pungent tang of camphor hovered around him, and a mild ointmenty smell from the chilblains on his fingers. The space beyond his bed swished and clanked, and squeaked with footsteps, and the alarming rhythmic groans from the man in the next bed. Even more alarming was the shrill rasp of his own breath cutting into his ribs like a bread knife.

Freddie was not reassured by the amorphous shape of a doctor in a white coat sitting uncomfortably close to him, and the starched apron of a nurse bending over him. Freddie had never been in a hospital and he was terrified. He struggled to see the nurse's face, and she was frowning like a bulldog. She had his arm in a vice-like grip.

'Keep still or this will hurt,' she said sharply and a stinging pain drove into his bicep. He heard a man's voice saying 'This will make you sleepy, Mr Barcussy.'

Blissfully it faded and he returned to the floating place, so warm and soft now that he no longer wanted to look down at his body lying there. He wanted to go with the man in a cream robe who smelled of meadow hay and boot polish, a shining man who was leading him down an avenue of lime trees. At the end of the avenue was an archway in a high wall with golden flowers hanging over the top of it. Freddie could see a familiar figure standing here, waiting for him. Levi!

He paused, then walked up to his father and looked deeply into the translucence of his eyes, old familiar eyes but different now. The weariness and the gloom, the frustration and the rage had gone, leaving a mysterious contentment. Freddie felt they were both weightless, suspended like feathers on the wind, and he sensed himself absorbing the essence of that sparkle in Levi's eyes.

'Now I'll tell you something,' Levi said in his normal voice. He put his hand on Freddie's left shoulder, its comforting warmth radiant like the heat from a flame. 'That Ian Tillerman. Don't you let 'im take your life. He's lying. He's lying, Freddie.'

Freddie stared into his luminous eyes and felt a change moving over him. Coral-coloured, it wound itself around his shoulders like the hug Levi was giving him now.

'I'm sorry, son. Don't you ever be like me.'

'I've forgiven you, Dad,' said Freddie, and Levi beamed, the smile magically bringing them closer than they had ever been.

Levi stood back and Freddie gazed beyond him into

the archway, curiously observing a garden where trees glittered like jewellery and everything danced with colours. Across it was a lattice of brilliant gold.

'No,' said Levi firmly. 'You gotta go back, Freddie. Go on. Go back.'

Freddie nodded. He turned and floated back, still light as air, the man in the cream robe drifting beside him. He looked back once and saw Levi watching him, waving, then melting into the webs of light. The tingle of his feet reconnecting with the earth made him stronger, but still he couldn't hear his footsteps. What he could hear, louder and louder, was a rushing sound in his ears, a voice speaking his name.

'Mr Barcussy. Come on. Open your eyes.'

He came back with a jolt into the body lying on the bed. The pain had eased and his skin felt cool and soft, his body relaxed on comfortable pillows. Gradually the nurse's face came into focus. She was smiling now, a slim glass thermometer in her hand.

'Welcome back,' she said. 'We nearly lost you.'

Freddie was ill for many weeks. After George had driven his lorry all the way to Gloucester and fetched him home, he lay in bed watching and listening.

His hearing was super sensitive and so attuned to the

land beyond the town that he could hear the quack of herons passing overhead at dawn, and the unearthly sharp yelping of foxes, and in the mornings the squeak of ice being broken and crisp leaves being crunched underfoot. At nine forty-five he listened for the cattle train passing through, and the distressed cries of sheep and cows crowded together, terrified, their faces pressed to the slatted openings, their noses sniffing the fresh turfy fields where they had grazed. He felt their desperation.

Annie lumbered up and down stairs with trays of home-baked meals. She brought him a new drawing book and a pencil, but he didn't want to draw. He just wanted to stare out at the winter sky. The clouds created curling images of faces and ferry boats, lions and angels. Strangely, the illness was a gift of time to Freddie's artistic soul, each change of the light adding to his storehouse of ideas waiting to be carved in stone. He dreamed of carving in marble or alabaster, his fingers coaxing a smooth translucence from the rough blocks.

At night he kept the curtains open to the starlight, watching and learning to read the night sky. His room faced west and he lay on his side and watched for the planet Venus, as Granny Barcussy had taught him in his childhood. 'Venus follows the sun,' she'd said, and her eyes had sparkled. 'And – it's the planet of love.'

So Freddie stared at it, and wondered if Kate was seeing it too. He'd shown it to her once, at Hilbegut Farm in the twilight when the western sky flushed pink, then duck-egg green smoothly blending into indigo, and they'd gazed at the big bright star together.

Thinking of Kate was too painful most of the time, but he had to do it. He had to plod his way through the pain until he had overcome it with his own strength. There was a molecule of hope in Levi's words, 'He's lying,' but Freddie didn't cling to it. Kate had stopped writing to him, she was far away making a new life, and, worse, she had cut her hair. That news in her last letter, had upset Freddie. He couldn't imagine Kate with short hair, yet she'd said it made her feel liberated. Liberated from what? Was being beautiful such a burden? Supposing he had carved a stone angel with short hair? It bothered Freddie in an inexplicably sensitive part of his soul, and when he dreamed of Kate it was always with the sensual memory of her hair twined in his fingers. At least, he thought, Ian Tillerman wasn't going to have that particular delight.

★   ★   ★

One morning just before Christmas, on the day of the winter solstice, Freddie sensed a change. At first light he got out of bed and stood at the window, watching the sunrise reflected in the windows across the street. The weather was mild and spring-like. He opened the window and breathed deeply, smelling the steam trains and the flooded Levels beyond. A song thrush was singing with its whole being, like an opera singer filling the awakening town with exuberant music. 'The first bird to sing at the turn of the year,' thought Freddie, his eyes searching until he saw the slim shape of the thrush high on the apex of a roof, the sun gilding its speckled breast, its beak lifted to the sky. It filled him with longing to carve a singing bird. But how would he put the song inside the stone?

Though his legs were weak, Freddie climbed into his clothes and dragged himself downstairs and out into the yard. There was his stone angel, illuminated by the sunrise, and it startled him to see it. Had he done that? He stood in front of it, filled with an overpowering sadness as he looked at Kate's beautiful face, captured in the stone, forever frozen, no longer laughing, no longer turning her big eyes to gaze into his face.

A maelstrom of negative feelings gusted through him. Bitterness, vengeful thoughts towards Ian Tillerman, a slow burning fury that made him want to raise an axe high in the air and smash the stone angel into hundreds of pieces. He let the thoughts pass through like a crowd of people stampeding to some event that didn't interest Freddie. He could turn his back and walk away. Those thoughts did not belong to him.

Blessed with the gift of peace, he stood thinking, his eyes exploring the blocks of stone waiting to be carved, and the red roof of his lorry still parked outside the garden wall, waiting for him. 'I gotta get on with it,' he thought. 'With or without Kate.'

And as he thought those words he was suddenly remembering another pair of eyes. Ethie's eyes. They were pale, pale blue with a cluster of yellow in the centre of the iris, yellow like the eyes of a sparrow hawk. Her eyes were focused on him, compelling him to interpret some silent message coded within that ring of yellowness.

Since his visions were usually of spirit people, Freddie was surprised to see Ethie in such a way. He frowned, concentrating on the deeper meaning, and saw that Ethie was lying on her back, looking at him, trying to ask him some question that smouldered on her mind. She was floating, and the river glistened as it carried her away, her face glaring at the sky.

'Freddie!' Annie cried out in surprise. 'You're up and dressed. At last.'

He turned to see his mother emerge from the bakery, drying her hands on a towel.

'Don't you get cold now,' she tried to hustle him inside.

'I'm all right,' he said. 'I gotta get on with it now. Earn some money.'

Annie looked tired out, he thought, sitting with her to share a breakfast of lardy cake and cocoa at the scullery table.

'It's been hard for you,' he said, 'having me laid up.'

Annie nodded. 'But worth it to see you better. I had enough disasters in the past so I can deal with this one. We shall get over it.'

'Thanks.' Freddie looked at her eyes and detected a subtle change, a shimmer of hope which hadn't been there before. 'Are you managing all right?' he asked.

'Joan's been helping me,' Annie said, speaking faster than usual, almost bubbling with some secret. Then she shut her mouth, brushed the crumbs from her apron, and looked at Freddie expectantly. 'You still want to do the stone carving, don't you?'

'Yes.'

'Well – Joan made such a fuss over your stone angel,

and she dragged the vicar down here to see it. Can't say I like the man, but there – he's a vicar. And he came in and sat down with me at this table and he ate a huge piece of lardy cake, got crumbs all over his whiskers. I've never seen a man make such a mess! He left me this letter to give you.' Annie went to the dresser and rummaged in the drawer. 'Here 'tis.' She handed him the white envelope, her eyes twinkling like they did on his birthday, watching him unwrap her hand-knitted present.

'The VICAR wrote me a letter? What the hell does he want?'

Freddie took a knife and slit the envelope, unfolded the letter and sat back sceptically against the chair to read it, his eyes getting rounder and rounder. Momentarily speechless he stared out the window at the stone angel.

'Did you know about this?' he asked.

Annie nodded and she had tears on the rims of her eyes.

'I got a commission,' said Freddie, incredulous, 'to carve a statue of St Peter. And they are going to PAY me – how about this, Mother? Twenty pounds!'

Annie gasped. They sat together smiling like two children.

'Can you do it?' she asked.

'I can do that standing on me head,' said Freddie, and the joy came in a huge dollop. He threw the letter up in the air and laughed out loud. 'I got a commission. Yippee!'

'You should say yes, Kate,' said Sally forcefully. 'Have some sense, girl.'

Kate sighed. She squared her shoulders and looked back at her mother with good-humoured assertiveness. 'I'm not going to marry for money. I shall marry for love.'

'You might never get such a chance again,' warned Sally. 'Ian Tillerman is a real catch. You'll want for nothing. And think of your children.'

'My children, when I have them, will be loved,' said Kate, 'and that's more important than being rich.'

'Well, you know what they say. When poverty comes in the door, love flies out of the window.'

'It's never flown out of our window,' said Bertie who privately thought that Kate was right. He didn't like the way Sally was pushing her to accept Ian Tillerman's proposal. In his opinion his beloved daughter had lost her sparkle since she'd been working at the racing stables. 'Leave her alone, Sally.'

'I only want what's best for her, and for Ethie,' said Sally, raising her voice a little. 'And it's madness to turn down an offer like that.'

'Better than that lorry driver,' hissed Ethie. 'Anyway Kate is too young to get married. I should get married first.'

'Who to? You're not exactly encouraging anyone, are you?' said Sally sharply. 'What is the matter with you, Ethie?'

'Nothing.'

'Then why is it you can't open your mouth without upsetting someone?'

It was Kate who saw the pain in Ethie's pale eyes, and she intervened before it turned to spite.

'I'm not going to marry anyone yet,' she said lightly. 'I want to be a nurse, you know that. This job is only for a bit of money, and I'm enjoying it. I love Little Foxy, not Ian.'

Ethie tutted. 'Horses!'

Kate grinned at her mischievously. 'You're just as bad, Ethie – only it's fish. You're always down at the river. You can't marry a fish.'

'And you can't marry a horse.'

Kate giggled. 'If I did, it wouldn't be to one of Ian's racehorses. It would be – Daisy.' Her voice trembled, she met Sally's eyes and then looked down at the table. The shoreline between coping with living at Asan Farm and homesickness for Hilbegut was fragile, always shifting like the estuary sand. 'When are Polly and Daisy being sent up here?' she asked. 'They'd be useful here, wouldn't they?'

Sally and Bertie looked at each other.

'You should tell her, Bertie. Go on, just come out with it,' said Sally rather fiercely.

Bertie shook his head. 'I can't.'

'I can,' said Ethie. 'It's time she knew.'

'She doesn't need to hear it from you, Ethie.'

Bewildered, Kate looked from one to the other, aware that some bitter truth was being withheld from her.

Ethie digested Sally's sharp comment huffily. 'Oh, so my words aren't good enough for precious little sister. Why has she always got to be cosseted? It's not fair.'

'Kate doesn't go around with a face as long as a yard of pump water,' said Sally, and immediately regretted it when she saw the dreaded flush of anger on Ethie's cheeks.

'I can't help my face,' stormed Ethie. 'We're not all born flawless like little Miss Perfect here. I didn't choose to look like I do. Do you think I like it? Do you think I enjoy having pimples?'

'That's not the point, Ethie. Stop taking it out on Kate. It's nothing to do with what your face is like. A smiling face is a lovely face. If you smiled instead of going round scowling at everyone, you . . .'

'DON'T keep telling me to smile,' shouted Ethie. 'That's all you ever say to me, isn't it? Do this, Ethie. Do that, Ethie. Do all the dirty work, Ethie. And smile. I don't want to smile; I'm not going to smile. Why should I smile? I'll smile if I want to, not when you tell me to.'

'Pull yourself together, girl,' said Sally desperately. 'It's hard enough for us here.'

'None of you know what it's like to be me,' raged Ethie. She dragged a chair out and slumped down on it, put her hands over her burning face and drew a savage breath into her lungs.

'Ethie, stop it,' pleaded Kate, putting her arm round her sister and rubbing her back gently.

But the kindness seemed to trigger Ethie into a final explosion, like a boil bursting. She clenched her fists and pounded the table with them. 'You don't UNDERSTAND,' she wailed, then jumped to her feet and slammed out of the room, returning seconds later with another slam. 'I'm going to feed the chickens. At least the chickens don't care whether I smile or not.'

Kate and her parents looked at each other.

'She's getting worse,' said Sally.

'No she isn't, Mummy, she's always been like it. We can't make her any different,' said Kate. 'We just have to look on the bright side.'

'What bright side? She hasn't got one.'

'She has,' said Kate. 'She works so hard. And she does laugh with me sometimes, when she hasn't got her nose in a book.'

'Some gloomy book, I don't doubt. What do you think, Bertie?' Sally looked at her husband who had sat looking uncomfortable.

'I don't get involved in women's disputes,' he said calmly.

'So what was it you were going to tell me?' asked Kate. 'About Polly and Daisy. I'd rather know.'

Bertie nodded, his eyes sad. 'We're sorry, dear, but Polly and Daisy had to be sold. We couldn't afford to bring them up here.'

Kate stared at him wordlessly. She thought about the gentle Shire horse she'd loved. She and Daisy had a special bond. The big horse had always been so careful and kind around Kate when she was little, standing like a statue, afraid to move her huge feet in case she trod on the little girl who loved her.

Kate noticed her parents' doleful expressions.

'Oh, I expect it's for the best,' she said, 'don't worry about me. I've got plenty to be happy about. Now I must be off to work or I'll be late. I'll take the toast with me.'

Bertie was looking at her with a perplexed expression in his eyes. He got up and followed his daughter's straight back out into the morning light. 'Wait a minute, Kate. I'll walk to the gate with you.'

She turned and gave him a smile that turned his heart over. 'Come on then, Daddy.' She linked her arm into his and they set off on the half-mile walk to the racing stables, Kate carrying Little Foxy's bridle which she'd been cleaning.

'I want to give you some advice, Kate,' said Bertie. 'If I can get a word in edgeways.'

'Of course,' she laughed.

'This is serious, Kate. I love you dearly, and you don't fool me. I know how upset you must be over those two horses. I admire the way you keep so cheerful, it's a wonderful gift you have, Kate – and – and don't waste it.'

'How could I waste it?' she asked, surprised.

'Don't waste it on someone you don't love. It's your life, Kate. I don't want you to suffer because you want to please us. You be true to yourself. Do you understand me?'

They stopped in a gateway, and Kate looked thoughtfully at her father. He always knew exactly what was in her heart.

'I never want to leave you, Daddy. You've been like a guardian angel,' she said. 'But yes, you're right, I've got some thinking to do.'

'You may have to leave me one day. But we'll always be close, Kate – even when I'm gone. I want to see you happy – truly deeply happy, dear, not just putting a pretty face on it. I've watched you, Kate, and I know – I know there's some deep-down thing bothering you. You've lost your sparkle.'

'Have I?'

'You don't have to tell me, Kate. But please – think about your life and your future. Don't let me, or anyone, hold you back, girl. You do what you've got to do.' Bertie was looking at her intensely and his words were full of passion as they stood in the gateway overlooking the estuary. 'If you love someone, you let them go, let them be free. You are a blessed gift to this world, Kate, you spread your wings and fly free.'

Kate's eyes stared past him, across the shining water to the distant hills, then back to the brimming flood of love and caring in her father's gaze.

'You're not responsible for Ethie, or me, or your mother.' Bertie gave her a little pat. 'You spread your wings and fly free.'

He wagged a finger and looked at her under his brows, a fixed stare that put a seal on his words.

'Thank you, Daddy. I'm glad you care so much.' Kate kissed him on his pale cheek and walked on by herself, swinging the bridle. She looked down at her legs in the long boots and riding breeches, and thought how lovely it would be to wear a swishy red skirt again and feel like a woman. She found herself slowing down, dawdling a little, listening to the hum of bees in the blackthorn blossom, and suddenly she remembered Freddie telling her the Innisfree poem, explaining to her about the 'bee-loud glade'. It had been a magic time.

'That's what I'm missing from my life,' Kate thought suddenly. 'The magic. The magic is missing.'

She remembered Freddie's story of how he had saved up and bought the lorry at sixteen. It inspired her. Surely if Freddie could do that, then she could 'spread her wings' and take charge of her own life, couldn't she?

Chapter Nineteen

THE TURN OF THE TIDE

'I'll be perfectly all right,' Ethie said impatiently to her father. 'I know the tides by now. I've been doing it for six months now.'

Bertie nodded, his face pale as he sat in the wicker chair by the stove. 'I wish I was well enough to go with you.'

'Well you're not,' said Sally, 'so stay there, Bertie, or I'll tell you off.'

Bertie grinned, and wagged a finger at Ethie who stood half in and half out of the door. 'Tonight is full moon,' he said. 'There'll be a spring tide, and big bore up the river.'

Ethie rolled her eyes. She didn't want to upset her father when he wasn't well, but she wished he wouldn't fuss over her and keep telling her the same things.

'Let her go,' she heard Sally saying as she closed the door. 'She loves the river. And I hope she does come back with a fish. We could do with it.'

Ethie scowled and trudged out into the clear March sunshine. She walked down to the river, swinging the metal bucket. She wanted to be alone, like she was now, free of the expectations and the jealousy. The walk to the river was a wooded path with chaffinches and chiff-chaffs singing and blackthorn in full blossom, the verges yellow with celandine and dandelion. Corners of the river shone blue through the branches, then the whole vista opened up between two gnarled old pines, their bristly foliage covered in new cones. Wooden steps made from railway sleepers led down to the narrow beach and Ethie bounded down them.

After checking that she was alone on the sand, she ducked under the steps, put her arm into a deep crack in the low cliff, and extracted the long-handled fishing net she'd hidden in there.

'Just check the putts, Ethie. Don't go trying to fish the pools,' her Uncle Don had said. 'You're not experienced enough for that.'

But Ethie had taken the net from the barn and hidden it. She'd use it to check the shallow pools that shone like opals in the sand at low tide. She found it more exciting than dragging a trapped fish out of the putts. Paddling up to her knees she often caught smaller fish, and once she'd gone triumphantly home with a conger eel in the bucket. How she had caught it was one of Ethie's many secrets.

In the warm March sunshine she stripped off her boots and socks, something else she'd been told not to do. The velvet sand and the chill of the water on her skin was soothing to Ethie. It cooled the eternal burning of her thoughts, the inner loneliness, the longing for transformation. She felt part of the river, a rare content-ment as she wandered from pool to pool, following ridges of hard sand encrusted with the myriad pinks and greys of tiny clamshells.

Far out in the estuary, close to the deep channel of the main river, Ethie felt dazzled by her freedom, as if she looked down on herself and saw her spirit like a flickering candle, reaching out, longing to escape from the body she hated. Why bother to catch a fish? It was hot for March and she was sweating in her heavy farm clothes. Why not strip naked, roll in the crisp sand and let the cool river heal her burning skin? She looked back

315

at her life and it was a switchback of rage and injustice, jealousy and pimples. It coiled after her like a poisonous snake. The only place she remembered being happy was in the water, swimming in the school pool, in the summer river at Hilbegut, rowing a boat across the winter floods with the white wings of water birds all around her.

Ethie lay down on the sand and allowed herself to be sucked into a whirling dream where her itchy clothes became the soft satins of forgiveness, where her hair was long again and rippling like waterweed. She lay on her back and gazed through the shimmer of the sky to whatever was out there, to whoever may know she was lying there, a pearl in the oyster shell of day.

'Why am I so horrible?' she shouted at the sky. 'Why have I got pimples and a fat body and a wicked deceitful heart? Why me? Why?'

She listened for an answer, but nothing came. Only the burble of the turning tide flooding into the pools and stealing over the sandbanks and mud flats, glittering as it came. And in the distance the roar of the Severn Bore, foaming, gathering height as it funnelled into the estuary.

Ethie sat up. She tasted salt on the wind. She looked

back at the beach and the line of putts, and saw speeding water where sand had been. She looked at her hand clutching the handle of the fishing net.

'What am I DOING?'

She scrambled to her feet in a panic, and saw that she now stood on a narrow island of sand. It was shifting and crumbling under her feet as the brown water came churning in ahead of the spring tide.

'Get back – get back.' Ethie heard her own voice rasping like a storm twisting a stalk of barley. Clutching the net, she waded into the current, feeling the water sucking sand away from her heels. She was a strong swimmer, thank goodness, she thought. She kept wading desperately, waist deep, the water bitter and fierce around her body, dragging her heavy clothes, lifting her now, her chin suddenly in the water, her mouth spluttering, gasping with the cold. Fighting the weight of her sodden clothes, she swam vigorously towards the line of putchers. If she could only reach them, she could scramble to safety.

In the hours she'd spent by the river Ethie had come to recognise the burbling roar of the Severn Bore. It excited her to watch the edge of creamy foam rumpling up the river hauling the tide like a great silver breath discharged from the lungs of the ocean. Hearing it now,

317

Ethie knew she was going to die, and she shouted to the sky.

'I'm sorry. I'm sorry, Mum and Dad and Kate. I did love you. I did.' And then she fought to stay afloat, the cold reaching deep into her bones, her breath lurching in her chest. She fought, and she cursed, and at last Ethie let go as the brown waters carried her swiftly upstream under the silent, watching, waiting skies.

She uttered a final curse at the sky.

'I'll be back,' she shouted, 'I'll be back.'

Kate and Sally stood one each side of Ethie's empty bed, looking at each other.

'Come on Mummy. We've got to do this,' said Kate.

'I know. It just seems so final.' Sally looked down at the neatly made bed with its white pillows and the green and black tartan rug that Ethie had always wanted. She was glad of Kate's bright strength there in the room with her. 'You're too young to have this happen to you, Kate,' she said, 'especially just now, after losing our home and with you worrying about Freddie.'

'I'm all right, don't you worry,' said Kate. Her toe touched Ethie's slippers which were under the bed. She picked them up tenderly and put them in the wooden tea chest with the rest of Ethie's things. 'Now let's start by folding the blanket.'

Once the blanket had gone, Ethie's bed looked ordinary, and the two women silently folded the heavy blankets and the starched sheets. Kate took off the pillowcases and added them to the laundry basket. Now they were looking down at the bare blue and white striped mattress and it seemed natural to sit on it and talk about Ethie.

'If there's anything of hers you want, you must have it, Kate,' said Sally. 'Her clothes perhaps.'

'I don't want her clothes.' Kate shook her head adamantly. To her, Ethie's clothes were gloomy, and touching them somehow connected her to all the unhappiness and the resentment her sister had emanated. 'But I'd like this.' She rummaged in the tea chest and took out a heavy navy blue book, its cover embossed with gold.

'Oh yes,' said Sally. '*The Water Babies*. It was her favourite book. She was always reading it, even when she was grown up. Ironic, isn't it? There must have been something in it, some truth that she needed.'

Kate put the book on the windowsill. Outside, in the home field, baby lambs were scampering and blackbirds were warbling. Through the trees glinted a silver strip of river, and she looked away, suppressing the twinge of longing for Hilbegut.

'We'd better turn the mattress, hadn't we?' Sally said, getting hold of the two fabric handles. 'Lift it up, then we'll put it on the floor and turn it.'

They heaved the mattress and slid it onto the floor. Then both women gasped. Lying on the brown Hessian that covered the bed base was a pile of little blue envelopes.

Kate went pale. She picked one up.

'Letters. My letters. From Freddie.'

Sally stood watching her, transfixed. Ethie had hurt Kate, even from the grave, and Sally felt devastated and ashamed. For the first time since Ethie's death, Kate was openly weeping, her face red with fury as she gathered the precious letters, each one beautifully addressed to Oriole Kate Loxley in Freddie's copper-plate script.

'How could she DO this? My own SISTER.' She wept and wept, clutching the letters close against her heart. 'How could she take Freddie's letters? And why? WHY?'

Sally put her arms round Kate and let her cry, but Kate whirled around out of the room and ran down-stairs to her father who was sitting on a bench outside in the sun. By the time Kate reached him, she couldn't speak for the sobs racking her body.

'Kate!' he said in surprise and held out his arms. She slumped onto his shoulder, the letters still tight in her hand.

'What is it? My lovely Kate. Come on, don't cry. I'm here,' Bertie soothed, alarmed to feel Kate shaking all over. He hugged her close and leaned his pale cheek on her hair. 'We're all grieving for Ethie,' he said, thinking he was sure to be right. But Kate sat up and looked at him, her cheeks flushed, her mouth twitching, and a look of burning fury in her eyes that Bertie had never seen before.

'Kate?'

But Kate couldn't speak. She held it in, knowing that if she did speak it would be a scream that would never stop. Fearing she might crush them, she put Freddie's letters down on the bench. Bertie glanced at them, his brow furrowed, then up at Sally who appeared in the door. He raised his eyebrows, questioning.

'Freddie's letters. Hidden under Ethie's mattress,' she mouthed.

'Come here.'

Bertie moved sideways to let Sally sit on the other side of him, and put his arms around both of them like the wings of an angel.

'Shh,' he said. 'No – don't try to talk. Let's just be quiet. Be quiet and listen. Shh.'

At first Kate could only hear the awful sound of her own sobbing, and with each sob, a pain that felt like broken glass. Then she heard her heartbeat loud and fast, and her father's slow, peaceful one, and Sally's rhythmic breathing. She heard the chickens having a dust bath, their wings flapping madly, the baby lambs bleating out in the fields, the distant throb of Uncle Don's tractor. She heard the blackbird singing and her father's watch ticking deep in his waistcoat pocket. And then she heard the bees. She was back in the woods at Hilbegut, looking so deep into the blue of Freddie's eyes as he told her the poem, and she felt love come flooding back into her being.

She dried her eyes on Bertie's hanky, and looked at her parents' concerned faces.

'What am I crying about?' she said brightly. 'I've got all these letters to read!'

'That's my girl,' said Bertie. 'My golden bird.'

'Letter for you.' Annie tutted, as she put the plump envelope on Freddie's plate. 'It's got a Gloucestershire postmark. That Loxley girl, is it? Took her long enough to answer your letters! Looks like she's got a lot to say. It's a wonder that envelope hasn't exploded.'

Freddie picked up the bulging envelope and turned it over and over in his hands. He'd left the pain of losing Kate far behind, back in that autumn time of cold rain and Ian Tillerman's eyes, and his motorbike going in the canal. He didn't want to go back there.

'Aren't you going to open it?' asked Annie sharply.

'Not yet,' said Freddie.

'I should burn it.'

'Burn it? Why?'

'That Loxley girl's hurt you enough,' Annie said fiercely, her arms folded over her bust. 'Just give me five minutes with her.'

'Kate doesn't deliberately hurt people.' The look in Freddie's blue eyes silenced Annie. She set about dishing up lunch, her cheeks twitching with disapproval. Freddie tucked Kate's letter into his inner pocket to read when his mother wasn't breathing down his neck. 'This looks good, thanks.' He rolled up his sleeves and tackled the steaming meal of steak and kidney pudding with purple sprouting broccoli and carrots. It calmed Annie to see him enjoying it. He knew she'd been trying to build him up after the long winter of illness, and it was working. It was good not to be hungry.

Kate's letter felt like a warm hand over his heart. Yet something was haunting him. Ethie! Those pale

323

---

tormented eyes kept staring into his mind. He didn't like Ethie. So why was she there, in his mind, wanting to tell him something? On his visits to Hilbegut Farm, Ethie had regarded him with smouldering resentment. It hadn't bothered him then, but now it hung on his conscience like a sparrow hawk.

Unable to concentrate on the stone carving, Freddie downed tools and headed for the hills in his lorry, drawn as always to the ridge of hill where he and Kate had picnicked. Still Ethie's eyes followed him as he drove through the scented, blossom rich lanes, past swathes of dog violets, stitchwort and primroses. He longed to have Kate there beside him on the beautiful April day, and by the time he reached the parking place, her letter was hot in his pocket. Before he even opened it, he felt powerless. She was his love. That hadn't changed and never could until the end of time. No matter how much he immersed himself in his work, his love for Kate was an eternal presence; it was both a wound and a passion.

Hundreds of butterflies bobbed and danced over the hillside. Orange-tips and yellow brimstones, hoverflies and bumblebees gathering nectar from the flowers. Kate would have loved it, Freddie thought, allowing himself the dream. He'd paint her a picture.

The sun was warm for April, and he sat on the ridge, gazing across the Levels towards the Bristol Channel. A sparrow hawk hovered right in his line of vision. Without warning it swooped like a deadly arrow and caught a linnet from a pair that were fluttering over the grasses. Freddie heard the bird scream, and saw its mate cowering in the grass, its wings trembling, its little voice cheeping in distress. He watched the hawk fly off with the tiny bird struggling in its claws, and Ethie's eyes again looked cruelly into his soul. With a sudden foreboding, he opened Kate's letter.

Dearest Freddie,

I hardly know how to tell you this, but your beautiful letters have only just reached me, every one since September. I sat down and read them over and over again, Freddie, and oh how I cried! Happy tears, and sad tears. I was distraught to find you had written me those interesting, lovely letters and I had not been able to respond. No wonder you stopped writing to me. You must have been hurt, and undeservedly so. I hope that the sad news I must tell you now will help you to understand and forgive me.

Two weeks ago my sister, Ethie, was out in the estuary, alone, checking the putchers as she always did.

We don't know exactly how it happened, only that she must have been caught unawares by the Severn Bore. She was swept away, tragically drowned, and when the tide ebbed, they found her body miles upstream.

Freddie stopped reading, the letter frozen in his hands. He looked up, and the sparrow hawk was there again, chillingly close, circling in a sky which was the colour of Ethie's eyes – pale blue with that leonine tinge of gold. His vision had been true. He'd never doubted or questioned his visions before, but this one had disturbed him at a very deep level. Finding it true was shocking. Why did he have this gift? Why hadn't he shared it? Could he have saved Ethie's life? Was that why her eyes were haunting him now? He dismissed the thought as quickly as it came. Nobody would have believed him, especially a rebellious young woman like Ethie. Had his parents been right to forbid him to speak of it? Wise, he thought, but not right.

Shaken, he returned to reading the bundle of numbered pages Kate had sent him:

My parents are terribly upset, of course, and so am I. Ethie was not a happy person, but we loved her. I hope and believe that she is happy now, and in a better place.

We held a quiet little funeral for her in the church at Lynesend, but we all wished we could have taken her home to Hilbegut. After the funeral we went down to the putchers and threw some flowers in the river. The tide whipped them away so fast, tiny daffodils and primroses looking so lost on that vast river. Mummy couldn't stop crying. She said that no one ever gave Ethie a bunch of flowers in her whole life and she had to die before she could have one. None of us understood Ethie, but she was secretly very clever and loved to read, and her favourite book was The Water Babies by Charles Kingsley.

This morning I had another shock. Mummy and I were clearing Ethie's bed, and there, under the mattress, were all your letters, unopened. Mummy said Ethie had always gone running to meet the postman while I was at work, and she must have taken your letters and hidden them. I was devastated to think that my own sister could have done that. Why, why did she want to hurt me so?

A rush of anger engulfed Freddie's mind. He visualised Ethie's pale sparrow hawk eyes and sent her a furious message with the power of his thought. 'Leave us alone, Ethie. Go into the light and don't ever come back. And if you try, I'll have something to say to you. I'll be waiting.'

He read on.

Please forgive my family, Freddie. They are part of me and I feel responsible. I'm sure that in time we shall get over it and that happy times will come again.

I would have loved to welcome you here on your new motorbike, but of course you didn't know that. Will you come another time? There's so much more I want to tell you, and I want us to have another picnic together, and next time we shall go to the sea. I want to be with you when you see the real sea for the first time! And I want to see the stone angel. Fancy you making it look like me!

I wish I could move back to Somerset, but I must stay and help my parents to get over Ethie's death. I hope you will write to me again, Freddie, and tell me all about your work and your life, and I hope that next time I shall write you a more cheerful letter!

Love and God Bless

From Kate xx

He read the letter again, this time extracting little sparkles of light and hope from it. She hadn't mentioned Ian Tillerman. And she'd called him 'dearest' Freddie.

Not 'dear'. 'Dearest'. That felt warm and special. He stared at the word for a long time, drinking in its meaning like a man in the desert with a beaker of cider. He stared at the 'Love and God Bless' and the two kisses. Then he folded the letter and stuffed it back into his pocket, over his heart. Despite its sad news, it was precious, with precious grains of hope like the heads of golden barley he had gleaned from that field so long ago. Grains of gold that would nourish and heal.

But be careful, he thought, and remembered another line of Yeats.

> *'But I being poor have only my dreams;*
> *I have spread my dreams under your feet;*
> *Tread softly, because you tread on my dreams.'*

Chapter Twenty

TREAD SOFTLY

Freddie reached under his bed and dragged out a small leather suitcase. He wiped off the dust with his hanky, and put the case on the table. It had belonged to Granny Barcussy, and as soon as he touched it he could feel the swift warm vibration of her. He'd rarely opened it since Levi had given it to him. The burning grief he'd felt was somehow trapped inside, so he'd put it away under the bed, and now his mind was on fire with the need to find something he hoped was in there.

He unclipped the two rusty clasps and lifted the lid. It squeaked and flopped back, releasing a faint scent of old lavender bags and damp. A few silverfish darted across the dark book covers, escaping from the light. Gingerly he searched inside the books, flipping the gold-rimmed thin pages; he shuffled through a box of letters and cards with crinkled edges. Nothing. Surely he couldn't have lost something so precious?

Disappointed, Freddie took everything out, laid it on his table and stared at the cream and brown emptiness of the case. Last to come out was a flat brown paper bag, the paper eaten away in little lines and blotches by the silverfish and the damp.

He heard Granny Barcussy's voice, clear as glass, and there she was, sitting in his chair, her crocheted green shawl around her small shoulders, her knobbly hands on the table, her eyes smiling at him. 'It's in the cloth,' she said, and her image melted away into an apple-green radiance that left Freddie feeling invigorated. He picked up the paper bag and carefully slid out the dark blue cloth. The satiny fabric had been beautifully ironed and he'd never dared unfold it in case he spoilt it.

Smoothing it with his hands he remembered watching Granny Barcussy sitting in the candlelight on winter evenings stitching the cloth with gold and silver silks, so close to the candle that it illuminated her hair like cobwebs of gold. She'd embroidered the sun, moon and stars in each corner, and little curly clouds and flying birds around the edges.

'What are you doing it for, Granny?' he'd asked, and she'd said, 'It's a poem cloth, a love story, about a man who dreams of marrying a beautiful woman. It's like a prayer, a prayer for your dreams.'

Freddie wanted the poem now with an intense spiritual hunger. It said everything he felt about Kate, and he could only remember the last three lines. He wanted all of it. Conscious of the rough, stained skin of his big fingers, he unfolded the cloth, spreading it out over his bed. In the centre, in perfect condition, was a piece of cardboard cut from a fag packet. Shaking with emotion, Freddie took it to the window to read the poem Granny Barcussy had inscribed on it in her tiny neat writing. That was it, he thought, satisfied. A prayer for his dreams.

He tucked the square of cardboard into his wallet. Then he took the dark blue cloth downstairs, past Annie who was asleep in her chair, and out into the summer twilight. The western sky was apricot and deep turquoise, with one bright star. Freddie put both hands on his carving of the stone angel and repeated the poem silently, and he could feel the words in his hands, percolating into the stone where he wanted them to stay forever. Then, with the deepest reverence, he draped the embroidered cloth right over the stone angel and left it there.

Like the ghost of a long ago ocean, the white layers of mist covered the Somerset Levels turning the hills to mystic islands. The windows of Monterose Hospital reflected the pale morning sunlight. It was an imposing building, looming over the summit of the town, and today it had an air of expectancy as if to welcome the attractive young woman who was walking up from the station, her red shoes tip-tapping smartly, her skirt swinging, her dark eyes alert with excitement.

Kate paused at the gates to smooth her clothes and pat her hair which was now shoulder-length again. Then she entered the building with a business-like strut.

About an hour later, she emerged, her eyes brimming with tears, her lips pursed tightly. She walked round to a bench on the other side of the clump of elm trees and sat down to compose herself out of sight of the hospital windows. Only then did she let go of the mixed emotions corked up inside her. She'd managed a dignified exit. Now she wanted to kick off her shoes and dance barefoot and exuberant around the twiggy trunks of the elms, the way she had danced at home under the copper beeches of Hilbegut so long ago. Another part of her wanted to cry and cry. For Ethie. For her family. For the parting of the ways which change must bring.

She had spread her wings, but flying free had happened with ruthless speed as if the west wind had been waiting to whisk her away. There had been no time to contact Freddie, no time to prepare herself for the confluence of emotions that welled up from her as she sat alone on the bench overlooking Monterose. Like folds of butter muslin, the mist retreated across the Levels towards Hilbegut, allowing Kate a glimpse of the tall chimneys and copper beeches.

'I've done it,' she kept thinking, and then she pictured her parents' grief-stricken faces. How could she tell them? How could she?

With the sun warm on her face, Kate sat listening to the sounds of Monterose. The town rang with voices and busy hammers, trotting horses and the scrape of cartwheels, but Kate was alert for the sound of a lorry. She tingled with the thought that she might see Freddie. Even to see him driving past would reassure her, just the sight of his profile, his cap, his big steady hands on the wheel, his expression calm and intent on driving. Even if he didn't see her, she would know he was all right, she would feel that blend of peace and magic his presence evoked.

But she didn't see him, and no lorries came up the hill past the hospital.

Kate took Bertie's watch out of her handbag and put it to her ear. It was still ticking, and she had just one hour before the train would take her back on the long trip under the Severn Tunnel and into Gloucestershire. Was there time for a quick visit to the bakery? Impulsively she set off, walking and running along the slippery flagstone pavements, hoping she wouldn't meet anyone who wanted to chat and keep her from the precious slice of time she might have with Freddie.

Annie was surprised to see the beautiful young stranger come into the shop. Her face was oddly familiar as she stood smartly behind the customer Annie was serving. Annie kept an eye on her while she wrapped bread and counted change, noticing how the girl's big eyes were looking everywhere, over the shelves, out of the window, up at the ceiling, and even trying to peer past her into the scullery. The girl looked alarmingly confident and womanly.

'What would you like?' asked Annie when the customer had gone and the shop doorbell jingled shut.

Kate stepped forward eagerly and held out her hand. Annie searched her bright eyes and saw they were velvety amber and compelling. Annie often disliked people on sight, but the girl had a magnetism, a glow of light around her and she was beautifully dressed in a black suit with a blouse of a strawberry red colour, red shoes and bag. She gave Annie such a radiant smile that she found herself smiling back.

'Are you Mrs Barcussy?' she enquired. 'Freddie's mother?'

'That's right.'

'I'm Kate Loxley. It's lovely to meet you at last.'

The smile vanished from Annie's face. That Loxley girl. Brazen hussy.

'What a lovely shop you have here,' said Kate enthusiastically. 'You must work so hard!'

Annie drew herself up proudly. 'I've always worked hard.'

'And you make all this lovely bread? My family are cheese-makers. We ought to get together, shouldn't we? Oh, and is this your DELICIOUS lardy cake? I must have a bit. I'll buy some to take home.' Unabashed by Annie's suspicious stare and blunt manner, Kate chatted on. She admired the arrangement of daffodils and catkins on the counter. 'Did you do this? I love pussy willow. It doesn't grow much where I live now.'

Annie stood there with her lips disappearing into her

face. She was furious with Kate Loxley. The girl had hurt her Freddie, not answering his letters, breaking his heart Annie thought bitterly. Making him go all that way across the ferry and have his terrible accident, and lose the motorbike he'd saved up for. Annie had worked herself into a fury against this girl who had the cheek to stand there, bold as brass, in her shop. She controlled herself with difficulty, wrapping the lardy cake a bit too vigorously and putting Kate's change down on the counter with a petulant click.

'Was there something else you wanted?' she asked.

'I'd like to see Freddie please. Is he here?'

'No, he isn't,' said Annie triumphantly. 'He's gone up the alabaster quarry with Herbie. He won't be back until late.'

Kate looked disappointed. 'I've only got half an hour before my train back to Gloucestershire. I can't stay. Will you tell him I called?'

'Oh yes. I'll tell him.' Annie thawed just a little when she saw the sadness in Kate's eyes.

'I did so want to see him,' she said, and her eyes glistened with some secret she wasn't sharing. 'But I've got a long journey home, and I must get back to my parents. Daddy is so ill, and they're grieving, we all are. My sister Ethie was drowned in the River Severn.' Kate's voice went down and down, to a whisper, and Annie stood in silence, a battle going on inside her mind as the angry bitter thoughts collided with an incoming rush of maternal understanding. Kate was a human being, a young girl who had lost her home, and her sister. Annie opened her heart like she opened the front door, just a crack, and began to let her in.

'I'm sorry about your sister,' she said.

'Thank you.' Kate looked into Annie's eyes, which were so like Freddie's, cobalt blue with flecks of violet, and full of wordless insight. Freddie's eyes were calm but Annie's had tinges of anxiety, similar to Ethie's, Kate thought. Anxiety masquerading as anger. 'Is Freddie all right?' she asked.

'He is now,' Annie replied proudly. 'And . . .' She hesitated. 'I should ask you in for a cup of tea. He'd want me to.'

'That would be lovely,' said Kate warmly, 'but I've a train to catch so I must go.'

Annie nodded. 'I've got some more customers coming up the road. But – there's something you should see, Kate, before you go.' She opened the door to the garden. 'You take a look out there and you'll see what my Freddie's been doing. Go on, it won't take you a minute.'

Kate stepped out into the garden and her mouth fell open in astonishment.

'Night and day he've worked,' said Annie, 'and that one there, that's St Peter and it was commissioned by the church. 'Tis not quite finished yet.'

'This is unbelievable.' Kate stood looking around at the display of stone carvings. There was an owl, a squirrel, a collection of stone faces, and a tiny singing bird. She looked closely at the statue of St Peter, marvelling at the way Freddie had carved the peaceful face, the drape of his robe, the bunch of keys hanging from his belt. 'It's marvellous. I can't believe Freddie has done all this. How exciting! I'm thrilled to bits. How wonderful. You must be so proud, Mrs Barcussy.'

Annie beamed, enjoying Kate's enthusiasm.

'And what's under that cloth?' Kate asked in a stage whisper, her eyes very bright as she walked round something on a pedestal, completely covered in a dark blue embroidered cloth. Her fingers itched to unveil it.

'Ah – I'm not to show you that,' said Annie secretively. 'Freddie said – he wants it to stay under that cloth that his Granny embroidered until – until . . .' She couldn't bring herself to say the words, not while she still held some of the anger and suspicion in her heart. 'You'll have to wait to find that out.'

'Ooh I do LOVE mysteries!' Kate smiled at Annie, then glanced at the time again. 'This is Daddy's watch! Oh dear, I've got to dash. Excuse me, won't you? It's been lovely meeting you. Thank you for showing me this – I know we're going to be good friends, aren't we?'

To Annie's surprise, Kate leaned over impulsively and gave her a warm sweet kiss on the cheek. Then she whirled out of the shop and went running down the hill to the station, her red shoes clopping and her hair bouncing as she ran. Annie was left at the shop door, staring after her, a lump in her throat, her cheek glowing. No one had given her a sweet kiss for years and years, she thought, not since her girls were little.

She couldn't wait for Freddie to come home.

'Guess who came here?' she'd say tantalisingly, and when he asked 'Who?' she wouldn't say 'that Loxley girl' she'd say, 'Kate' as nicely as she could manage.

'That's a good 'un,' said Herbie, smoothing the chunk of freshly quarried alabaster Freddie had loaded onto the back of the lorry. 'Got plenty of pink in it. That's what you want, that deep rose pink, 'tis hard to find in a stone. Want a fag?'

'No thanks.' Freddie took off his cap, rolled up his

shirtsleeves and plunged his face into the stone trough of clear spring water that welled up from the hillside. He cupped his hands and drank, then splashed it over his hair. 'Beautiful water this,' he said. ''Tis a mystery where it comes from.'

'An underground lake,' said Herbie, lighting up his fag and sitting up on the back of the lorry. 'Look at yer shirt – soaking wet. My missus'd be after me if I did that!'

Freddie didn't care. It was steaming hot in the alabaster quarry, a suntrap deep in the hills where the rare translucent stone was being hacked out by teams of men, and hauled away down the wooded lanes, covering the trees in dust. At the end of the day the workers were stacking their picks in the long shed, and leaving on an assortment of bicycles or hitching rides on the stone carts drawn by heavy Shire horses.

'You're steaming like a pudding now,' laughed Herbie as Freddie sat beside him on the lorry.

'I gotta get back,' said Freddie.

'Ah – you gonna write that letter?' Herbie wagged a finger and looked under his heavy brows at Freddie. 'You do it, lad, or you'll lose her. 'Tis like fishing – always the best ones get away and you end up wishing you'd hauled 'em in while you got 'em.'

'I don't want to make the same mistake again,' said Freddie.

'Pah! Mistakes,' said Herbie fiercely. 'I made plenty of they. And if I hadn't I wouldn't have learned nothing. You gotta give love a chance, lad. You win some, you lose some. Don't you let mistakes stop you.' He ground his fag end into the dust.

Freddie looked at him gratefully, thinking that Herbie's rather brusque friendship had done more for him than any of his family. He'd helped him discover his gift for stone carving. Every time he needed a push, Herbie seemed to be there, encouraging him, and now he was reinforcing what Freddie knew in his heart. He had to respond to Kate's letter. Forget Ian Tillerman, and give love a chance. But first there was something he needed to do.

At the end of the hot afternoon he stood outside the pawnbroker's shop looking in the window, searching for something he couldn't see there. He pushed the door open and went in. A woman was in there haggling over the price of a silver teapot she was pawning. Freddie padded around, waiting and thinking about Herbie's advice. He hadn't yet replied to Kate's letter. It needed thought, and he was being cautious, holding back his feelings. He didn't want to upset Kate any more, and he didn't want to make the same mistake again. Until he knew about Ian Tillerman, he wasn't going to bare his soul.

He was busy, helping Annie with the bread in the early mornings, then doing as many haulage trips as he could with the lorry, and working far into the night on the stone carving. The statue of St Peter was nearly finished, and then he had to start on Joan's commission, two stone eagles for her gateposts.

Intuition had brought him back to the pawnbroker's. He watched with empathy as the woman left her silver teapot in the shop and departed with a meagre amount of cash in her hand, her eyes downcast. Back in January he'd stood there, miserable and penniless, and pawned the diamond ring he'd bought with such hope and joy.

'Have you still got the ring?' he asked, pushing the receipt across the counter. The pawnbroker peered at the receipt and opened a slim drawer in the cabinet.

''Tis that one,' said Freddie, his heart soaring as he spotted the black velvet box, and he felt proud of the way it stood out, brand new amongst the collection of scruffy ring boxes. The pawnbroker seemed to enjoy creating suspense by pretending to search through the boxes, turning them over to look at numbers.

'Have you got the money?' he asked, finally putting the box on the counter, keeping his hand on it.

'Would you open it, please – check the ring is in there,' Freddie asked, and the box was opened. Both men gazed in silence at the sparkling diamond.

'It's a beauty. Got a bluish quality to it,' said the pawnbroker. 'I hope she's worth it.'

'She is.'

Freddie handed over the money and left, jubilant, with the box safe in his heart pocket again. It had survived his long wet journey, his accident and his illness, and its time in the pawnbroker's shop. A symbol of hope, he thought, feeling that he could now try to answer Kate's sad letter. And he still had money in his pocket.

'I promise you, you won't die of fright, Annie,' said Joan as the two women stood on the pavement outside the bakery. Annie was clutching a willow basket filled with flowers in one hand and Levi's walking stick in the other. Her eyes were dark with fear and the pulse was racing in her temples.

'I can see how afraid you are,' Joan said kindly. She looked into Annie's eyes. 'The fear isn't going to go away. It's like childbirth, Annie. The only way out of it is through it.'

Annie looked at her gratefully. She hung on to those words like a mantra. 'The only way out of it is through it.'

'Don't fight it,' said Joan, 'let the fear come, you can't stop it. Let it come and let it go. It will take about ten minutes. My husband says these attacks of fear only ever last for ten minutes because the body can't sustain that level of fast breathing and racing heartbeat. The body will calm itself down, Annie, if you let it. And use the stick. If you get that giddiness, push the stick into the ground, and it will anchor you.'

'But what will people think of me? Using a stick like an old woman?'

'Does it matter?' asked Joan. 'Does that really matter MORE than you getting better?'

'I suppose not. No.'

'Every step you take is one step towards your freedom.'

Annie was quaking inside and she could feel the sweat prickling in her hair, but she started to do what Joan had taught her in the garden. Three steps, breathe in, three steps, breathe out.

'Well done,' cried Joan.

'Shh! I don't want the whole town to know.'

'Keep going,' said Joan in a gentler voice. 'I'm with

you but if I hold you it doesn't count. You have to do it on your own.'

Annie kept going doggedly, walking and breathing as Joan minced along beside her.

'I don't want Freddie to know,' she said. 'Not until I'm sure I can do this.'

'That's fine. I won't say anything,' Joan promised. 'Look, we're nearly there, Annie.'

It was about a hundred yards to the church, and Annie was surprised to find herself standing in the porch.

'There!' said Joan triumphantly. 'Do you want to sit down?'

'No.' Annie smiled and her soft eyes twinkled. 'I want to dance!'

She put some flowers on Levi's grave, and then the two women spent a happy hour inside the church arranging the tall spikes of larkspur, lilies and marigolds from Annie's garden. Joan had brought a bunch of antirrhinums and some foliage.

'That looks beautiful, doesn't it?' she enthused when they had finished. 'You've done that pedestal very cleverly, Annie, I'd never have thought of doing it like that.'

'I wanted to be a florist,' Annie said, gathering up the

stray leaves and stems from the floor. 'I enjoyed doing that.'

Joan gave one of her shrieks, 'Look at the clock! I can't believe it's ten past three. I promised to drive Susan to an interview for a job. I'll have to dash. You go home on your own, Annie. You can do it. I'll see you tomorrow.'

She ran down the church path, leaving Annie standing at the door, a look of horror on her face. Joan had abandoned her. Or was it deliberate? She'd never trusted that Joan Jarvis in the first place. Annie sat down on the porch, hoping the vicar wouldn't turn up and find her there, hoping Freddie might come past in his lorry and see her. Then she remembered he wouldn't be home until late. She couldn't sit there for hours.

Trembling with anger and nervousness, Annie took her basket and Levi's stick and set off down the path, counting her steps and chanting the mantra in her mind.

But when she went through the gate into the street, her throat closed up, her heart raced like galloping hoof-beats, and the whole street rocked and swayed, the buildings toppling, the pavement gyrating around her.

Annie was terrified.

'I'm going to die, here on the street,' she thought.

But Joan's words rang in her head. 'The only way out is through it.'

'Are you all right, Mrs Barcussy?'

Annie looked up and saw the vicar looking down at her like an inquisitive heron. She stood up straight and puffed herself up proudly. 'I'm very well, thank you. Just on my way home. Good afternoon.' And she walked on, her head held high. One, two, three, breathe in. Four, five, six, breathe out.

She arrived home in a state of utter exhaustion and despair. She collapsed into the old rocking chair where she rocked and cried and rocked and cried until she fell into a deep sleep with one thought blazing in her mind.

'I'm never, EVER going out again.'

Chapter Twenty-One

TRUSTING THE DREAM

On 19 June 1930 Freddie was standing in the church porch helping to set up his statue of St Peter. With the twenty pounds stashed in his wallet, he felt satisfied as he viewed the statue from all angles, turning it to catch the light. A beam of sunlight was filtering through the tall pines and poplars that grew along the wall of the churchyard.

'Like that?' he said to the vicar who was earnestly inspecting the statue. 'It needs a bit of sunlight.'

'Yes, yes. You're right,' the vicar agreed. Then he looked at Freddie the same way as he'd looked at the statue. 'You really are a very talented young man. You've carved the face so beautifully – and the bunch of keys – that can't have been easy – in stone.'

'It wasn't.'

'Those are the keys to the kingdom. Did you know that?'

'Yes. *Through gates of pearl*,' quoted Freddie, thinking about Levi standing by the archway in the wall. Through that archway he'd seen a golden web of light. He wanted to tell the vicar, but he felt ill at ease with him, so he asked him a question instead. 'Do you believe in life after death?'

'Of course I do. Jesus came to teach us that.'

Freddie frowned. 'Then why is it wrong to talk about it?'

'What exactly do you mean?'

'Well – I'll give you an example. You knew my father, didn't you? You did his funeral. So do you believe he's still alive?'

'He's with God.'

'But do you believe that my father is alive?'

'Yes, of course I do.'

'So why is it wrong for me to tell you if I see him?'

'Do you see him?' The vicar's eyes hardened and he looked intently at Freddie.

'I'm not saying I do. I said IF I see him, why is that wrong?' persisted Freddie.

The vicar looked flummoxed.

'I've known you a long time, Freddie,' he said, 'ever since you were a rebellious young boy at your father's funeral. You're obviously a deep thinker aren't you?'

'You still haven't answered my question.'

'Do you need an answer?'

Freddie didn't want to fall out with the 'Holy man' who had just paid him twenty pounds and a lot of compliments. So he said pleasantly, 'Not today. We'll talk another time. I've gotta be on my way now.'

The vicar looked relieved. He disappeared into the church and Freddie strode down the path thinking about his next haulage job: collecting sacks of grain from a farm and delivering them to the mill. The stationmaster had caught him yesterday as he was driving out of the yard. 'Two parcels arriving for you on the mid-morning train, Freddie. Can you be here?'

'What are they?' he'd asked.

'I don't know – but they're from Lynesend. I would guess a truckle of cheese – or a salmon maybe?' Charlie had winked at Freddie and rubbed his hands together. 'Something that nice young lady has sent you, I would guess.'

It was mid-morning now, but he wanted to fetch the

grain first. The parcels would wait, he thought, pausing at the gate of the church to listen to an unfamiliar bird-song, a plaintive warbling melody coming from somewhere in the churchyard. Intrigued, he searched the trees and a flash of gold caught his eye, in the rippling foliage of the black poplars. He stood motionless, watching, and the bright yellow bird flew down and perched on the wall right in front of him.

Freddie held his breath. A golden oriole. There in Monterose on the church wall. A rare sight, a rare visitor.

And then he remembered. Those words! Words given to him in the night, a long, long time ago.

'When the golden bird returns, you will meet her again.'

From far away in the cutting through the hills came the shrill whistle of a train. The mid-morning train from Gloucestershire.

Freddie leapt over the church wall and ran down the road to the bakery, started his lorry and drove off, leaving Annie standing open-mouthed in the doorway. Freddie was a grown man now, a six-footer, slow moving and thoughtful. What could have caused him to run, and to rev his precious lorry like that?

Freddie's heart was racing as he drove down Station

Road, and he was cross with himself. Why was he being an idiot? Rushing about like that. Trusting a dream!

The train was already steaming into the platform. Freddie sat in the cab of the lorry, watching the gates, watching the passengers emerging, the young boys scurrying to carry luggage as he had done. He watched and searched for a little dark-haired beauty with the face of an angel. He waited and waited, but she didn't come. Disappointment settled over him. He'd made a fool of himself.

Now the train was leaving, the passengers walking away up Station Road. Freddie saw Charlie pop his head round the gate and look over at him, with a thumbs-up sign. He sighed. Better go and collect the parcels, whatever they were.

He swung down from the cab and loped across to the entrance.

'Here you are, Freddie. This is yours.' Charlie led him up the platform to a trolley where a truckle of cheese sat, wrapped in a cloth. It had a label in Kate's writing which said, *'With love to Annie and Freddie, from the Loxley Family at Asan Farm'*. It smelled heavenly, he thought, pleased. Annie would be thrilled. He lifted the trolley handle to wheel it out.

'Don't go without the other parcel,' said Charlie who seemed to be bursting with some mysterious joke. 'It's here, in the waiting room. 'Tis a big 'un.'

'Right.'

Freddie pushed open the varnished door. The room was empty except for a young woman who stood with her back to him looking at a poster on the wall. Her hair was shoulder length, thick and glossy, and she wore a summer dress with emerald greens and touches of red, and a velvet bottle-green jacket. She stood with her feet neatly together in smart black shoes and stockings with straight seams.

Freddie stood there, frozen, and the door creaked shut behind him. The young woman swung round, and the room filled with light.

'Kate! My Kate!'

Freddie went to her quietly and stood basking in her smile. She was laughing.

'How's this for a parcel?' She twirled around and stood still again, gazing up into his eyes. 'It's lovely to see you, Freddie. I'd forgotten how tall you are.'

'You look – radiant,' said Freddie, trying to detect the sadness in her eyes from losing Ethie. But he saw only sunlight and humour. 'And very smart,' he added, suddenly conscious of his own scruffy clothes covered in stone dust and oil. 'I'm in me working clothes. I didn't know you were coming.'

'I LOVE surprises,' said Kate. 'And you look fine. You're a working man, that's something to be proud of. And guess what? I'm a working girl now. I've got a JOB, at Monterose Hospital. I'm going to train to be a NURSE.'

'Oh well done. So, you'll be living here then? Where are you going to live?'

'In the nurses' home. I'll have my own room, and we get all our meals, and bed linen, and I shall make lots of friends. The matron's a bit of a dragon, but we'll get over that. I'm used to dragons. I'm looking forward to it.'

'Well – I hope you don't go all stiff and starchy,' said Freddie with a twinkle in his eye, and listened in delight to the peal of ringing laughter, a sound he'd missed.

Charlie knocked on the window and peered in cheekily. 'Told you it was a big 'un!' he shouted. 'Now I'm off to taste me cheese.'

'Was he in on the secret?' asked Freddie.

'Yes,' said Kate, 'and I brought him a little round truckle of Mummy's cheese in my bag. He was pleased as punch.'

She chattered on about her journey and the people

she had made friends with on the train, and Freddie stood there in a hazy dream, breathing in the loveliness of her presence. It was like standing under a cherry tree in full blossom on a hot day, wrapped in its wordless glory. He imagined being married to her. It would be like being married to a piece of music, he thought, and the haunting song of the golden oriole came into his mind. He wanted to tell her about it – but first –

'Kate – before we go any further, and I hope you understand what I mean, I need to ask you something.'

'Go on, then.' She smiled into his attentive blue eyes, concerned to see anxiety in there.

'What about – Ian Tillerman?'

'Oh him,' said Kate contemptuously. 'I'm afraid Ian is like a little boy. He went around telling everyone I was his fiancée, and he was lying. When I found out, I told him to go to Putney on a pig.'

Freddie laughed with her, feeling his troubles rolling away like barrels down a hillside.

'Well now – I'll tell you something, Kate,' he said. 'What do you think I saw this morning? A golden oriole!'

Her mouth fell open.

'Well I never,' she said.

'I bet you don't believe me.'

Kate looked at him, her eyes full of that searching, caring expression he loved. 'I do believe you. I'll always believe you, Freddie,' she said emphatically. 'I trust you utterly and completely.'

'So – you won't tell me to go to Putney on a pig then?'

'No. Never,' she said staunchly, and linked her arm into his. 'Now, I want you to look at this poster with me. See? It says you can go to WEYMOUTH for a day trip. Shall we go one day? It would be lovely, Freddie. You wait 'til you see the sea.'

Freddie looked at her expectantly, waiting for the next bit, and he wasn't disappointed.

'It SPARKLES like DIAMONDS.'

He thought about the diamond ring in its box, hidden under the floorboard, and he could feel it sparkling, coming to life in the dark place. The magic is back, he thought, the magic is back in my life. I'm so lucky.

'Of course we'll go,' he said. 'We've got all the time in the world. And – I might even dig out that poetry book again.'

Annie soon became aware of the difference in her Freddie. He moved around with new energy, he was whistling and singing, and his eyes had changed. They were mysteriously alive now, as if he had found some secret light, and Annie couldn't help being pleased. She even began to feel better in herself. She had to admit that Kate Loxley had brought a new bright spirit into both their lives. The entrenched anxiety began to crumble, day by day, and her feelings warmed towards the brave, happy girl who was coping with a new life and the rigorous demands of a nurse's training.

'What's Kate's favourite colour?' Annie asked Freddie as he was heading out to start the lorry.

'Red,' he replied without hesitation. 'I'll see you later, Mother – about six.'

Annie stood at the gate watching him drive off in a cloud of dust. 'Red,' she thought, and glanced up the hill at the hospital where Kate was working, its windows a soft amber in the afternoon sun. She looked down the road and she could see the wool shop. Her fingers itched to get her hands on some lovely red wool and knit Kate a cardigan. A red cardigan.

She walked inside and looked at herself in the mirror.

'All your life, Annie Barcussy,' she said to her reflection, 'you've been standing at the gate expecting other folks to run your errands. Now it's time you changed.'

She'd vowed never to go out again, yet now she

found herself putting on her hat, taking some money from the bakery box, and wrapping her hand around Levi's walking stick. What would she do if the panic started? She couldn't be bothered with it. All she could see was the excitement of coming home with a basket of red wool, and a pattern for a cardigan.

Annie opened the gate and stepped out, her basket over one arm, squared her shoulders and walked steadily down the road to the shop.

On a blazing hot Saturday in July, it seemed to Freddie that the whole day was encapsulated in one moment of time. It was like the centre of a sparkle, where all the rays of light converged, focusing the essence of his dreams into one intense minute of pure light.

All day he'd waited for the moment to come. He could think of little else as he and Kate travelled down to Weymouth. They got off the train, walked hand in hand down the street towards the clock tower, and arrived at the promenade railings. Seeing the sea for the first time stunned Freddie into silence. The water heaved and glittered before him like the sequinned gown of an opera singer; it had the same massive, mysterious power as the undiscovered half of his consciousness.

For once, Kate was quiet as she watched his reaction, and waited for him to speak, but he didn't. He was far away, under the waves, following exotic fish into caves, watching shoals of them catching the light as they twisted and turned.

'Well, say something!' Kate prompted him after ten minutes of contemplative gazing.

'Ah – well – words might spoil it,' he said. 'I didn't expect it to be so blue, well blue-green like a kingfisher. And I didn't know it would be so vast.' He pointed at the horizon. 'That sharp line, 'tis like the blade of a knife. What would I see if I went out there?'

'France,' said Kate.

Freddie digested that information as he followed her down some steps to the sand. France had been pink in his geography book at school, and that was all he knew about it.

As usual, Kate kicked off her shoes, looked at him bewitchingly, and went running across the sand to paddle in the edge of the sea. He struggled out of his boots and socks, rolled up his trousers and sprinted over the velvety sand into deliciously cool crystal-clear water. Together they paddled, watching the sunlight marbling their skin.

'Taste it. It's SALTY.' Kate offered him some sea

water in the palm of her hand. He dipped a finger, tasted the salt, then looked into her amber eyes. Is this the moment? he thought. No wait. Wait and be sure.

Someone was guiding him that day, Freddie knew. The same feeling of being in a bubble of light with Kate lingered all day as if they were cupped in the womb of a shining angel whose wings covered the sea. He fancied there were golden ribbons in the air around them, winding, binding them together. He wanted to tell Kate, but it was hard to find an opportunity. She was so busy introducing him to the wonders of the seaside, collecting shells, popping seaweed, and building sand-castles. Then came the picnic, leaning against the hot sea wall, the taste of butter and cucumber, the burn of the sun on his white feet.

The moment came just one hour before the train home. They were sitting on the end of a wooden jetty, dangling their feet in the water, and Kate was playfully trying to link her toes with his. Her sunburned arm kept brushing against his, and the sea-breeze was blowing through her hair. The sunlight was sparkling on the water.

'Kate.'

There was something compelling in the way he lowered his voice an octave, and the way his eyes looked at her, unwavering and deep. Kate stopped giggling and paid attention.

'Now I'm going to tell you something,' he began, and he reached out and took her hands in his. 'In all of my life, I've never done anything major without thinking about it first, and I've thought and thought about this, Kate. I've loved you ever since I saw you riding down the lane on Daisy. I've kept an eye on you, in secret, all those years, and when I got the chance to meet you that day at the station, I saw something in you that is very rare and beautiful. No, don't say anything – hear me out.' Freddie's voice deepened with the passion he was feeling, and Kate listened, spellbound by his intensity. 'I don't just mean beautiful to look at, Kate, because you are, but it's something beyond that, some magic in your eyes. You're a beautiful person. You're kind and full of life and – and hope. I think you are pure goodness. And when you went I was – devastated. I put my heart and soul into carving the stone angel, and her face is your face because I carried you in my heart all those years, Kate.' Freddie paused and squeezed her hands. He looked at the sunlight in her eyes and knew from the way she was listening that he could say everything in his heart. 'No one else knows this, but I can pick up feelings from touching stone, as if it's a storehouse of everything that has happened close to it. So when I'd finished the stone angel, I stood out there in the twilight, with the planet Venus bright in the west, and I put my two hands on the stone angel and recited a poem, one that says everything I feel about you, Kate, and I could feel the stone absorbing my words like a prayer.'

'What was it? The prayer?' Kate asked, her eyes never leaving his face.

'It's W. B. Yeats again.' Freddie took out his wallet and extracted a dog-eared square of cardboard, cut from a cigarette packet covered in tiny neat handwriting.

'My granny wrote this out for me when I was a lad,' he said, 'with a quill pen she'd made from a chicken feather. She'd got a dark blue tablecloth she embroidered with white and gold, and she'd done the sun, moon and stars on it, and the clouds. I got it now – and I put it over the stone angel to keep the prayer in there until you saw it. 'Tis a lovely old thing, I treasure it, and she made it because she liked the poem. Have you read it?'

'No – you read it to me, please,' implored Kate. 'I love to hear your voice.'

'Oh all right.' Freddie studied the poem for a moment, then slowly read it in a voice so quiet and deep that it blended with the whispering of the sea.

'Had I the heavens' embroidered cloths
Enwrought with gold and silver light,
The blue and the dim and the dark cloths
Of night and light and the half light,
I would spread the cloths under your feet:
But I being poor have only my dreams;
I have spread my dreams under your feet;
Tread softly because you tread on my dreams.'

'That's beautiful,' she breathed.

Freddie took a deep breath. He sensed the golden ribbons being wound around them. He was almost there – almost.

'Now I've got to ask you a question,' he said intently.

'Go on, then.' Kate smiled encouragingly.

'Do you – do you think you can love me, Kate? The way I love you?'

The answer came warm and swift, carrying him effortlessly into the moment he'd waited for all day.

'But I DO love you, Freddie. With all my heart,' said Kate warmly.

Freddie looked at her joyfully. He let go of her hands, reached into his heart pocket and slowly withdrew the velvet box. He hoped he wasn't going to cry, but his voice broke a little as he gave it to her.

'Freddie!'

'Open it, Kate.'

She lifted the velvet lid, and gasped as the sun caught the diamond and the facets winked with the colours of sunlight.

'I want you to have it, Kate. Because you are the diamond in my life. I'd like it to be an engagement ring – if—'

'Freddie!' Kate whispered, again, and her eyes brimmed with happy tears. She took the ring out, held it up to the light and then slipped it onto the ring finger of her left hand. 'How wonderful. I've always loved you, and hoped you would love me too. I've truly – never, ever felt so blessed.'

They stared at each other, and the humour came dancing back into Kate's brown eyes.

'And now,' she said bossily, 'you are going to kiss me, aren't you?'

Freddie took her into his arms. She felt warm and her tears tasted salty like the sea. The long slow kiss melted them together, there by the sparkling water, for one moment of time.

Chapter Twenty-Two

ONE YEAR LATER

Daisy stood patiently in the stable at the back of Herbie's yard, wondering what all the fuss was about. She was an old horse and she'd done everything from ploughing, hauling timber in the woods, dragging hay carts, and being paraded at shows and carnivals. She'd done it all obligingly and carefully, she'd endured being muddy and wet and tired, or tolerated being dressed up in jingling brasses. Now there were three people round her: Freddie, who was grooming her vigorously with a brush, Herbie, who was shampooing her huge legs, and Joan, who was standing on a box plaiting her mane into little braids, looping them and tying in brightly coloured ribbons and tassels.

'She's looking good!' Herbie grinned up at Freddie. 'Look how white her socks are. Don't know how I'll ever get them dry.'

'I've never done this before,' said Freddie who was enjoying polishing the big solid horse's coat, leaning his weight on the brush until she shone like a conker. Daisy seemed to like what he was doing.

'Oh I have,' said Joan brightly. 'My parents had show horses. Now – where are those brasses?'

'In that box.' Freddie handed her the clinking box of horse brasses Annie had spent hours polishing. 'They still smell of Brasso.'

'Never mind the Brasso. This is hoof oil going on now,' said Herbie, sloshing it on with a paintbrush. 'She's going to use up the whole tin with hooves this size.'

'Hadn't you better go and get ready?' Joan looked pointedly at Freddie. 'You've got one hour.'

Herbie turned and winked at Freddie. 'Go on. Don't be late.'

Freddie put the brush down and stood back to gaze in awe at Daisy's transformation from a shaggy muddy carthorse into a proud, gleaming show horse. Daisy lowered her great head to him, as if she knew everything. He reached up and rubbed one of her silky ears. 'Thanks – Daisy,' he said, and the horse nodded graciously.

'Cheerio, Freddie – and good luck!' Joan called after him as he headed down the road in long strides, his clothes smelling of horse, his eyes watching the swifts and swallows diving and sweeping in the skies about Monterose.

Down at the station, Charlie sat on his bench in the morning sun, his green flag rolled up beside him. He was energetically polishing a trombone to a mirror-like shine, buffing and buffing it until he could see reflections of the station footbridge and the walnut tree and the cerulean blue of the June sky. One more train to meet, then he could go. His band uniform was hanging up in the back of the ticket office and his fingers itched to be playing that tune and marching up the street with the band.

He'd seen more posh hats that morning than he'd ever seen in his life, he thought, watching the ten-thirty train come steaming in. More women in fancy hats and men in grey top hats and tuxedos got off and strutted past him. He was glad to see the relief stationmaster jump down from the train.

''Ello, Sid.' Charlie handed over the green flag, the whistle and the timetable. Then he changed quickly into his band uniform, dark green with a smart green

Sheila Jeffries

and gold cap, gold epaulettes and buttons. Hyped with excitement he set off for the Jarvises' house where the procession was assembling in the courtyard. All Charlie wanted was one special smile that day from a girl he had secretly admired ever since she came to his station as a bright-eyed schoolgirl with red ribbons in her plaits.

In the town hall, Betty and Alice were bustling up and down the trestle tables, arranging napkins and plates of ham. There were jars of pickles, plates piled high with boiled eggs, tiny sandwiches and wedges of cheese, round bowls of ripe strawberries and cherries, dishes of clotted cream, and a tray piled high with fresh lardy cake.

George was pacing up and down the hall, checking his pockets and looking at the clock.

'Come on, girls. We'd better get up there,' he said.

'What about Mother?' asked Alice.

'What about her?' said George. 'She won't come. 'Tis no good trying to drag her.'

'We won't DRAG her,' said Alice huffily. She went to the mirror and arranged her blue and white hat. 'Leave her alone. She never is going to go out. I hope I don't get like that.'

'I hope I don't either,' echoed Betty.

★　　★　　★

372

It had been an effort for Bertie and Sally to make the trip to Monterose, especially going over the ferry and thinking of Ethie being swept away in that fierce tide. They'd taken some roses and thrown them overboard when the boat reached the middle of the river. Bertie was ill, but determined, and Sally felt the time had come for her to stop working and give him devoted care. She was glad of the support of the extended Loxley family around them, but she missed her daughters, especially Kate.

'I'm going to cry when I see Kate in her dress,' she said, as she and Bertie waited, sitting in two basket chairs on Joan's veranda.

At last the door opened and Kate emerged, beaming, in her long cream silk bridal dress. It was simple but beautiful, and instead of a veil she had chosen a dramatic wide-brimmed hat trimmed with tiny flowers and a white ostrich feather.

Bertie stood up, speechless as he gazed at his beautiful daughter.

'You look – perfect,' breathed Sally, 'just perfect, dear. Now – here's your bouquet.'

'Twelve red roses,' smiled Kate. 'It's what Freddie wanted – and his mother has made it up. Hasn't she done it beautifully?' She sniffed one of the cool roses. 'It smells divine. I can't WAIT to find out how I'm getting to church. You've all been keeping it a secret!'

Bertie and Sally looked at each other happily. 'You won't have to wait long,' said Sally and as she spoke Joan swept into the room in a flurry of ostrich feathers and mustard-coloured silk.

'Your carriage awaits!' she cried. 'Oh, you look marvellous, Kate!'

Bertie held out his arm. 'Here we go.'

Kate linked her arm into his, and gazed into his pale face. His eyes were bright with anticipation. Leaning on his stick he took her through the house to the front door. Standing patiently in the drive was a Shire horse in full regalia, jingling with brasses and bobbing tassels, her coat gleaming in the sun. The horse turned her head and saw Kate. She whinnied in greeting.

'DAISY!'

Kate forgot about looking elegant. She went to Daisy, flung her arms around the huge neck and cried.

'Kate, your DRESS!' roared Sally, and Kate giggled.

'Quite like old times,' said Bertie, laughing out loud.

'Don't let Daisy eat those roses.' Sally rescued the bouquet, and the three of them stood together laughing and making a fuss of the dear old horse who had been part of their happy family.

'I'd have had a bouquet of carrots if I'd known.' Kate laughed. 'And LOOK at this carriage she's pulling! Is this yours, Joan? It's magnificent. I'll feel like a queen!'

'Are you ready, Miss Kate?' Charlie appeared in his band uniform, a trombone shining in his hands. 'Got the town band here to escort you. And the music is what Freddie wanted.'

He got the smile he'd been hoping for. Kate and Bertie climbed into the highly polished carriage and the procession began. The band started its music with a drum roll, then marched forward to the tune of 'I'm forever blowing bubbles'. Daisy loved music. She arched her neck and stepped out majestically, her hooves clopping time to the music. She was an old horse now, too old to work, but today she was full of life and pride.

Left alone in the bakery, Annie squeezed her feet into some new shoes. She trimmed her posh hat with a few flowers and put it on in front of the mirror. Then she pushed her face up close to the mirror and looked into her own eyes.

'You,' she said, pointing at herself, 'are going to your son's wedding.'

She opened the door and went out. In the distance she could hear the town band and the clip-clop of Daisy's hooves. Straightening her back proudly, Annie walked confidently down the road and into the church.

Acknowledgements

Thank you to Barbara Large and the Winchester Writers Festival, my amazing agent, Judith Murdoch, my wonderful editor, Jo Dickinson and all the team at Simon and Schuster UK. A special thank you to my local writers group, my husband, Ted, and my family for their kindness and support.

A Note From the Author

THE BOY WITH NO BOOTS is fiction, but it is based on the true stories my late father told us about his early life. The stone angel and many of his carvings are in homes and churches around Somerset, some of them still in the family. Monterose and Hilbegut are fictitious places, typical of towns and villages in my home county of Somerset. If you're good at anagrams, you could work them out! You might even discover a small grey village church where Dad's statue of St Peter still stands in the porch.